THE Rodenburg GIRL

THE Rodenburg GIRL

JOURNEYS OF THE HEART BOOK 3

a historical romance by

SHAELA KAY

Other books in this series

A Heart Made of Indigo
Scoundrel In Disguise

Published by Blue Water Books
Richland, WA

Cover design © Blue Water Books

© 2019 Shaela Kay Odd
Visit the author at www.shaelakay.com

This book is a work of fiction. While great care has been taken to ensure historical accuracy of dates and locations, characters and events in this book are products of the author's imagination and are represented fictitiously. Any likeness to any person, living or dead, is purely coincidental.

This book is dedicated to the countless readers who have written to me and asked for Lady Rockwell's story.

I hope you will find it has been worth the wait.

Chapter 1

There is something delicate and soothing in the sound of the harp. When the thick, tight strings are plucked in just the right order, a beautiful symphony of sound pours forth that calms and quiets even the most nervous of minds.

Which is precisely why Greta preferred the pianoforte.

She knew how to play the harp, of course. Music was like air to Greta. She had never known a time in her life before music, and she could not imagine living a single day without it. But unlike the harp (which her mother preferred), or the dulcimer (which her sister preferred), when Greta placed her hands on the smooth white keys of the pianoforte, the music came alive. What was written on the page before her did not matter. Whatever notes she played, whatever song she practiced, she infused the melody with the feelings of her sixteen-year-old heart. The music became a living, breathing extension of Greta herself.

The third movement of Johann Sebastian Bach's *Concerto No. I in D minor* was a passionate piece, and it suited Greta's mood perfectly. Her fingers were a blur as they flew over the keyboard, striking the notes with forceful precision. The pins in her carefully coiffed tresses slipped with every shake of her head, until an errant lock of honey-blonde hair came loose and bounced erratically around her face. She ignored it. The music increased in tempo, coming to a crescendo as she pounded out the last few measures.

The final notes hung in the air like rich perfume, fading softly as the seconds ticked by. Taking a breath, Greta allowed herself a smile, and reached up to brush the unruly curl away from her face. It bounced back with frizzy determination.

"Our mother would like to see you, Margareta."

Greta looked up at the sound of her younger sister's voice. Katarina's face was pinched in a frown, which could only mean that their mother was in a good humor. Usually when Greta was summoned to her mother's bedchamber it meant that she was in trouble, which would have been cause for Trina to gloat.

"I shall be right there."

Katarina turned on her heel and flounced away. Smiling ruefully, Greta stood from her seat and carefully arranged her skirts, ensuring that her panniers were straight and her petticoats were smooth. She swept through the marbled hall and ascended the grand staircase, stopping in the corridor outside her mother's chambers to check her appearance in a mirror. Her eyes narrowed as she scrutinized the prodigal curl, which her mother would surely notice. Sighing, she tucked it behind her ear until she could properly pin it back.

Turning from her reflection, Greta knocked quietly on the door of her mother's room.

"Come in."

Dorothea Rodenburg was sitting at her dressing table, in an evening gown of midnight blue taffeta. She looked every bit the Prussian princess—a title which she clung to, despite its relative worthlessness. The wars that had plagued the Holy Roman Empire for the last century had resulted in an overabundance of new city states, and an overzealous appointment of Prince Regents to rule over them. So while Heinrich Rodenburg's wife *was* a Prussian princess, she was only a third daughter, and a penniless one at that. It was to her very great advantage that she was a remarkable beauty, or else she might never have married at all. As it was, Heinrich Rodenburg—wealthy, if not handsome— had taken a fancy to her, and she consented to marry him after knowing him only a few short weeks. Having attained what she had been raised to do, her purpose in life shifted. She was a pretty wife with pretty manners who played her role well, intent on teaching her daughters the same principles, and, for the most part, she was happy with her success.

Except that Greta refused to be taught.

Frau Rodenburg's maid was combing and looping her mistress's hair into an elaborate *tête de mouton*, with short curls on the sides of her head and the nape of her neck, and the rest smoothed into an elegant bouffant on top. Greta was always amazed at the amount of work it took to tame her mother's hair, which was as curly as her own. But curls were only fashionable in certain instances, and Frau Rodenburg was determined to beat her unruly mane into submission.

Frau Rodenburg looked at her daughter's reflection in the glass. "Margareta, we have a guest joining us for supper today, and I want you to take exceptional care with your appearance. Your maid has been instructed as to your attire, and Trueden will be doing your hair."

Her gaze slid back to view her own reflection once more, leaving Greta standing shocked and speechless by the bedroom door. When her eldest daughter made no move to withdraw, Frau Rodenburg turned and spoke sharply.

"Really, Margareta, do not stand there like a goat with your mouth open. Did you not hear what I said?"

"Yes, Mama," Greta stammered. "But who is coming to dine? You look as if you are dressed for court."

"Don't be impertinent."

"Forgive me, Mama."

Her mother resumed gazing at herself in the glass. "An English ambassador, the Viscount Ellsworth, has been invited to stay with us, by your father."

"An Englishman?"

"Yes. He is a man of influence with considerable property, and I wish you to be on your best behavior." She looked at Greta's reflection, which was a miniature of her own, and raised her eyebrows. Greta nodded slowly, and her mother appeared satisfied.

"That is all. You may go now. I will send Trueden to your room shortly."

Greta's head was reeling as she returned to the staircase and descended to the second floor. What was an Englishman doing in Strausberg? And what business did her father have with him?

Greta chewed on her bottom lip as she entered her chambers, throwing herself backwards onto the bed.

"Lisbet," she called to her maid, who was busy in the adjoining dressing room. "Do you know anything about the visiting ambassador? Have you heard anything below stairs?"

"Only that your mother wishes to make a good impression, Fräulein."

Greta rolled over and propped herself up on her elbows as Lisbet walked in, carrying a larger set of panniers. She placed them on the floor next to Greta's bed.

"I wonder what he is doing here," Greta murmured, eyeing the contraption beside her with loathing. "Mama said he has influence and is very rich—which explains why she wishes to make a good impression," she added, rolling her eyes. "I wonder how much he is worth?"

The matronly servant smiled affectionately at her mistress. "Perhaps you should ask him at dinner," she teased.

"Mama would be furious," Greta mused. Suddenly a wicked smile flashed across her face. "But what a marvelous idea, Lisbet! I believe I shall."

"Fräulein, you mustn't!" Lisbet cried in alarm. Greta laughed at her maid and rolled onto her back once more. Lisbet clucked her tongue.

"Your mother had a new gown sent up for you, special for the occasion. But I have half a mind to keep it from you now, after your teasing."

Greta shot up from the bed. "A new gown? *Zeig es mir!*"

Lisbet chuckled, retrieving a flowing garment of lavender silk from the dressing room. Greta cried out in delight, hugging her

5

maid and crushing the new gown between them.

"Fräulein, the dress!" Lisbet cried.

"Oh, Lisbet, is it not beautiful?" Greta took the garment from her maid and held it to her figure, twirling in a circle. "Wait till Hans sees me in this," she breathed, admiring herself in the glass.

"No one will see you in it until you put it on," Lisbet said, all business once more. "Come now, let us get you dressed. Trueden will be here any minute to do your hair, and your mother will want to see you in the gown before you go down. It will not do to keep her waiting."

Frederick Greenwood, the Viscount Ellsworth, stole yet another glance at the young lady seated beside him. There had only been time enough for a brief introduction in the drawing room before supper, but even those few minutes had piqued his interest in Herr Rodenburg's eldest daughter. He knew that his host had three children, but he was not expecting any of them to be as charming—nor as beautiful—as Greta.

Greta reached for her glass and glanced up at him. Frederick smiled and quickly looked away, only to find his eyes drawn to her a moment later. She was still looking at him.

"I hope you had a pleasant journey, Your Excellency?"

Lord Ellsworth was pulled from his thoughts by Frau Rodenburg's voice.

"I did, thank you," he replied.

"Do you come to Prussia often?"

"Not often, though I have been before."

"And have you been to Brandenburg?"

"No, Your Highness." His eyes flickered in Greta's direction as she coughed, hiding a laugh. His brow furrowed—what had he said?—but he looked back at Frau Rodenburg. "This is my first time in this part of the country."

"And what is your opinion of it thus far?" Herr Rodenburg asked, taking a sip from his glass.

Frederick turned to the man on his other side. "Brandenburg is beautiful. It reminds me very much of home, though perhaps a bit drier."

"Ah, yes," Herr Rodenburg chuckled. "You English are forever drowning in rain and mist over there."

Frederick inclined his head.

"Does it rain *all* the time?" Greta asked. It was the first time she had addressed him directly since the meal began.

"No," he said, pleased with her attention. "But it rains a fair amount of the time. It is very green."

Her head tilted ever so slightly to the right—just enough to dislodge a lock of golden hair, which curled across her brow with maddening charm. He watched, waiting for her to reach a hand up and brush it back into place, but she did not. His lips quirked up in a smile.

"I understand you hail from Kent, Your Excellency," Frau Rodenburg said, breaking into his thoughts once more.

"The earldom is located in Kent, but I hold an estate of my own in Leicestershire."

Greta paused with her soup spoon halfway to her mouth. "The earldom? I thought you were a viscount."

Frau Rodenburg cleared her throat, shooting her daughter a

look.

Frederick inclined his head. "Indeed, Fräulein. But my father is the Earl of Rockwell."

"Oh." The renegade curl fell into her eyes, and she brushed at it carelessly.

A bell rang, indicating the end of the first course, and Frederick dragged his eyes away from her face. *Pull yourself together, man. She is naught but a child! And you are here on the king's errand.* He turned himself deliberately to face his host as the dishes were removed, the table linens replaced, and new dishes brought forward. Frederick made light conversation with Herr Rodenburg while they waited, but when he turned back to his plate, he noticed Greta watching him. Her expression was open, curious even, and her full lips were parted slightly, as if on the verge of a smile.

"Fräulein," Frederick said, raising his brow expectantly.

"Lord Ellsworth," she said, "I have a question for you which you may find impertinent. But I cannot help but ask it."

His surprise nearly caused him to laugh, but he checked himself when he caught Frau Rodenburg's poisonous look. It was aimed not at him, but at her daughter, who could not see her mother's face.

"I doubt there is anything you could say that I would find to be improper, Fräulein."

Her eyes brightened. "Shall I take that as permission to speak freely, my lord?" He nodded, and her look grew more earnest. "Have you always lived in England?"

Her question surprised him. "Yes, all my life."

"*You have never lived on the continent?*" she asked, slipping into French.

He grinned. "No. Though I have spent considerable time in various countries, my home has always been in England."

"And your parents—they are both English?"

"Decidedly so."

She narrowed her eyes, but said no more as she turned back to her meal. Frederick's own curiosity was piqued, and after a moment of silence he asked, *"Puis-je demander pourquoi vous voudriez savoir?"*

Greta looked up at him. "I ask because you barely have a discernible accent. Your German is near perfect."

His startled eyes crinkled when he smiled at her. "Thank you, Fräulein. That is a great compliment, coming from one such as yourself."

She laughed—a warm, rich sound, like melted chocolate. "From me? Oh, but I am no one, *Your Excellency*," she said, her eyes dancing.

Before Frederick could ascertain whether she was teasing him or laughing at him, her mother spoke.

"No one!" Frau Rodenburg exclaimed. "Margareta, do not discredit your heritage, nor your own accomplishments. You are a Rodenburg, and your mother is a Keyser. You are most certainly someone."

"Yes, Mama." Greta pinched her lips together, reaching up to tuck the curl behind her ear.

"Not only do you come from such impressive lineage, but your own accomplishments add to your merit. Lord Ellsworth, were you able to hear her from the study this afternoon? She is quite a remarkable musician."

The viscount nodded to the woman smiling tightly at the end of the table. "Yes, I was fortunate enough to have had the pleasure."

"Greta surpasses even her lovely mother in her musical abilities," Herr Rodenburg added. "Now, if only she applied herself as willingly to her other studies, eh?"

Greta grinned at her father, who smiled indulgently at her.

Frau Rodenburg sniffed. "In my opinion, a young lady has no need to be filling her head with numbers and figures and foreign languages. She would be far better served learning the lessons of obedience and docility."

"Yes, because needlepoint is so very important," Greta mumbled.

"Margareta." Frau Rodenburg's voice cut through the air like a dart.

Greta snapped her mouth shut and dropped her eyes. Frederick observed the tightness of her jaw as she reached for her knife and fork. Her knuckles were white as she gripped her utensils.

Herr Rodenburg cleared his throat. "Obedience is certainly a very great virtue," he said, addressing his wife. "But I must disagree with you, my dear, on what you feel to be impractical numbers and useless learning. There is a great deal of usefulness in what Greta is being taught."

Frau Rodenburg pressed her lips into a crimson line. "Just as you please, then. I am sure you know best how to raise our daughter."

"Dorothea—"

"Forgive me," Frau Rodenburg simpered, rising gracefully from the table. Frederick nearly knocked over his chair in his haste to rise as well. "Your Excellency, please excuse me. I must see to my younger children at present."

She smiled sweetly at the viscount before leaving the room, sparing not a glance for either her husband or her daughter. When she had gone, Herr Rodenburg sat down with a huff.

"My apologies, Lord Ellsworth," he said, raising his glass to a footman to be refilled, "but as you can see, my wife does not always share my views on what constitutes a proper education for young ladies."

"She is not alone in her feelings, I am afraid. Many English women feel the same," Frederick said, taking his seat again.

"Is that so?"

The viscount nodded.

"Hm." Herr Rodenburg swirled his drink, watching his guest over the rim of his glass. Frederick cleared his throat and glanced at Greta, but she was looking at him with the same intense, gray eyes as her father. He flushed.

"What do *you* think about the education of women, Lord Ellsworth?" Greta asked.

Her father laughed. "*Schatz*, do you wish to frighten away our guest with a heated argument on his first day here? Should you not inquire after the weather or the state of the roads?"

Greta's eyes shone with impish delight. "My dear Papa, you cannot possibly think that His Excellency, the Viscount Ellsworth, would be remotely interested in such mundane topics as the weather and transportation." She shot him a look. "Are you?"

Frederick looked between the two expectant faces—the father's, full of gentle humor, and the daughter's, brimming with mischief—before laughing nervously. "I find that such

11

conversations depend entirely upon the person with whom I am speaking, Fräulein."

Greta sat back, disappointed, but Herr Rodenburg chuckled. "A diplomatic answer if ever I heard one," he said, raising his glass.

Frederick inclined his head, willing himself not to glance beside him for the hundredth time that evening. But he could feel Greta's piercing gaze on his face, and at last he turned to meet her eyes.

She did not look away.

Chapter 2

Hans Schneider straightened his cravat and knocked firmly on the front door. He counted the seconds silently in his mind while he waited. *Eins, zwei, drei...*

The door swung open, and the Rodenburg's butler stood before him.

Seven seconds. Exactly as many as the week before.

"*Guten Tag*, Herr Schneider. Please, come in."

Hans followed the butler to a small salon on the first floor. His eyes narrowed as he glanced up at the intricate mural painted on the ceiling and the gilt chandelier hanging below it. He shook his head—the opulence of the estate never ceased to disgust him.

"Please be seated. Fräulein Rodenburg will be in shortly."

Hans nodded as the butler retreated. A pile of books, a stack of paper, and a silver-plated writing service sat neatly on the table across the room. Two chairs were drawn up in preparation for their lesson, but instead of seating himself to await Greta's arrival, Hans made his way to the large paned window on the other side of the table.

The view was breathtaking. Though not as structured and formal as the English kept their gardens, the grounds around the estate were beautiful nonetheless. A long, wide avenue stretched from the house to the orchard and fields beyond. In the middle of the avenue, near to the house, a narrow pool reflected the sky overhead. Wide green lawns and manicured hedges were punctuated with large outcroppings of wildflowers and trees. Hans leaned a hand against the window, glaring at the prospect.

The door opened behind him and he turned, allowing his expression to clear. Tall and willowy, Greta floated into the room, followed by her maid. Despite the resentment that still burned within him, Hans could not help but smile at his friend.

"*Guten Tag*, Hans," Greta said brightly. Her maid *tsk*ed and shot her a sharp look, which she ignored.

"*Guten Tag*, Fräulein," Hans bowed. "You look lovely, as always. Is that a new dress?"

She flushed with pleasure. "Yes, it is."

Greta's maid shot Hans a look as well, which he returned with a saucy wink. She huffed and shook her head, seating herself across the room from them with her mending basket.

Hans chuckled, turning his attention back to Greta, who was looking up at him expectantly. Her large gray eyes were thickly framed with heavy lashes, giving her the slightly wide-eyed appearance of a child. His look softened. How well he knew those eyes!

"Are you ready to begin our lesson?" he asked.

"Yes, please."

He held the chair for her while she arranged her skirts and sat down. Seating himself beside her, he reached for one of the books.

"Let us begin with a bit of translation."

He flipped through the pages until he found the chapter he was looking for. Placing the volume in front of Greta, he pointed to the spot where she should begin. "Translate this passage into French."

Greta reached for a quill and a sheet of paper. Glancing at the book, she began moving her hand smoothly across the page. Ribbons of ink blossomed beneath the nib, and for several minutes the only sound was the scratching of the quill on the paper.

Soon Greta set the pen down, blew gently on the words she had written, and looked up at Hans. He pulled the book towards him and nodded at her.

"Now, read what you wrote."

Greta's voice was clear and strong, and she did not hesitate over her words. Hans's eyes darted across the page of the book, following along.

"*Sehr gut*, Fräulein," he said when she had finished. "But you made a few mistakes. Let us try this part again." He glanced down at the page. "*He was called upon to introduce his guests.*" He nodded at her.

Greta bit her lip. "*Il a été invité à présenter ses invités.*"

"*On lui a demandé de présenter ses invités,*" Hans corrected her.

Greta leaned towards him to look at the book again, quietly repeating the phrase in question to herself. "Oh yes, I see now," she said brightly, looking up with a smile. "Thank you, Hans."

15

"*Bitte schön*, Fräulein."

Greta rolled her eyes. "Hans, why do you insist on addressing me as Fräulein during our lessons? You call me Greta everywhere else."

He shrugged. "What if your father were to come in?"

"Better he than my mother."

Hans smirked. "Had another run-in with Her Highness?" he asked.

Greta sniffed. "No, I did not." She paused. "At least, not today."

He laughed, the echoes of his rich bass voice filling the room like cathedral bells. Greta smiled. She loved to hear him laugh.

"Oh! Did you hear? There is an English ambassador staying with us. He joined us for dinner last night."

Hans raised his brow. "An Englishman?"

She nodded.

"For how long? What is his purpose here?"

"I am not sure. He is a viscount, so it is likely something political. But Mama gave me a new dress for the occasion."

"*C'est la robe que vous êtes portée?*"

Greta laughed. "Of course not! This is a morning dress. I wore a lavender evening gown last night."

"I see. Well, you must wear it to the dance next week so I can see it for myself."

Greta's eyes brightened at his comment, but Hans did not notice. He was leafing through another one of the books on the table, his mood darkening.

"Politics," he muttered, pushing away from the table.

Greta looked surprised. "Is something wrong?"

16

"Why do you even want to learn all this?" he said suddenly, bitterness leaking into his voice like acid. "I do not understand why your father insists on these lessons."

"I like learning French," she answered, surprised at his sudden outburst.

"And geometry? Philosophy? Do you like those as well?"

Greta frowned. "Do you not enjoy our lessons?"

Hans shoved the book away from him. "For what Herr Rodenburg pays your private tutors, he could build a school in Strausberg to teach everyone's daughters, not just his own."

"Not everyone wants their daughters to be taught, Hans."

"But everyone would like their sons to be taught."

"Yes, but there is already a *Volksschule* in Strausberg for them. And the girls are welcome to attend as well."

"What about secondary school? Why does your father not build one of those, for further learning? If he cares so much about *education*," the word sounded like an expletive, "why are only the wealthy allowed to continue their studies?"

Greta tipped her head to the side. "It is not only the gentry. You were able to go, and your brothers."

"Only because we sit in your father's pocket," Hans muttered.

Her eyebrows shot up. "That is not true."

"Is it not? Why then can Ernst not attend school in Berlin, as I did?"

Greta sighed. "Ernst has no need for further education. He is going to be a blacksmith."

"That is precisely what I mean," Hans said, shaking his head. He stood abruptly. "You don't need my help anymore, Greta. Your pronunciation is nearly perfect and your comprehension is good.

That is all you need to know."

"But, Hans—"

"Tell your father to find another French tutor. I cannot help you anymore." He strode swiftly to the door, scowling at the velvet carpet beneath his feet. His hand was on the brass before Greta's voice called him back.

"Hans, wait!"

He turned to see her crossing the room towards him, holding her heavy skirts out of the way.

"When will I see you again?"

"We are not children, anymore, Greta. We cannot run off to play like we used to."

"I know that," she answered petulantly. "But if we do not continue our French lessons, how can I be assured of seeing you each week?"

He let out his breath in a sigh that was nearly a growl. "Considering that my father is now teaching me to manage the estate, you will likely be seeing me just as often."

"Oh Hans, at last! That is wonderful!" Greta's face broke into a delighted smile.

"Wonderful?"

"Of course. As steward, you will have so many more privileges and freedoms. Why, you could take the dogs out hunting whenever you wished!"

A smile tugged at the corner of Hans's mouth. "I do that already, Greta."

She lowered her voice, glancing at her maid. "I know, but when you are my father's steward you will not have to sneak them off and hide all traces of the hunt."

He laughed, and it felt good. Being in this house always angered him. The opulence, the extravagance... the Rodenburgs enjoyed a life of privilege few would ever know, and it vexed him. What made them better than his own family? Or any other family in Strausberg, for that matter? Could not their wealth be shared, for the betterment of the entire community? He sighed. It angered him, yes. But Greta's quick wit and ready smile always had a way of soothing his nerves.

"Well, that is true," he conceded.

"I have complete faith in you, Hans. You will learn it all in no time," Greta replied confidently. "And you will be a marvelous steward."

"We shall see."

He opened the door, and Greta laid a hand on his arm. "Are we really done with our lessons?"

Her eyes pulled at him, pleading, and for a moment, he was transported back to their childhood. She looked just as she always had, with her head tipped back and her eyes wide, looking up at him as if he carried the moon in his pocket. Despite his frustration, he could not help but smile.

"Ah, Greta," he said. "How can I deny you when you look at me like that?" He reached up and touched her chin with his thumb, memories swirling inside as she smiled at him. "I suppose we can have one more lesson."

Greta's face blossomed, and his breath caught in his chest. She had always been like a younger sister to him, but now she verged on womanhood. When had she grown up? When had he?

He shook his head, dropping his hand. "I shall see you next week."

"What is it that you plan to do while in Strausberg, Lord Ellsworth?"

It was early afternoon on a beautiful July day. The two men were gathered in Herr Rodenburg's study, having retired there after the midday meal. Frederick set down his glass and turned to face his host.

"Observe, for the most part. His Majesty King George would like a report on conditions in Eastern Europe, and I was assigned to visit the city states here in Brandenburg. We are concerned for the welfare of our former allies, and wish to know if there is anything we might do to assist them."

Herr Rodenburg barked a laugh. "Anything *England* might do to assist *us?*"

"Of course. The nature of the relations between—"

"Any relations Prussia had with England were dissolved years ago, Lord Ellsworth. Surely you must know that," Herr Rodenburg said, shaking his head.

Frederick studied the man before him. Heinrich Rodenburg was tall and thin, with a large, hooked nose and a pointed chin that jutted out. His dark hair, which was pulled back and tied neatly together at the nape of his neck, was only just beginning to gray at the temples. In the popular style of the time, his face was clean shaven, and as he peered at his guest, Frederick saw that his eyes were the exact same shade of gray as his daughter Greta's.

The viscount took a sip of his own drink. "I know that dealings between England and Prussia have been somewhat," he paused, searching for the word, "*strained,* since the Anglo-

20

Prussian alliance was dissolved."

"Since you withdrew all support and left us at the mercy of Austria, you mean."

Herr Rodenburg spoke mildly, but there was a note of caution in his voice. He drained his glass and set it down with a sharp tap.

"Lord Ellsworth, you gave me a very diplomatic answer when I asked what your intentions here were. But do not mar my good opinion of you by insulting my intelligence in such matters. You and I both know that England is far less concerned about Prussia, and far more concerned that you no longer have any political allies on the continent."

Frederick watched him warily.

"It is my understanding," Herr Rodenburg said, "that England is concerned about France."

Frederick stood and paced to the window, clasping his hands behind his back as he looked out on the view. "Can you blame us?" he asked.

"Not at all. Ever since they joined the colonists in fighting against the British, there has been nothing but talk of revolution in France as well. Which would not bode well for England. Or any of Europe, for that matter."

"*You* seem to have recovered sufficiently from the mid-century wars."

"We have recovered to an extent," Herr Rodenburg replied, joining Frederick at the window. "But Prussia is treading more cautiously now. We do not want to find ourselves in the middle of another argument."

"Especially not with Russia."

Surprised, Herr Rodenburg looked over at his guest. Frederick smiled. "Your frankness does you credit, Herr Rodenburg. If you will forgive my initial reluctance, I will speak candidly from now on."

Herr Rodenburg nodded, pleased. "*Gut.* I have great admiration for men who do not mince their words. Yes—we are concerned about Russia. And Austria. We are hanging in a delicate balance; any major shift elsewhere in the world may tip the scale."

Silence settled over them as they gazed out the window together, watching the sunshine dance across the surface of the reflecting pool. A movement on the lawn off to the right drew their attention, and soon Greta and Katarina came into view. The former frolicked across the lawn, her step light and swift. Her sister, however, had her nose in a book, and followed behind Greta at a more sedate pace. The men watched as the sisters drew near to the reflecting pool and stopped. Greta perched herself on the low wall and leaned over the water, while Katarina sat primly on the edge and continued reading. Herr Rodenburg sighed.

"I worry for my children, Lord Ellsworth," he murmured. "What sort of world will they be raising their own families in?"

Frederick shifted beside him. "In whatever state the nations of Europe are to be found, you can rest assured they will be well prepared to handle it. Especially since you are having not only your son, but your daughters educated as well."

"Yes. I am a firm believer that women have just as much right and ability to be educated as men. I may not be able to get them into a university, but I have spared no expense in securing private tutors for them. I refuse to raise ignorant children."

"What subjects are they studying?"

"History, philosophy, science, and mathematics, as well as French, English, and Latin. And politics," he added, almost as an afterthought.

"Politics?"

"Of a sort. It is not something I am having Katarina or Johann taught at this time—they are still too young—but I am giving Greta lessons in government and political science myself."

Herr Rodenburg returned to his seat, and Frederick turned his attention back to the young ladies outside. Katarina was now on her feet, shouting at her elder sister. Half her dress was drenched, so he could easily guess what the trouble had been.

"Are they good students?" he asked, not turning away from the window.

"Trina is. And Johann can be when he has a mind to, but he is still very young."

Frederick watched as Greta, who looked as though she had fallen into the pool, pulled out a sodden handkerchief and held it out to her sister with a look of contrition. Instead of taking it, Katarina tossed her head and stomped away.

"And your elder daughter?" the viscount asked, just as Greta drew back her arm and launched the soaking article at her sister's head.

Herr Rodenburg swirled the liquid in his glass. "Let us just say that Greta has not yet learned the importance of polite international relations."

Chapter 3

The township of Strausberg was one of the oldest cities in Prussia. Founded in the twelfth century, it had a high stone wall which completely encircled the town. In the very center, a castle made from the same stone as the wall was erected for the overseer to live in, but the reigning noble family had long since abandoned it for a larger, more modern establishment without the wall. After their removal, the original castle had been converted into a public assembly hall. There, the community came to witness trials of court, to participate in weddings and other ceremonies, and to gather in times of war or distress. At present, the *alte Burg* was brilliantly lit and decorated with fragrant garlands of flowers, in preparation for a late summer's ball.

Greta was trembling with excitement as their carriage pulled up in front of the ancient building. She and Lisbet had spent hours in her room that afternoon, primping and polishing in preparation for tonight. Her hair had been teased into an elegant arrangement that added nearly six inches to her stature, with curls and ringlets cascading from the sides and back. She was wearing her new silk dress, hoping that Hans would remember his request, and know that she wore it for him.

Herr Rodenburg handed his wife down from the carriage and led her into the building, leaving Greta to take the viscount's offered arm. She placed her gloved hand delicately on top of his own, looking up at him with a brilliant smile. He smiled in return, his heart beating faster at her touch.

"Have you ever been to a Prussian ball, Your Excellency?" she asked.

"No, but I imagine they are very similar to English balls."

She cocked her head. "Do you think so? I have never been to England, and therefore cannot tell you. What are they like?"

"The balls in London are incredibly crowded, so much so that there is hardly room to dance. And many of the attendees are insufferable social climbers or snobbish gentility, intent on their own aspirations and heartless to any who get in their way."

"And which are you?" she asked with a coy smile. "An insufferable social climber or a snobbish gentleman?" She laughed when his ears turned pink. "If it is really as you say," she continued, "then you have naught to fear. Our balls are nothing like that. Strausberg is a small town, and we are all friends. Nearly everyone attends."

That surprised him. "Everyone?"

She grinned as they stepped into the hall. "Everyone."

Though somewhat outdated, the ballroom was still magnificent. Four massive chandeliers hung from the ceiling, illuminating the mirrored walls and high, coffered ceiling. The room was warm, not only from the pressing bodies but from the sheer number of candles hanging overhead. Greta floated across the room on the viscount's arm, scanning the crowd for Hans's familiar profile. The floor beneath her feet was dented and scratched, but polished so highly that it reflected the rainbow of petticoats that swirled above its surface.

Lord Ellsworth led Greta to the far wall. Two velvet ropes stretched across the width of the ballroom, creating three distinct areas for dancing. Though the city of Strausberg was a tightly knit community, where gentry and peasantry mingled and communed at will, tradition mandated that formal public functions such as this required a far more distinct separation of classes. The Rodenburgs, being the only noble family in the city, occupied the farthest section of the ballroom. Gathered with them were a few families of the peerage and gentry from their corner of the province. The largest collection of persons were between the two cordons, and represented the middle class, or *bourgeoisie*. On the far right side of the ballroom, as far from the gentility as space would allow, were the peasantry.

Greta withdrew her arm from Frederick's as soon as civility allowed. He was pleasant enough, but he was her father's guest, and therefore she did not give him much thought. It was not for him that she had prepared so carefully. Searching the faces mingling on the other side of the barrier, she finally spotted Hans. He was standing with a pretty village girl named Julianna, whom Greta also knew. Before Greta had a chance to catch their attention, her mother called her name.

"Margareta," Frau Rodenburg said, a hint of exasperation in her voice. "They are waiting for you to begin the dance."

With a sigh of resignation, Greta moved away from the cordon and took the viscount's outstretched hand. She had forgotten that she was now expected to lead the dance in her mother's place. Smiling absently at Lord Ellsworth, she allowed him to lead her to the top of the room.

All along the length of the ballroom, couples were forming into sets for a Prussian folk dance. Greta watched Hans lead Julianna to the floor, and at the far end of the room, she saw another friend, Ernst, standing across from a redheaded young lady. When he saw Greta watching him he flashed her a smile.

Ernst's enthusiasm was contagious, even from across the room, and Greta found herself grinning as the orchestra finished tuning their instruments. She might not be dancing with Hans, but as the song began, a current of excitement coursed through her. Music had always had that effect on her. It wove its way into her very soul, capturing her heart with the beauty of its spell.

It did not take long for the spell to break. For all his wealth and influence, the viscount was an awful partner. He moved awkwardly beside her, with hesitant steps that never seemed to land on cue.

"To the left, Your Excellency," Greta murmured. "Now to your right. Good."

Frederick obeyed, his brow furrowed in concentration. "Thank you, Fräulein."

"When you were explaining about the balls in London, I did not realize you never actually danced at them," she teased.

He laughed nervously. "Oh, but I do. I quite enjoy a ball."

Greta raised her brow, her lips twitching as he took another misstep. "The other way, Lord Ellsworth."

He sighed in frustration. "Forgive me," he said, correcting

27

himself. "I am not familiar with the movements of this dance. We do not have it in England."

His confession surprised her. She had not considered that the viscount would not know the steps to the opening dance, and she suddenly saw the terror hiding behind his eyes. She laughed.

"And here I was, thinking you were merely a terrible dancer."

He laughed awkwardly beside her. "I am sure that to your eyes, I am. Your mother insisted that the dance was simple enough to learn, but in spite of Her Highness's assurances, I feel that I am quite the blundering partner at present."

Greta frowned. "You need not call her that."

"Pardon?"

"My mother. You need not refer to her as Her Highness, nor address her as Your Highness. Everyone knows her nobility means nothing."

Frederick's face registered his shock for only a moment before he composed himself. "I was not aware she could be addressed any other way. She has never corrected me."

Greta snorted in a most unladylike fashion. "Of course not! You are the first person to treat her with such deference in years. Why would she wish to correct you?"

"Is she not respected in the community?" Frederick's voice could no longer hide his surprise.

"Respected, yes. Reverenced, no. The Prussian nobility are more prolific than rabbits in May. Everyone knows that."

They were silent for the remainder of the dance. Greta, annoyed at the viscount's obvious admiration for her mother, wished it was over. Anyone impressed with Frau Rodenburg was not worth Greta's concern, let alone her regard. She thanked him politely when the music had ended, but sailed away before he could engage her once more.

Though the dancers were forbidden from joining the arena of another social class, there was nothing preventing them from visiting with their neighbors over the cordon. All along the length of the ropes, friends and associates were conversing with one another. Being positioned in the very middle of the room, the *bourgeoisie* had the advantage of being able to speak with practically all members of the community. The gentry and the peasantry, of course, were not able to converse at all, an anomaly which Greta had always found strange, considering how often they otherwise interacted.

Greta stood in the corner near the barrier, trying to catch Hans's eye as he danced—again—with Julianna. She was wearing the lavender gown they had discussed during her lesson, and she wanted to hear his opinion of it. She imagined the way his eyes would light up with admiration as he looked her over. Reaching down, she smoothed the folds of her skirt, waiting for Hans to see her. He and Julianna spun and twirled, but no matter how many times they turned her way, his eyes never found Greta's.

While Greta was attempting to draw Hans's attention, another pair of eyes were watching her. From his position on the far side of the room, Ernst kept glancing in her direction. At nineteen years of age, he was only a few years older than she. That, combined with the fact that he was Hans's best friend, meant that he had known Greta practically all her life. It was only the vast distance between their classes—so much farther than the space between the cordons—that prevented him from going to her now.

He eyed the barrier separating him from the *bourgeoisie* with contempt. He hated the barriers. Why the town insisted on such a meaningless tradition at such events was beyond his comprehension. His gaze slid over to where Herr Rodenburg stood. *Gut,* he was distracted with the English ambassador. So swiftly that it was done before anyone saw, Ernst slipped over the side of the barrier and began casually walking along the wall to the top of the room. He was nearly at her side before Greta recognized him.

"Ernst!" she exclaimed in a shocked whisper. "What on earth are you doing here? Someone will see you!"

"Not if you keep your voice down. Really, Greta, if you did not sound so surprised no one would even know I was here."

Ernst angled himself away from the curious eyes around them and casually clasped his hands behind his back, rocking backwards on his heels. He raised an eyebrow at Greta, who smiled reluctantly.

"There's a good girl. Now tell me, what are you moping about for? Has nobody asked you to dance?"

"I am *not* moping."

"You're moping."

Greta's mouth twitched, and then she laughed. "Ernst, you are positively insufferable."

He bent forward in a mock bow, grinning at her. "Thank you, Fräulein."

Greta rolled her eyes, and he winked at her.

"It is not that I have been unable to secure a partner, but there

30

is no one with whom I wish to dance at present," she said, craning her neck to peer back at Hans.

"No one at all?"

"No one with whom I am allowed to dance."

A huge grin stretched across Ernst's face, but Greta did not see it. Slowly his smile faded. He glanced over his shoulder to where she was looking, and his eyes landed on Hans and Julianna, turning together. His grin turned mocking. "Ah! Could it be that the person you wish to dance with is a certain acquaintance of ours, presently engaged with a certain daughter of our dear Herr Schoeneman?"

Greta's head jerked away, a hint of color creeping into her cheeks. Ernst laughed.

"Hans is quite a handsome catch, if you like blue eyes and curls, I suppose." He watched her face for a reaction, but she remained stoic beside him. "I prefer gray eyes myself," he added with a sly smile.

Greta's eyes snapped to meet his. "Of all the presumptuous, arrogant things to say!"

"Arrogant? How is that arrogant?"

"Because, because..." Greta sputtered beside him, her cheeks turning crimson.

Ernst frowned. He had only been teasing her, but judging from her reaction he must have struck a nerve.

"Greta, I'm sorry." In an instant, he had slipped under the rope and clasped her arms. "Forget what I said. I was only trying to make you smile. Please, don't carry on so. I did not mean it—whatever it was."

She shook him off. "You should not be here, Ernst. Go back

31

before someone sees you."

"But, Greta–"

"Oy! You there!"

They turned, just as a man grabbed Ernst roughly by the arm. "Gottfried, you're not welcome here."

Ernst laughed, a faint flush on his cheeks. "Am I not? I thought it was a ball to celebrate the anniversary of the Peace of Westphalia, and that the whole town was invited. As we are every year."

"*Ja*, but you know the rules. No one crosses the barriers."

Ernst sighed dramatically, carefully removing himself from the man's grip. "Such a silly rule! Why should this be any different than meeting together in the town square, or talking over a cup of tea? Fräulein Rodenburg herself was even wishing—"

"Oh no, Ernst, please! Just go."

The dance ended, and several people now looked on the exchange with interest. Greta knew where this was headed. Of all her childhood friends, Ernst had always been the most volatile. The only son of the village blacksmith, he was doomed to a life of hard labor, little food, and weekly beatings. Though he put on a smirk and a devil-may-care attitude, she knew that underneath his swagger was a deeply embittered man, one who was prone to violent outbursts and not afraid to stand up to authority.

Greta saw the set of his jaw, and desperately cast her eyes around the room before things got out of hand. Oh, where was Hans!

He materialized as if out of nowhere. Stepping over the rope, he caught Greta's eye, and she knew he was thinking the same thing.

"Ernst!" he called, coming up beside them. "Come along, friend. Let us get some refreshment." He reached for Ernst's arm, but Ernst jerked it away, stepping back.

"Coming to save me from myself again, eh, Hans?"

"Ernst—"

"But why do I need saving? Why am I not allowed to be here? What is so special about this place that suddenly puts Greta out of reach? I speak with her in town all the time—why am I not allowed to do so now?"

All eyes in the room were now focused on the two men. Hans's eyes narrowed.

"Come on, Ernst, you know the laws. Stop being so belligerent and just come with me."

"I want to dance with Greta."

At this declaration, a collective gasp went up from the crowd, and an excited buzz filled the air. Greta felt sick.

"Please, Ernst, go with Hans."

"Go with Hans?" Ernst looked between them, his mood darkening. "Oh, yes. Why would you want to dance with me, now that Hans is here?"

"Gottfried!"

All heads turned at the sound of Herr Rodenburg's voice. "You can leave calmly or you can be taken out by force. Make your choice and leave us in peace."

Ernst glared at him, venom seeping into his look. Greta bit her lip. She looked imploringly at Hans, and was shocked to see the look on Ernst's face mirrored on his.

"Come on, Ernst." Hans's voice shook with the effort to control it. He rested his hand on his friend's shoulder, but Ernst

33

shrugged it off, turning abruptly and forcing his way through the crowd. Greta watched him go, sagging with relief.

"Thank you, Hans. I was afraid he would get violent, and then…"

Her voice trailed off when she saw the look in his eyes. Hans stood a full head taller than her, and she had to look up to see into his face. He was not smiling.

The musicians began another song, and slowly the crowd drifted off—some to dance, some to take refreshment, some to gossip over the scene they had just witnessed. Greta glanced at her mother, whose tight lips were white with displeasure.

"Hans?"

Hans shook his head, as if he were striving to rid himself of a fly. "I must be getting back."

"Thank you, Hans."

They stared at each other for a long moment, until finally his face relaxed. "*Bitte schön*, Fräulein." He glanced at her gown. "Nice dress."

Greta grinned, and the corner of Hans's mouth turned up before he moved to walk back around the barrier.

Chapter 4

The next morning dawned bright and warm. Fleecy clouds raced each other to the horizon, leaving an empty canvas for the sun to paint in colors of crimson and gold. Greta came to breakfast in spirits to match the day.

"*Guten Morgen*, Mama. *Guten Morgen*, Papa. Your Excellency," she said, dropping a curtsy at the viscount. She leaned over and planted a kiss on the top of her brother's head, then took her seat two chairs down, leaving a space for Katarina between them.

"*Guten Morgen*, Margareta. You look very nice this morning," her father said.

"Thank you, Papa."

Her mother remained silent, which meant she found nothing to censure.

Breakfast was an informal affair, as it was the only meal during the day when the entire family ate together. The conversation was random and lighthearted—Katarina entertained the viscount with a description of the new book she was reading, Greta and her mother exchanged pleasantries about the weather and their plans for the day, Johann chattered to no one in particular, and Herr Rodenburg watched them all with the look of one supremely pleased with himself. Every once in a while, five-year-old Johann would feed bits of toast and bacon rinds to the German pointer sitting at his feet. Throughout the meal he cast sly glances at his mother, and though she never paid him any mind, he once caught a stern look from his father, which successfully put an end to his antics.

"Margareta," her mother said, near the conclusion of the meal, "we will be going to town today, to distribute food among the poor. Frau Schoeneman mentioned to me last night that she has several loaves of bread she needs to dispose of, and we have produce from the gardens as well."

Greta's look brightened. "Of course, Mama."

Greta always enjoyed spending time in the village. At home, the lines drawn between herself and the servants were clear and never crossed. In town, however, among her friends and acquaintance of the *bourgeoisie*, societal lines were blurred.

The viscount looked up with interest. "At the ball last evening, I was surprised at how freely the members of the various social classes conversed with each other. I understand that you interact with one another on a regular basis?"

"Yes," Herr Rodenburg said. "The town relies on all of its citizens—gentry and peasantry alike—to flourish and thrive."

"Of course. But I have rarely seen such camaraderie among the classes in England. It is heartening to see such Christian charity and goodwill in practice."

"As the reigning family, it is our responsibility to set the example," Frau Rodenburg said, her voice like silk. "Though I wish we were not on such familiar terms with *all* of the city's occupants."

"I have business to conduct this morning," Herr Rodenburg said, addressing their guest. "But perhaps you would care to join my wife and daughter in town, Lord Ellsworth?"

"Unfortunately, I have business to see to as well," Frederick replied. "I must pay a visit to Rüdersdorf this afternoon. But I would be happy to escort them to town on my way."

Greta suppressed a groan, but her mother smiled as she rose from the table. "Wonderful. I shall call for the carriage, and we will leave directly."

The trek into town took only a quarter hour. Hans often joked that it took longer for Frau Rodenburg to get her skirts settled in the carriage than it took for the horses to make the three-mile journey. Greta, forced to sit beside the viscount due to her mother's voluminous petticoats, knew not what to say to him. She had exhausted her supply of polite conversation yesterday at supper, and without a real interest in either the viscount or his holdings—which her mother seemed vastly interested in—she spent the majority of the time staring out the coach windows. Rolling fields of corn and wheat grew in bright, orderly rows, fenced in by rutted dirt roads and low rock walls. Trees dotted the landscape, their dark green canopy blotting out the sky as the carriage passed underneath. Wildflowers, springing up alongside the road, streaked past in flashes of red, purple, and gold. As they drove, Greta only listened with half an ear to what her mother and the viscount were talking of. She hummed quietly to herself as her fingers drummed rhythmically against the glass, tapping out one of her favorite songs on an invisible keyboard.

Frederick stole glances at Greta now and again as they traveled through the countryside. An idea was beginning to form in his mind about the bright young woman seated beside him, but it was nebulous and vague. He needed time to reflect and consider, before deciding on a course of action. The two-hour drive to Rüdersdorf would be the perfect opportunity.

At last they rattled through the gates and into the town, where street after street of tidy little homes passed in a blur. As they approached the center of the village, the tall spire of the Lutheran church came into view, pointing heavenward.

The carriage stopped at the end of a short, narrow street in front of the churchyard. Greta climbed out of the vehicle and glanced around. Across the way, Julianna Schoeneman and her mother were talking with another woman. Julianna looked up as the trio emerged from the coach, and Greta waved a friendly greeting.

"*Guten Morgen*, Greta," Julianna called.

"*Guten Morgen*, Juli," Greta answered, crossing over to her.

"I see you brought the Englishman with you," Julianna said with interest.

"He is not staying. He has business in Rüdersdorf."

"Oh? What business?"

Greta was spared from responding by the approach of the priest. "*Guten Morgen*, Fräulein Rodenburg. Fräulein Schoeneman," he said, nodding at them. They chorused their greetings in reply, and he gestured to the building behind them. "Shall we go inside?"

Several tables had been placed in the main vestibule of the church, and to these he led the young ladies. Greta helped Julianna take in the baskets of bread, placing them on a table in the center of the small room. Lord Ellsworth soon came in, followed by Frau Rodenburg, who was supervising a team of servants carrying baskets and sacks of fresh produce. The viscount looked around with some interest.

"I have never been inside a Lutheran church," he said.

Greta and Julianna exchanged glances. Julianna giggled.

"You sound surprised, Lord Ellsworth," Greta said, looking more like her mother than ever with raised brows.

"I suppose I am, a little. I understood that the majority of the Holy Roman Empire was Catholic."

"The majority, yes, but not the entirety. Strausberg is mostly Lutheran, though there is a small Catholic church on the other side of town."

"I see."

Greta glanced at the priest, who was speaking with her mother. "Will you be joining us for Sunday services, Your Excellency? I am afraid there is no assembly of the Church of England here." Her lips twitched, hiding a smile.

"I should like that very much."

Frau Rodenburg and the priest crossed over to where they stood. "Pastor Wegner, may I present His Excellency Frederick Greenwood, the Viscount Ellsworth."

The gentleman shook hands, and Pastor Wegner smiled. "Welcome to Strausberg, Your Excellency. Will you be here long?"

"As long as it takes to fulfill my assignment, sir."

"Wonderful. I hope we will see you at Sunday services then."
He raised his brow expectantly.

"Indeed. Fräulein Rodenburg has just extended an invitation,
and I am looking forward to it." They turned to look at Greta and
Julianna, who were finishing setting out the food on the tables
provided. Pastor Wegner excused himself, and went to welcome
the others who were arriving.

Greta positioned herself on the far side of Julianna, helping
her hand out bread to the poor who came into the church. From
the corner of her eye, she watched her mother simpering and
smiling next to the viscount at another table.

"Tell me about the Englishman," Julianna whispered to Greta.

Greta shrugged. "There is not much to tell. He is an
Englishman. And a terrible dancer."

Julianna giggled. "But he is staying with you? For how long?
What is he doing here?"

"Those are questions for my father, since I know not the
answers."

There was a brief pause, as the widow Frau Gehr came into
the vestibule, stumping along with her cane. Greta smiled and
handed her a small loaf, which the old woman tucked into the
basket on her arm. She shuffled towards another table, where
Frau Schoeneman was passing out last year's apples.

"He's certainly handsome."

Greta glanced up. Julianna was eyeing the viscount with a coy
smile. Greta snorted.

"You think every foreigner is handsome, Juli."

"What is wrong with that?"

The girls looked up as Frau Rodenburg came towards them.

40

"Margareta, I am going with Frau Schmidt to visit the Voeglers and the Braacks and take them some baskets. Please see to it that all the bread and vegetables are handed out."

"As you wish, Mama."

Greta watched as the women left, carrying baskets on their arms. Julianna nudged her shoulder. "Look who's coming," she whispered.

Greta grimaced at her friend as the viscount came to the table. Planting a smile on her face, she looked up at him.

"Will you be in Rüdersdorf long?" she asked.

"No, I shall be back tonight." He hesitated. "Will I see you at supper?"

"Of course," Greta said, surprise coloring her tone. "Where else would I be?"

Frederick laughed softly. "I don't know. I suppose I wondered if you would be engaged elsewhere."

"Oh."

Greta frowned. What could he mean, asking if he would see her at supper? She glanced up at his face, which was clean shaven, like her father's. His hair and eyes were a warm brown, and when he smiled a cleft appeared in his chin. She looked away. He certainly *was* handsome, though she hated to admit it. Handsome, and wealthy, and titled—everything her mother found admirable. Suddenly Greta's eyes grew wide, alarm growing in her breast.

"*Guten Morgen*, Fräulein Rodenburg."

Startled, Greta pulled herself back to the task at hand, focusing on the woman now standing before her. "Oh! Forgive me. *Guten Morgen*, Frau Krämer." She shook off her thoughts of the

41

viscount, who still stood beside her. Why did he not leave?

"Say hello to Fräulein Rodenburg, Jakob," Frau Krämer said.

Greta ducked her head, addressing the little boy clinging to the woman's skirts. "*Guten Morgen*, Jakob."

"*Guten Morgen*, Fräulein," he mumbled, his face buried in the folds of fabric.

Greta laughed. "Would you like a sweet?" She reached into her pocket and pulled out a stick of hard candy. His eyes brightened as she handed it to him across the table.

"Oh! Bless you," Frau Krämer said, her voice catching. Greta smiled kindly at the woman, who was only five or six years older than herself.

"Think nothing of it. Here," Greta said, handing her a basket of produce. "Be sure to get some bread from Julianna. And Frau Ackerman has eggs, just over there." She indicated across the room.

"*Danke*, Fräulein Rodenburg," the woman said, ducking her head and turning away.

Greta watched her go, feeling a lightness in her breast.

"You have such a way with these people."

The lightness evaporated, and a stone of unease settled in her stomach. She glanced up at the viscount. "Thank you. I take my responsibilities very seriously."

"I can see that."

She cleared her throat, attempting to smile. "Speaking of responsibilities..." Her voice trailed off expectantly, and he laughed.

"Yes, yes, I must go. Thank you for the reminder. I will see you tonight."

He tipped his hat to her and strode off, leaving Greta wondering what to make of him, and hoping her assumptions were wrong.

Greta was waiting for Hans the following morning when he came for their last French lesson. She was wearing a pretty dress of forget-me-not blue, knowing it was his favorite color. He sat down in the chair beside her and grinned.

"*Guten Morgen*, Fräulein," he said.

"*Guten Morgen*, Hans."

"Did you have a nice time at the dance?"

She gave him a sour look, and he laughed. "I thought not. Was it Ernst who ruined it for you?"

"It was more than that, but yes, Ernst was part of it."

"What else went wrong?"

"For one thing, you never came over to talk with me."

Hans rolled his eyes. "We talk all the time, Greta."

Greta looked hurt. "That might not signify to you, but if you had no one else to speak with but stuffy, status-seeking gentlemen and ladies, surely you would understand."

He shrugged. "Balls are for dancing, not talking."

"The only dancing *I* did was with the English ambassador."

Hans looked up from the quill he was sharpening. "What is wrong with that?"

"Did you *see* the way he danced? It was a nightmare!"

"So the man cannot dance—what is that? I do not care for dancing very much myself."

"You seemed quite content to be dancing with Julianna," Greta mumbled, crossing her arms.

He grinned. "*Ja*, Juli makes dancing tolerable."

Greta slumped in her chair. "If we did not have to be separated by class, I am sure I would have enjoyed myself more. I could have been amongst my friends."

"Ernst would certainly agree with you about that."

She snorted. "Oh, Ernst. He deserved to be thrown out."

"Why? Because he wanted to dance with you? You just said it would have been better without the separation of classes. You cannot have it both ways, Greta."

"I know that," she answered, picking at a thread on her skirt. It was clear that Hans had no interest in taking her side, and had obviously enjoyed himself in Julianna's company. She knew that Hans and Juli were friends—were they not all of them friends?—so it should not bother her. It *would* not bother her. But even still, Greta felt the seed of envy begin to grow in her heart, and it made her quite uncomfortable. She did not want to argue with Hans, though, not today. Sitting up in her chair, she folded her hands delicately in her lap. "Shall we begin?"

Hans nodded, pulling a newspaper from his satchel. He spread it on the table before them.

"Where did you get a French newspaper?" Greta asked, surprised.

"*Stille!*" Hans cast a swift glance at the maid in the corner. "Never mind that now. This will be our lesson today."

He scanned the page quickly until he found what he was looking for. "Begin here," he said, pointing to a spot on the bottom half of the page.

44

Greta glanced up at the headline of the article. *Bretagne perd aux colons, cherche de l'aide européenne.* She frowned, but began reading the piece out loud. When she came to the phrase "*...la rumeur indique que les Britanniques chercheront bientôt des mercenaires en Autriche et en Prusse,*" Hans interrupted her.

"Do you know what this means?" he said excitedly.

She frowned. "The colonists in America will win the war?"

"No! It means that the British are still hiring soldiers to fight with them against the colonists."

She stared at him blankly. "So?"

"So, most of us thought they were done. Recruiters have not been seen in Brandenburg for months."

Greta was still confused. "But what does that have to do with us?"

"Greta," he said, folding up the newspaper once more. "The war in America affects all of us. France is already on the verge of revolution—do you have any idea what that would mean for the rest of Europe? For Prussia? If the British are able to squash the rebellion in America, things might settle down here." Hans grinned. "What an adventure it would be!"

Greta's head was spinning. "Wait..." She gasped. "Hans, are you saying that you want to join the army and fight for the British?"

He shrugged. "Why not?"

"Why not! Hans, you would be joining a losing battle—on the wrong side! The colonists have already declared their independence, and despite their earlier disadvantage, they have consistently driven the redcoats back. England is too proud to admit defeat, but everyone knows they no longer stand a chance.

45

If you join them..." She shuddered. "Hans, you could be killed!"

"Since when do you know so much about politics?" he asked, annoyed.

She arched her eyebrows. "You know perfectly well that my father has been giving me lessons for quite some time."

"Women should not concern themselves with such things," he snapped.

Greta recoiled as if she had been struck. He saw the stricken look in her eyes and sighed. "Greta, forgive me. But you cannot deny that your *education* has been quite biased. Clearly your father has not seen fit to inform you more fully."

"I certainly seem to be more *informed* than you," she spat.

Hans glared at her. "At least in joining the army I would be doing something with my life."

"You are already doing something with your life!"

"Oh, yes," he said, not hiding the bitterness in his voice. "Learning a trade that has no real value, forced to wipe the noses and clean up after those who are too rich and lazy to do so themselves."

Greta gasped. "That is not true! You know it is not."

"Do I?"

"Of course you do! Hans, do you see your father wiping our noses or cleaning up after us? The duties of a steward are far more important and respected than that."

"I do not think so," he said abruptly, standing. He grabbed his satchel and bowed stiffly. "*Auf Wiedersehen*, Fräulein."

Without another word, he turned on his heel and left the room.

Chapter 5

"Lisbet, will you lay out my riding habit? And fetch me some tea, please."

Greta was still fuming over her argument with Hans the next morning. She needed to clear her head and come up with some way to stop Hans from joining the army. Really, the idea was completely ridiculous, and why he could not see that was beyond her ability to comprehend. Rather than stew over the problem in the breakfast room, under the ever-watchful eye of her mother, Greta sent a request to the stables to have her horse saddled.

Lisbet laid out the clothing requested and helped her mistress to change. Greta ran a hand down her arm, admiring the feel of the fabric beneath her fingertips. She had always loved her riding habit. It was a deep midnight blue, with brown velvet trim on the collar and cuffs. The dark outfit complimented her lighter hair and eyes, and the trim matched her leather riding boots perfectly. She smiled to herself as Lisbet finished buttoning her boots, remembering when she had ordered the outfit. She and Katarina had their habits made up almost identically, with only one variance: Katarina's included a long petticoat of the same midnight blue fabric as the jacket, while Greta's consisted of trousers.

What a fight had ensued when she requested the culottes instead of a skirt! Unbeknownst to her mother, Greta had been riding astride for years—something which Herr Rodenburg had not only been privy to, but had even encouraged. When the argument between mother and daughter over her new habit had escalated to the point of intervention, Herr Rodenburg had come to Greta's aid, explaining to his wife that riding astride was far more safe than sitting sidesaddle, and that it was not at all improper, as Frau Rodenburg was wont to imagine. So seldom did Herr Rodenburg stand up to his wife that he nearly always got his way when he did, so the skirt was commissioned for Trina, and the trousers for Greta.

After mounting her horse and declining an escort, Greta took off from the stables. Her horse pranced and pawed beneath her seat, sensing her restlessness, and when she came to an empty stretch of road she let him have his head. Greta clung to the reins as the wind whipped at her hair and stung her eyes, but the thrill of flying so fast removed all thought from her mind. Reining in her horse at the end of the lane, she took a deep breath and patted his neck.

"There now, was not that nice? Would you like to go again?"

Her horse whinnied, and Greta laughed, reaching up to brush away the curls that had come unpinned from underneath her hat. She nudged her horse into a quick trot, taking the road to Strausberg. A ride through the woods was just what she needed at present.

As she came around a cluster of trees, she saw another horse and rider standing still in the middle of the road. By the time she realized who it was, it was too late to turn around—she had already been seen. Greta walked her horse up beside the viscount and stopped.

"Good morning, Fräulein," Frederick said, a tone of surprise in his greeting.

"*Guten Morgen*, Your Excellency."

"I had not anticipated meeting with much company this early."

"Nor did I."

They looked at one another, and Greta smiled smugly as his eyes darted to her saddle. *Women in England must not often ride astride*, she thought.

Clearing his throat, the ambassador looked behind her. "Have you no groom?"

Greta stiffened. "I am quite old enough to ride without a chaperon, Your Excellency."

Frederick bent his head in acknowledgment. "Of course, Fräulein. Have you been out long this morning?" he asked.

"I am not ready to return, if that is what you are asking."

He smiled. "It is. Would you like to continue our exercise together?"

Greta bit her bottom lip. She did not particularly wish for the viscount's company, but as she considered, the conversation with Hans came back to her. She wondered if the viscount, being an Englishman, knew more about the war in America. Perhaps in discussing it with him, she could form a plan to keep Hans in Strausberg.

At last she gave a brief nod. "I was planning a ride through the woods around the lake. Is that agreeable to you?"

He nodded, and motioned for her to show the way. Prodding her horse into a walk, she continued down the road leading to town, with Frederick beside her. As they neared the village, they turned and headed north, in order to go around Strausberg to the lake and woods on the west side of the city. Greta urged her horse into a trot, and Frederick followed suit.

"You are very quiet this morning," Frederick said.

"I was not anticipating conversation when I left the house."

Frederick chuckled. "I suppose that is true. Still," he glanced at her face, which she kept stubbornly turned towards the road ahead of them, "you are not usually so quiet."

Greta pulled her horse to a stop, looking at him soberly. "Your Excellency, I believe I must ask you a question before we can continue."

Frederick pulled his horse to a stop as well. "Of course."

"Your honesty would be greatly appreciated, and your answer is absolutely vital."

The intensity of her gaze gave him pause. He must tread carefully if he wished to remain in her good graces. He nodded, and she took a breath.

"What exactly is your purpose here? Why are you in Strausberg?"

Frederick relaxed. "I am an ambassador to the English crown," he said. "My sovereign has sent me to Prussia in order to further the relations with our former allies here."

It was clear from her reaction that Greta had not anticipated his response. "Oh," she said. "Then… you are here for political reasons?"

"Yes, Fräulein."

Relaxing her grip on the reins, Greta nudged her horse into motion once more. "I am glad to hear it."

Frederick followed her lead, watching her intently. She was a fascinating study, and he hoped the plan he had begun to entertain would prove fruitful.

"May I ask," he said at length, "the reason for your inquiry? You looked so serious, for a moment I wondered if you would ask my advice on a personal matter."

Greta looked over at him, frowning. "Are men in England always so forward?" she asked.

He grinned. "Perhaps not. But neither are the ladies in England so difficult to read, as you are at times."

To his surprise, she laughed. "My mother will be pleased to hear that," she mused. "She is always telling me that a woman ought to be mysterious and coy. But I find that I prefer to be frank."

He nodded. "I enjoy candor myself."

"Do you really?"

"Yes."

"In that case, Your Excellency, I—"

"Frederick, please," he interjected. "There is no need to call me 'Your Excellency.' Everyone knows my appointment means nothing."

It took Greta a moment before she understood his meaning. Not until she saw his mouth twitch did she realize he was teasing her, using the same words she had censured *him* with at the ball. She pursed her lips together, hiding a smile.

51

"Lord Ellsworth," she continued, with mock exaggeration. He chuckled. "I would like your opinion on a matter of political interest. If you would be willing to discuss it with me?"

His face registered surprise for only a moment. "Of course, Fräulein."

"I understand that the British are looking to recruit more mercenaries in the fight against America," she said, watching the road ahead of them. "Do you think that wise? Will it change the course of the war?" She could feel his gaze on her face, but she refused to meet his eyes.

"Might I ask your source for such information?" he said carefully.

She hesitated. Her father had said nothing about the British recruitment in her lessons, and she was not sure how the viscount would accept Hans's authority. Especially since it came from a French newspaper. "My source is reliable," she said at last. "Of that you may be certain."

"I see." He cleared his throat. "Though I am no expert on the art of warfare," he said slowly, measuring his words. "I believe that it would be near impossible to change the course of the war at this point. Even with the help of mercenary soldiers."

Greta's heart sank. "Not at all?" she asked, turning to face him.

The look on her face gave him pause. It was the most vulnerable glance he'd ever beheld. Her eyes were wide and frightened, begging for reassurance, and he wondered what she was worried about. He held her gaze, waiting for her to look away.

She did not.

"Not at all, Fräulein," he said at last. "I am sorry."

She turned away then, her stricken look melting into a façade of apathy. "Thank you."

By now they had journeyed around the north end of town, and the massive stone wall that encircled the city was visible on their left. Ahead of them, a dense forest grew right up to the edge of a vast lake. As they entered the pines, Frederick cast his eyes across the surface of the water, admiring the view.

The *Straussee* was a long, skinny lake shaped somewhat like an elongated *S*. It hugged the forest on the west and bordered the town on the east, making it nearly impossible to see until you were directly upon it. From their vantage point at the edge of the wood, the stones of the city wall were beautifully reflected in the calm waters of the lake. Splashes of orange and red amongst the brown and gray stones dotted the wall, which reached as high as a two-story home.

Greta was still mulling over Frederick's answer when he spoke out of the silence.

"You have a beautiful horse, Fräulein," he said, as they continued into the woods. "And you handle the reins very well."

"Thank you."

"Do you ride often?"

"Nearly every day. My love of riding is second only to my love of music."

"Which is immense, I understand."

Greta bent her head in acknowledgment.

"Your father says you are a very talented musician," he continued. "How many instruments do you play?"

"At present, I can play five with accomplishment."

Frederick whistled, long and low. "I do not believe I have met another lady as musically inclined, nor as talented, as that."

She shot him a curious look. "Are ladies in England not so accomplished as to be able to play and sing?"

"On the contrary—most young ladies are. The ability to entertain is one of the most fundamental skills they are taught. But from those of my acquaintance, only a handful can do more than play and sing for company. And of those, only a few play the harp or lute in addition to the pianoforte."

Greta fidgeted, uncomfortable with his praise. She searched her mind for a way to turn the conversation. "My father tells me that you are one of the king's newly appointed emissaries, and that this is only your third assignment," she said at length.

Frederick laughed. "Yes, I am still quite wet behind the ears."

She frowned. "Wet behind the ears?"

"Yes—it means that I am still inexperienced."

"Oh! You mean you are green." She grinned. "In German we say *grün hinter den Ohren*."

Frederick repeated the phrase to himself a few times, committing it to memory. Greta watched him thoughtfully.

"It is still surprising to me that you do not have much of an accent, Lord Ellsworth."

"I have worked for many years to perfect my pronunciation."

"Do you speak any other languages?"

He nodded. "Yes, a few."

She waited, but he supplied no other response. Raising her eyebrows expectantly, she asked, "And how many are a few?"

He shifted in his seat. "Eight. But only six fluently."

"Eight!"

"Only six, fluently."

Greta stared. "I cannot believe it! Eight!" She shook her head, her curiosity getting the better of her. "Which languages?"

"English and German, obviously. Also French, Italian, Latin, and Greek. I am learning Spanish and Portuguese as well.

"*Ach du lieber!* I certainly understand why your king wished to engage you in his service."

Frederick hesitated. "Yes. But my appointment was as much an escape as it was a duty to my king."

Greta cast a sidelong glance in his direction. An escape? From what?

"I have always wished to see the world," Frederick continued. "But I have never been very military-minded. I was far more studious, more interested in learning the languages and the cultures of the world than in conquering their armies and navies."

"But you clearly possess an understanding of politics and world economics," she said. "Surely that is required of your position as well."

"Of course. But *I* seek to study and understand, rather than criticize and control. That is a very different mindset than one of a commanding general."

The path through the trees became more and more narrow, and their conversation more erratic, allowable only when the path widened enough to admit them both to ride side by side. As much as Greta hated to admit it, her curiosity about the viscount had been piqued, and she was glad when the trail turned out of the woods and back onto the road.

"Have you any brothers or sisters, Lord Ellsworth?"

"No, I am an only child."

"What must *that* be like," Greta murmured, more to herself

than to her companion. Frederick chuckled.

"I take it that you are not overly fond of your siblings?"

Greta shrugged. "Johann is still a baby. And Trina and I are not good friends. We are as different as fire and ice, as Papa says."

"You seem to have an exceptionally close relationship with your father."

She smiled. "Yes, we are very close."

"I confess that it surprises me. It seems so very unusual, in this day, for a father to attach himself to a daughter in such a way. If you forgive me for saying so."

"I forgive you. But why do you find it so unusual? Are you not at all attached to your own parents?"

Greta hoped he would reveal more about his family life, given the mention he made of wanting an escape. He was silent for a moment before answering.

"I am quite attached to both my mother and father, Fräulein. They are wonderful parents."

His response was even more bewildering, and Greta's thoughts somersaulted over one another in an attempt to sort themselves out.

"Why did you want to escape, then?" she finally blurted.

Frederick studied her for a moment. "You look very much like your mother, Fräulein. Except your eyes. You have your father's eyes."

Greta knew not what to say.

Chapter 6

A letter was waiting for her when Greta arrived home after the ride. Recognizing Hans's handwriting, she tore it open, eager for his message. But it was short and disappointing: only a note to remind her that he would not be coming for their French lessons anymore, and a request to please refrain from mentioning the newspaper to anyone.

Her sour mood returned in full force, and she marched down to her father's study to discuss the matter with him.

"Yes, Hans sent me a letter last week, informing me of your progress in French and that he felt you no longer needed his tutelage. He assured me that your knowledge and understanding of the language were equal to his own, and that he could no longer teach you anything," Herr Rodenburg said.

"But how am I to retain what I have learned if there is no one with whom to speak French?"

"*Schatz*, there are several people with whom you can practice your French. Your mother, of course. And myself. And Katarina.

She could certainly use your help in her own studies."

"But I need a *master* to converse with. Someone who knows the language and can correct me when I mispronounce or misinterpret something. Hans always corrected me," she added, grasping at straws.

Herr Rodenburg considered her. "Hm, that may be true. I will speak with Hans and see what he suggests."

It was not the answer she was hoping for, but it was the best she could hope for. Having no further business with her father, Greta was forced to turn to her lessons for the day. She endured history, suffered through mathematics, and strove not to yawn during her Latin lesson, which was taught by her mother.

It was a very long morning.

But after the midday meal came Greta's favorite time of day: the hours she spent in her music room. She no longer took formal music lessons, having out-mastered all of the tutors who had been hired to train her. Instead, she practiced on whatever instrument struck her fancy and mood at the time. Most often she spent the entire afternoon on the pianoforte, playing not only her favorite songs, but original compositions as well. She loved it there— losing herself in her music was the only place she felt truly free in her own home.

As she made her way to the music room, she passed by a small parlor, whose doors stood ajar. Normally she swept through the corridor, anxious for the refuge of her music, but upon hearing voices, she paused to investigate.

Hans's curly head was bent over a table, fashioning something with his hands. Beside him, Johann bounced on the balls of his feet, his five-year-old voice chattering incessantly as he watched.

Greta smiled, wrapping her arms around herself and leaning against the door frame.

"Have you made many of these before?" Johann asked. "I've never seen one. Is it not grand? I shall ask Papa for another one. Don't glue your fingers together!"

"I may have to glue your mouth shut if you cannot keep quiet," Hans said with a grin. He looked up to ensure that Johann knew he was teasing, and caught sight of Greta standing by the door. "Greta!" The smile on his face faded.

"What are you working on?" she asked, coming forward to investigate.

"It is a gift from Papa," Johann cried, a grin stretching from ear to ear.

Greta came to the table and peered over Hans's shoulder. An assortment of small wooden pieces were scattered across the tabletop, and a jar of paste was open atop a spread of paper. In his hands, Hans held what appeared to be half of a carriage.

"What is it?" Greta asked.

"A coach and four!" Johann whooped. "Papa had it sent up for me, and Hans is helping me build it, aren't you, Hans?"

"It appears that Hans *is* building it for you," Greta said with some amusement.

"I've been helping some," Johann replied, deflated.

"Here now, I need your help again," Hans said. Johann immediately perked up. "See if you can find me another piece like this—we need it for the rear axle."

The little boy went to task like a bloodhound, scouring the table left and right as he searched for the missing piece.

"It was not already assembled?" Greta asked.

"No—it is a model. Half the fun is putting it together, is it not?"

He looked up at Greta, and she smiled. "I knew there was still somewhat of a little boy left in you," she said. Hans grinned.

"I always wanted something like this when I was a child."

"Perhaps Johann will share," she teased.

"Not likely. Have you heard the way he is going on about it?"

Greta laughed, and her look softened. "It is very kind of you to help him with it. I am sure you have more important duties you could be attending to."

"Not really. Your father gave me the afternoon off."

"A whole afternoon? And you are spending it with Johann?"

Hans shrugged. "I do not mind. Besides, it gives me a chance to spend it with you, too." He smiled, but then his look grew serious. "I am sorry about yesterday. I did not mean to quarrel with you."

Greta sighed. "I need to apologize as well. I think we both let our passions run away with us." He nodded, and Greta's heart lifted. All was well between them again.

Greta and Hans had always had their disagreements, but they never lasted long. They'd been friends all her life, and Greta often felt more at home in Hans's large family than she did in her own. Hans had taken to calling her *Schwesterlein* when they were growing up, and the term of endearment had thrilled her. She *hoped* he no longer thought of her only as a sister, though. Especially since her own feelings towards him were anything but sisterly.

She took a step closer, leaning over the table to watch him. His eyes were narrowed in concentration, and his dark hair fell across his forehead in careless curls. She trembled, wanting to reach up and brush it out of his eyes.

Hans turned to look up at her, and suddenly their faces were inches apart. Greta froze, wondering if the surprise she saw in his eyes was reflected in her own. Could he see how much she loved him? How much she had always loved him? Did he realize the hold he had upon her?

He did not move away, and she saw his gaze flicker from her eyes to her lips and back again. Blood rushed into her face, blossoming on her cheeks and pounding in her ears.

"Greta?" he murmured, his voice unsteady. A flicker of doubt crossed his face.

"Yes?" she breathed.

He was watching her intently, and when his lips gently parted, she closed her eyes.

"Found it!"

Johann's triumphant shout startled them both, and the tension between them broke. Hans turned to offer his congratulations and accept the piece in question, while Greta straightened, pulling at her sleeves and striving to slow her pounding heart. Disappointment coursed through her, fizzling into irritation at the horrible timing of her youngest sibling.

"Can we put the axle together now, Hans?" Johann asked, oblivious to the tension in the air.

"Of course," Hans said brightly, stepping back to make room for Johann beside him. He looked up at Greta, his cheeks slightly pink. "Greta? Will you join us?"

But Greta shook her head. "Thank you, but no. I shall leave the builders to their work, and see to my music." She turned to leave the room, but paused at the door, looking back.

Hans was watching her, and as their eyes met, he smiled. Greta grinned, dizzy with elation, and walked down the hall to her music room.

Chapter 7

For the next several nights, Greta dreamed of Hans. It was not so unusual, since she dreamed of him often, but for him to star so prominently each night following what she was sure had almost been a kiss, left her wondering if he, too, was dreaming about her.

She sat down to the harp one afternoon, wishing to refresh herself in the event she were called upon to play by her mother. She positioned herself on the cushioned stool and pulled the harp towards her, resting the heavy instrument on her shoulder. Plucking the strings to ensure it was in tune, she began to play.

It was a mournful song she chose; Robert Ap Huw's *Song of St. Silyn*. By the time she reached the second movement, her fingers were sore. She had not played the harp for so long that the callouses on her fingertips had softened, and her fingers were red and throbbing. Her arms ached too, although her daily rides kept them stronger than they might otherwise have been.

Her thoughts drifted to Hans as she sat massaging her hands, and she closed her eyes, remembering the moment they had shared earlier in the week. Her lips tingled, and she reached up, brushing her fingers against them.

"Why did you stop?"

With a start, Greta opened her eyes to see Lord Ellsworth standing just inside the room. He was holding his gloves and riding whip in one hand, obviously having just come from the stables.

"How long have you been standing there?" Greta asked, bristling. To have the viscount appear when her thoughts were on Hans felt like an intrusion of the most personal kind.

"Please, do not be angry. I was on my way to my room when I heard the harp. Normally you play the pianoforte, and the sound of the harp made me curious. It was such a beautiful melody— almost haunting—that I had to stop and listen. May I come in?"

Greta frowned. "This is a common room, Lord Ellsworth. You do not need my permission to enter."

He smiled. "It may be one of the family rooms, but it is *your* sanctuary, is it not?"

The truth of his words unnerved her, and she knew not whether to be flattered or alarmed at his observation. Finally, she lifted the harp and rested it gently on its feet, then stood and smoothed her skirts. "Of course you may come in."

Frederick inclined his head in thanks and made his way to where she stood. She felt awkward as she waited for him, and that made her angry. Who was he to make her uncomfortable in her own home? And why was he always around when she wished to be alone? Was he not here on business with her father? When he reached her side, she lifted her chin and looked him squarely in the eye, ready to tell him precisely how she felt about his presence there.

It was not what she should have done. His warm brown eyes were alight with wonder, and the admiration she saw there surprised her. Before she could arrange her thoughts, he spoke.

"I have lived with music since I was a child, but never in my life have I been so captivated by a melody as I have been in this house," he said. "Tell me—how old were you when you began to play?"

She hesitated. "Which instrument?" she finally asked.

He laughed, and the sound was rich and warm to match his eyes. "Any—pick one. Which did you learn first?"

"The pianoforte. I was three years old."

He shook his head; a smile stretched across his face. "Astounding. When did you learn your next instrument?"

"When I was five I began lessons on the lute. The harp, mandolin, and viola came after that."

"But you prefer the pianoforte."

It was not a question, and his tone surprised her. "Yes," she said slowly. "I do."

She frowned, struggling to find the words for what she was feeling—something between pleased and embarrassed, flattered and angry. He watched her, his own smiled fading, until he finally ducked his head.

"Forgive me, Fräulein, I did not mean to be presumptuous."

Greta sighed. "It is nothing. Your words surprised me, is all."

"Well, considering that you have been nothing *but* a surprise, I suppose it was time I returned the sentiment." He smiled, indicating the pianoforte behind her. "Please, would you play something now?"

She nodded, grateful to be done with words, and moved towards the instrument. Before she sat down, however, Katarina came into the room. She slowed when she saw the two of them together, and a sly grin flashed across her face. She quickly crossed over to them.

"Lord Ellsworth," she said sweetly, dropping a curtsy. "My father would like a word with you. He is in his study."

"Thank you, Fräulein, I shall go directly."

Frederick bowed to Greta and left the room. They watched him go before Katarina turned and smirked at her sister.

"Looks like you have yourself a foreign beau, Margareta," she said in a singsong voice.

"You don't know anything, Trina," Greta said, rolling her eyes and turning away.

"I know plenty more than *you* do. I know that Mama wants you to marry him, and even you cannot deny that if Mama wants the match, Papa will surely comply."

Greta turned to face her younger sister, who had just celebrated her fourteenth birthday. "Go away, Trina, and mind your own affairs."

"I will not. You cannot boss me around, and this is not your room to make me leave."

Shooting her sister a poisonous look, Greta spun on her heel and stalked off. Katarina followed behind, continuing to tease her.

"Are you not at all impressed with the viscount, Margareta? He is handsome, intelligent, and Mama says he is even more wealthy than Papa."

"Is that all you care about, Trina?" Greta asked, whirling around. She stopped so abruptly that Katarina almost ran into her.

"You are just like our mother—not caring what sort of man we marry so long as he is wealthy and titled."

Katarina gasped. "I shall tell Mama you said that!"

"I hope you do!" Greta said, fury loosing her tongue. "What do I care? You think you are so clever, Trina, but just you wait until it is your turn! Wait and see how sympathetic I will be when you are in my shoes!"

Greta stormed off, taking the stairs two at a time until she finally came to her bedchamber. She threw the door open and slammed it behind her, not knowing or caring whether Trina was still hot on her heels.

"You wished to see me, Herr Rodenburg?"

"Lord Ellsworth, yes. Please come in."

Herr Rodenburg stood as the viscount entered his study. He held out a folded piece of paper to his guest.

"What is this?"

"A letter. It was mixed with my own mail. I apologize for the delay in getting it to you—I am only just now sorting through my business from yesterday."

Frederick broke the seal and unfolded the paper as Herr Rodenburg pulled out his favorite pipe. He tamped in some fresh tobacco, watching the viscount.

"What do you hear from England?" Herr Rodenburg asked, lighting his pipe.

Frederick was quiet, reading the letter. When he finished, he folded it up and placed it in his pocket. He was not smiling.

"More political unrest?" Herr Rodenburg prodded. Frederick shook his head.

"No. It is not from a colleague. It is from my father's steward."

Herr Rodenburg puffed thoughtfully on his pipe. "And what news does he send from Kent?"

Fredrick walked to the window and clasped his hands behind his back, looking out on the lawn. "My father's health is failing."

"Oh. I am sorry to hear it."

Frederick made no reply.

"Will you be traveling home to see him, then?"

"No. He does not have much time left. We knew this, and said our goodbyes before I came to Prussia. I will not be leaving my assignment at present."

Herr Rodenburg frowned. "Surely your king will understand if you wish to see your dying father," he said, puffing on his pipe.

"Perhaps. But my father would not wish to see me."

"Not wish to see you!"

"No. Not under the circumstances." Frederick glanced over his shoulder at Herr Rodenburg, who was lounging in an armchair near the fireplace. "My father has a great deal of affection for me, but an even greater sense of duty. He knows the commitment I made when I entered into the employ of my king, and he would never forgive me for breaking the vow of service I made to my sovereign."

"But surely, when your father passes on…" Herr Rodenburg lifted his brow.

Frederick sighed. "Yes. Then I shall go. But not before." He looked out the window, past the lawn and hedges, to the wild forest beyond. "I will be duty-bound in another way, then," he said, almost to himself.

The men were silent, and Frederick allowed his mind to consider again the idea that had been percolating in his mind for the last fortnight. With his father's failing health, it was now a very real possibility. But how would his plan be received? He glanced behind him at the other gentleman. Herr Rodenburg was watching him, and when their eyes met, the older man stood.

"And when your father passes on? What do you plan to do then?"

Frederick resumed gazing out the window. He was not averse to the idea of getting married, but it had never been a priority for him. Now, with his impending inheritance, he knew the time had come.

"What plans have you for your eldest daughter, Herr Rodenburg?" he said slowly.

"Greta? She is still being tutored, and while I had hoped to send her to university, I do not believe my fellow countrymen are ready to embrace women in the academic world. And with the current political climate throughout Europe, I am averse to sending her somewhere foreign."

"Have you no desire to see her married?"

"In due course, yes. Given her mother's title and my situation, she will not want for suitors when the time comes."

"And when is that to be?"

Herr Rodenburg frowned at the viscount, who was looking intently at his host. "Not for several years, *mein Freund.* Why do you ask?"

Frederick looked out the open doorway, towards the silent music room.

"I wondered if you would consider engaging her in marriage to myself."

"Marriage! She is only sixteen!"

"Plenty of women marry at sixteen, Herr Rodenburg."

Herr Rodenburg was silent, rubbing his chin. "That is true. But, Greta is so young! And stubborn."

"And I am a bit older, and slightly less stubborn," the viscount grinned. He then sighed, and shook his head. His look turned serious. "Would you at least consider it, Herr Rodenburg? You know my situation, and know that it would be a very advantageous match for her. For your whole family."

"And for you?" Herr Rodenburg asked, raising an eyebrow.

"With my father's failing health, I can no longer ignore the duty I have to my family," he said, rubbing his eyes. "Some day I must marry, Herr Rodenburg, and while I can return to England and enter the marriage mart there," he made a face, "I would much rather settle the matter before my return. My duties to both my family and my country will be better balanced with a wife by my side. Fräulein Rodenburg is bright, energetic, and willing to learn. I cannot think of any finer qualities suited to my future wife."

Herr Rodenburg sighed. "I will think about it, Lord Ellsworth," he said. "But I will make you no promises."

Frederick nodded. "That is all I am asking."

Chapter 8

Greta awoke early the next morning, intent on walking to the Schneider's home to visit with Hans before her lessons. Sparrows, starlings, and magpies all cried for their breakfast, their songs broken by the occasional cry of a crow. The sunlight filtered through the trees like speckled gold, and Greta breathed in the soft, warm air. It smelled of earth and clover.

Cutting through a nearby field, Greta heard a familiar voice on the road up ahead. She quickened her pace, her heart racing out ahead of her.

"*Fuss!*" Hans called. A pair of pointers were frolicking ahead of him, but turned and walked beside him at the command. He crooned at them in praise, but he stopped short at the sight of Greta approaching from the meadow. The surprise on his face quickly gave way to a grin.

"Greta! What are you doing here?"

"I was on my way to see you. Are you taking the dogs for a hunt?"

"Training, per your father's request. Marta is an old hand, but I am hoping she can teach her pup Rodolfo here a thing or two. Eh, Rolo?"

He tousled the larger dog's ears and patted him firmly on the side. The silver shorthair yipped and rubbed against his leg.

Greta smiled. "Papa says you are the best trainer the dogs have ever had."

Hans ducked his head. "Anyone can train a dog. You just have to know how to speak their language."

"And what language is that?"

"The same language for every creature," Hans said, dropping to one knee to rub the dog's belly. "Kindness, affection, loyalty."

"Love?"

He looked up at her, and Greta flushed. Had she been too bold? *No*, she thought. *Surely he knows how I feel.* She waited, her hands clasped in front of her, her eyes willing him to speak.

For a moment Hans said nothing, then he dropped his eyes. "Yes, love is certainly a universal language."

He glanced up again, and their eyes met. The longer she looked at him the faster her heart beat. He got to his feet in one fluid motion, and she tipped her head back, not breaking his gaze.

"Greta," he said, his voice hesitant. "About the other day…"

"Yes?"

He was standing closer than he had been, and Greta could count the curls on his forehead. She forced herself to breathe, not daring to look away from his face. He was no longer smiling, and his eyes looked troubled. Did he want to kiss her? Was he worried about her reaction? She smiled at him—gently, encouragingly, and reached her hand towards him.

But Hans stepped back, rubbing the back of his neck and blowing out his breath. Smiling crookedly, he looked back at her. "Has Johann broken the carriage yet?"

"The… carriage?"

"The model we built the other day. Is it still in one piece?"

"Oh." Greta tried to gather her tangled thoughts, forcing her disappointment away from her tone. "I am not sure. I have not seen him with it."

"That is a good sign. You are sure to hear his cries if anything should happen to it," Hans chuckled.

He whistled, and the dogs came to stand beside him. It was clear that he wished to go, but Greta was not ready to say goodbye.

"Your father was at the house this morning," she said, grasping at anything to keep him talking, keep him standing there, beside her.

Hans raised his brow, an amused smile on his lips. "My father is often at the house, Greta."

"Yes, of course." She blushed, twisting her hands together. "I overheard him talking with my father the other day. It appears he would like to retire in a year or two."

The smile on Hans's face faded. "He may wish to retire, but it does not follow that I will be the one to replace him."

"Why ever not? What else would you do?" She frowned. "Surely you are not still considering entering the military…"

Her voice trailed off expectantly, but he said nothing as he crouched down again, rubbing the hounds and speaking to them softly. After a moment he looked up.

"Ernst is considering it. He would like to escape his lot in life

73

as well."

"Ernst is the son of a drunken blacksmith. Anyone would wish to be out from under his father's thumb."

"Why does that make his choice valid but not mine? Are only those consigned to a hopelessly destitute fate allowed the privilege of dreaming of another life?" Hans was on his feet again, his eyes flashing.

"But Hans, think of it! You have a brilliant future ahead of you —a life of comfort, respectability, and relative ease. Why on earth would you wish for anything else?"

"You should talk! All your life, you have fought against the future you have been prepared for. If your mother has her way, you will become the worthy and admirable wife to a man both titled and wealthy. Is that not what every girl dreams of? Yet you have fought against her tooth and nail!"

"It is not the same," Greta said. "I am a woman—I can do nothing of myself; I can have no merit of my own! If I were a man, I would—"

"You would feel exactly the same way, Greta," Hans said firmly. She shook her head, and his look softened. "I *know* you, Greta. I know your independence. Being a woman has very little to do with how you feel. If you were born the eldest son, you would feel just as trapped, just as rebellious as you do now. Even knowing the life of privilege and honor you would have; knowing that you would inherit all that your father owns... you would be just as resentful towards your duty and your lot in life as you are now."

The words hung heavily in the air between them. Greta bit her lip, striving to hold her tears in check. Hans watched her looking anywhere but at him, and at last he sighed, rubbing his eyes. "Forgive me, Greta. You know I have a habit of speaking my mind too plainly in your presence." He smiled softly. "Old friends, you know."

She made no response, and he continued. "All I ask," he said, more gently this time, "is that I be allowed the same courtesy as you, or Ernst, or anyone else dissatisfied with their lot in life. If there is an opportunity for me to make a different life for myself, one of my *own* choosing, can you blame me for wanting to take hold of it?"

Slowly she shook her head, and he let out his breath. "Thank you, *meine Freundin*. I am happy to have your understanding at last."

He bridged the gap between them in one stride, bending down and brushing a kiss on her cheek. Grinning, he touched the brim of his hat and strode off, calling to the dogs, who had wandered into the surrounding brush.

Greta remained motionless, the shock from his kiss still frozen on her face. Slowly she reached a hand up and touched her cheek, tracing her fingers along the place where his lips had been.

An hour after she left, Greta returned to the house, humming to herself. The encounter with Hans carried her through the rest of the morning in the highest of spirits. She floated through her lessons without a single rude comment or deliberate mistake for the first time in weeks. Dinner, likewise, was a happy affair. Lord Ellsworth was polite and attentive, and Greta was still so elated from Hans's kiss that she could not help but reciprocate. Frau Rodenburg was practically purring with delight as she watched their exchanges over the meal, and Herr Rodenburg was no less pleased. Though he contributed to the conversation when necessary, he was more inclined to silently observe both the viscount and his daughter. What he saw must have encouraged him, for he called Greta into his study shortly after the meal.

"You wished to see me, Papa?"

"Yes, *Schatz*. Please, come in."

Greta chose a comfortable chair by the window, carefully arranging her skirts before sitting down. Herr Rodenburg paced in front of her, puffing on his pipe.

"Margareta, my dear, there is a serious matter I wish to discuss with you."

"Yes, Papa?"

He stopped and took a long draw from his pipe, considering her. Greta's face was turned up expectantly, her lips slightly parted in a gentle smile. He coughed.

"Greta, I am wondering how you feel about… marriage."

She blinked. "Marriage?"

"Yes." Herr Rodenburg began pacing again, relieved that the subject had been broached. "How do you feel about it?"

Greta frowned. "Papa, I am only sixteen."

"Yes, yes, but I want to know how you feel about it in general. The entire institution of marriage. Is it something you are looking forward to?"

A whirlwind of thought and emotion raged inside of her as Greta considered his question. At the forefront of it all was Hans. "I… I would like to be married someday, Papa," she said,

76

flushing slightly.

"*Das ist gut!* I am sure you know that your mother and I would be pleased to see you happily married and settled in a comfortable home of your own someday."

"*Someday,*" Greta said forcefully, suddenly nervous.

"Yes, *Schatz*, someday," he chuckled. "In a year or two, or perhaps even three. After you have completed your studies."

Greta relaxed. The ambassador would return to England long before then. If they were talking about some distant day in the future, perhaps they were speaking of—

"Of course, when you will be married will depend largely upon your own wishes."

A flurry of excitement began to build inside her. She thought of Hans's kiss on her cheek, of the moment they had shared in the parlor, and her excitement burst into a flame of desire. She wondered how his strong arms would feel clasped around her, pulling her close. She closed her eyes and imagined his lips on her mouth, and suddenly she found she could hardly breathe.

Swallowing, she opened her eyes and glanced up at her father. He was looking away from her, puffing on his pipe. "I think the timing of my marriage will depend upon the gentleman in question," she said.

"Precisely!" Herr Rodenburg said as he turned, pointing his pipe at her. "Not every man is worthy of my dear Margareta. He must be a man of sense and intelligence—"

"—who is passionate and kind," Greta broke in.

"Respectable, honorable, and acquainted with the customs of our people," Herr Rodenburg added, nodding.

"And handsome," Greta grinned.

Her father chuckled. "Ach, *Schatz*, looks are not so terribly important! But I believe we shall have no trouble finding a handsome husband for you."

Greta was trembling with excitement. They had described Hans perfectly. Was it possible that her father knew her so well as to be able to read the deepest desires of her heart?

"If we could find such a man, Papa," she said slowly, "I would not be so averse to marrying young."

"*Wirklich*? I thought you were concerned that you were only sixteen?"

"Plenty of women are married at sixteen, Papa."

Herr Rodenburg puffed his pipe thoughtfully, a smile playing about his lips. "Yes, I suppose they are."

He moved to the window and looked out across the park. Greta watched the smoke drifting in lazy clouds around his head, her heart hammering in her chest. At last he turned and made his way back to the desk. Putting out his pipe, he set it down and took a seat in the chair across from her.

"Greta," he said slowly, taking her hands. "You know how much I care for you."

"And I you, Papa."

"Yes." He squeezed her hands. "*Schatz*, I believe I have found the type of man we have been describing. You know him quite well, in fact."

Greta smiled.

"He has come to me with a proposal to consider."

An image of Hans and Peter Schneider shut up in her father's study the week before flashed into her mind, and her chest constricted.

"Margareta, he asked if I would arrange a marriage between himself and my eldest daughter—that is to say, with you."

He paused, and Greta stopped breathing.

"At first, I was not convinced it was a good idea. You are so young, after all," Herr Rodenburg said, smiling at her. "But after our discussion just now, I am far less concerned. It is clear that you are mature beyond your years, and eager to fulfill your duties as a wife and mother."

"Yes, Papa, I am," Greta said, breathless.

"*Gut.* I shall have the paperwork drawn up for a formal betrothal tomorrow, and you and Lord Ellsworth shall be married in two months' time."

Chapter 9

The silence in the room lasted merely a moment. It took Greta only half a second to realize that her dearest dream had morphed into a terrible nightmare. In the very next instant she was on her feet, shouting at her father.

"I will do no such thing!" she cried. "Marry Lord Ellsworth? *Nie!* Never!"

Herr Rodenburg stared at his daughter, completely dumbfounded.

"How could you even suggest such a thing? Papa, he is nearly twice my age!"

"Greta," Herr Rodenburg said, having at last found his voice. "I do not understand. You said you wanted to marry him!"

"I never said anything of the sort," she said, the fury she felt causing every inch of her body to tremble. "I thought you were speaking of Hans!"

"*Hans*? Hans Schneider? Really, Greta, the very idea!"

She glared at him. "Why not? Hans is every bit the gentleman and possesses every quality you listed as necessary in a suitable husband."

"I hardly thought it necessary to stipulate that the gentleman you marry must also belong to the gentry, Margareta," he said bitingly. "I thought you understood that."

"And I thought you understood *me!*"

Greta dropped into a chair and buried her face in her hands. Great shuddering sobs wracked her body as she struggled to breathe. "I cannot marry him, Papa, I cannot. I do not love him. I love Hans."

Herr Rodenburg's mood had swiftly soured. He fished around in his pocket for a handkerchief and thrust it at her.

"For heaven's sake, calm down, Margareta."

She took the handkerchief from him and blew her nose. Herr Rodenburg took up his pipe again and relit it, puffing furiously.

"If you continue in this manner there can be no reasoning with you," he declared. "Go back to your room and think it over."

"I do not need to think it over, Papa. I will not marry him!"

"*Ich glaub mich knutscht ein Elch!* I have heard enough!" he said, finally losing his patience. "Have you forgotten who is the head of this house, Margareta? Have you forgotten that I alone make decisions for this family? Leave me now; I will hear no more."

He strode swiftly to the door and opened it, standing back to let her pass. Greta lurched to her feet and tore from the room, tripping over her skirts and stumbling on the stairs. She ignored the concerned exclamations of the servants she passed, thinking only of gaining the refuge of her room and never coming out again.

Greta was so hasty in her flight that she nearly ran headlong into her sister as she emerged onto the second floor corridor. Katarina cried out in indignation, but stopped short when she saw her sister's face.

"Why, Margareta!" she exclaimed. "What is the matter?"

"Nothing to concern *you*, Trina," Greta said, pushing past her. "Let me alone."

Greta reached her bedchamber and slammed the door behind her. Lisbet, who was sitting by the window mending one of Greta's dresses, jumped at her mistress's violent entrance.

"Fräulein! What a fright you gave me! What is wrong, child?"

"My father has arranged a marriage for me," Greta choked out, dropping onto her bed.

Laying down her work, Lisbet went to her side and pulled Greta into her arms. Greta rested her forehead on her maid's shoulder and wept.

"There, there, Fräulein. It will be all right."

"I do not see how," Greta sniffed. "Papa was simply horrid. He would not listen to a word of my argument—he insists that I marry him!"

"May I ask whom the gentleman in question is?"

"That English ambassador, Lord Ellsworth."

There was a sharp rap on the door and both of them turned. Greta sat up as Lisbet rose to answer it.

"If it is Trina, tell her to stick her fat nose in a book and let me alone," Greta said.

But when Lisbet opened the door, it was Frau Rodenburg standing there.

"Leave us," she commanded, sweeping into the room. Lisbet

curtsied and left, shutting the door behind her.

"Margareta," her mother began. "Your sister just informed me that you ran up the stairs in a terrible state a few moments ago. What has happened?"

Greta dried her eyes and swallowed the remainder of her tears. "I was upset by something Papa told me, that is all."

Frau Rodenburg's eyes narrowed. "What did he tell you?"

If Greta had received no sympathy from her father, she certainly did not expect any from her mother. She lifted her chin and looked her squarely in the eye. "He wishes to arrange a marriage between myself and Lord Ellsworth."

There was silence in the room as the women stared at one another. At last Frau Rodenburg moved to a chair and sat down.

"This has upset you, *meine Kind*. Why?"

"Because I do not love him!"

Her mother waved a hand dismissively in the air. "Marriage is not meant as an institution of affection, Margareta," she said. "It is our duty as women to marry, bear children, and run the households of our husbands. Love and affection, if they come, are a blessing to a marriage, not a foundation for it."

The calm manner in which she delivered this sermon rankled Greta, but she knew she could not speak her mind to her mother as she had to her father. She sighed and shook her head, choosing her words carefully.

"Mama, I know that you and Papa were married when you barely knew one another, but I do not want that for myself. If I am to spend the rest of my life with a man, I intend to know and love him before I marry him."

"It does not work that way, Margareta!" Frau Rodenburg said, losing her patience. "Marriages are arranged by the parents, to be both suitable and advantageous to all parties. Lord Ellsworth is perfectly suited to you, and you would do well—"

"We hardly know him! How can you say that we are suited to one another when we have only known him for a few weeks' time!"

"Margareta," her mother said, rising from her seat. Her voice was dangerously low. "You will marry Lord Ellsworth, just as your father has arranged, and that is the end of it."

She sailed out of the room without a backward glance. Furious, Greta grabbed a pillow and pressed it to her face, screaming into the feathers.

Greta passed the remainder of the day in her room. She refused to join her parents and their guest for supper, and in turn, Frau Rodenburg refused to allow the servants to take a meal up to her. When at last the sun began to set and the candles had been lit, Greta crept from her chambers and made her way silently down the hall, toward the far end of the house and the servants' staircase there. She paused at the top, listening, then continued swiftly down. She encountered no one. Slipping outside, she gathered her skirts about her and sped off into the dusk. Greta's stomach growled as she made her way down the lane, but food would have to wait.

She had to see Hans.

Several windows were lit in the little manor where the Schneiders lived. She knew the house well, having spent many happy days there in her youth. Hans had been her principle playmate as a child, and though he was four years older than she, they got along splendidly. Greta had always been happy to go along with any of Hans's schemes, whether it was climbing up trees to gather birds' nests, or sneaking off in the dark to fish by moonlight. She smiled at the memories that flooded her mind as she stepped up to the front door and knocked. After a moment it was opened by one of Hans's younger brothers, Gregor.

"*Guten Abend*, Greta," he said.

"*Guten Abend*, Gregor. Is Hans at home?"

"You just missed him," he replied, hitching a thumb over his shoulder. "He and Ernst walked back to town with Julianna."

Greta's stomach clenched. "Julianna?"

"*Ja*. She and Ernst were here for supper, but they had to get back to town before the gates close for the night."

"I see. Thank you, Gregor."

She started down the lane again, her heart sick. "You are being ridiculous," she told herself, trying to shake the leaden feeling in her gut. "Juli is as much your friend as she is Hans's."

She took the road leading to town at a brisk pace. The sun was now below the horizon, and Greta wished she had brought her cloak. A half mile down the road, Hans came into view, and Greta gratefully called out to him. He hastened his pace until he stood beside her.

"Greta! What brings you here?"

Looking up at him caused a lump to form in her throat. The breeze had mussed his hair so that the dark curls fell across his brow in perfect disarray. Even in the dim light, his eyes were smiling at her, and the grin stretched across his face spoke straight to her heart.

He was perfect, and she loved him so much she felt as if her heart would burst.

"Hans," she said, relief flooding her voice. "I am so glad to see you."

"Is something wrong?" he asked, an edge of concern creeping into his voice.

She swallowed. "Yes, but no one is hurt or ill. Come—will you walk with me?"

She took his arm and they turned back, walking in silence for a few minutes, until Greta slowed to a stop. Hans stopped beside her, and for the first time he noticed that she was trembling. He shrugged out of his jacket and threw it around her shoulders.

"Thank you," she said quietly.

"*Bitte schön*, Greta. But why are you out without a cloak? The night air is chilly—we must get you home."

"No, Hans, wait." Greta took a deep breath. "I cannot go home."

"Why? What has happened?"

Greta's eyes filled with tears, and she threw herself into his arms. "Oh, Hans! My father has arranged a marriage for me," she sobbed. "He insists that I marry that horrid English ambassador, Lord Ellsworth."

Hans did not know whether he was more shocked by her news, or to find Greta in his arms. He held on to her awkwardly, not quite sure what to do.

"I told Papa that I would not marry him, but he would not listen. My mother has wanted the match all along, so naturally she says I must comply. But I cannot marry him, Hans, I cannot!"

She clung to him, sobbing, until he dug a handkerchief out of his pocket and held it out for her. She took it, stepping away to dry her eyes. Relieved, Hans took a step back as well.

"There now, Greta, why all the fuss? He seems a decent fellow —why can you not marry him?"

She stared at him. "You cannot be serious, Hans. Marry him? *Him?* How can I possibly marry *him* when you know full well that I love—" She stopped, suddenly afraid. Had she misjudged him?

"Not everyone marries for love, Greta," Hans said gently.

Greta bit her lip. "Perhaps not," she said. "But I have always wished to marry for love, Hans. Is that not what you want as well?"

"Of course it is."

"And I do not wish to marry a stranger."

"Nor do I."

She relaxed. "Oh Hans, I am so glad to hear it. I was afraid…" She stopped again. The image of Hans and Julianna dancing together thrust itself upon her mind, but she shook it off, smiling up at him. "But it does not signify. Not when we both want the same thing. I knew I could count on you. That is why I came in search of you this evening. You are the only one who can help me, Hans."

"Help you?"

"Yes." Taking a deep breath, she reached for him. "I love you, Hans, and I have no desire to marry anyone but you."

Hans's mouth dropped open, and Greta's face flushed scarlet. There—she had said it. She took another breath, gathering her courage.

"Hans, I am sure you knew that I loved you. How could you not? Ever since we were children, I have loved you. And I *know* you care for me. Please, Hans—can we not run away? I know that our relative situations are such that—"

"Greta…"

" —we cannot expect the blessings of our parents, but what need have we of them? If we love each other, Hans, we can—"

"Greta!"

She stopped, her eyes glistening. Though his look was tender, his jaw was set. "Greta, you cannot be serious. Run away together? It is madness!"

"But why not? You said yourself that you wished for a different life—here it is! We can go to France, or even as far as Spain if you like. I do not care where we go, so long as I am with you. I love you, Hans."

She reached for him again, but he took a step back. Dragging a hand up through his hair, he looked away. His curls were now standing on end, and he blew out his breath.

"Greta," he said, searching her face. "I *do* care for you. I do. We have known each other all our lives—how could I help but care for you? But, Greta, it is only that. I feel for you the affection of an older brother; nothing more. I do not love you, Greta—not in the way you think I do, not in the way you wish for me to."

"You… do not love me?"

Hans forced himself to look in her eyes. They were huge, staring up at him in desperate disbelief. He closed his eyes.

"No, Greta. I do not love you."

Chapter 10

Greta felt as though she were underwater. She heard his words and saw his face, but it was through the murky lens of disbelief. She shook her head slowly, trying to gather her bearings.

"I did not know," she murmured. "I thought... I always thought..." Her voice trailed off, and she reached up to brush at the curl on her forehead.

"Greta, I'm sorry," Hans said gently.

"Sorry? For what? Oh," she said, her voice trembling slightly, "sorry that you do not care for me in that way? It is nothing."

Hans's sympathetic look tore a hole in her already gaping heart.

"It is natural that you should care for me like a sister. Were we not raised together as such? It was so long before I had siblings of my own, you know. And you have ever so many—younger siblings, that is. And you care for each of them. Just as you care for me."

She was rambling, desperately trying to hold herself together long enough to escape him. She took a step backwards, pasting a smile on her lips.

"Greta, you do not have to pretend."

"Pretend? Pretend what?" She forced a laugh, but it came out more hysterical than disinterested. She coughed in an attempt to hide it.

"I cannot marry you, Greta," Hans said gently. "But that does not mean you cannot marry the viscount. He must be a good man, if your father approves. He will make a fine husband for you."

The delicate thread holding reason in place snapped in Greta's mind. "A *fine husband?* Hans, he is nearly twice my age!"

"Come, Greta, do not exaggerate. He cannot be more than thirty."

"And *I* am sixteen."

"That is no great difference. When you are eighty he shall be only ninety-five."

His attempt at humor did not sit well. She glared at him, and he sighed. "Greta, it is your duty as the daughter of nobility to marry whomever your parents choose for you. You know that— everyone knows that! Marriages are arranged all the time.

"I know you think that you will be happy if you marry someone you love, but that is not always the case—just look at what happened to Ernst's parents. The surest way to happiness is by doing your duty. Listen to your parents. They love you, Greta, and they want what is best for you. If you marry the viscount, I am convinced that you *will* be happy, if for no other reason than knowing that you did your duty."

Greta's eyes flashed. "What right have you to speak of duty to me? You will not even acknowledge your own duty, let alone accept the responsibilities that are yours to perform."

"In joining the army I shall be doing a great service to my country," he shot back. "It is my duty as a citizen of Prussia to take up arms in defense of my fellow countrymen."

"Hans, we are not at war with anyone at present—least of all the Americans."

Without a word, he turned on his heel and strode off. What little light remained was only just enough for Greta to follow after him. She stumbled in the dirt, tripping on the hem of her skirts in her haste to catch up.

"Please, Hans, forgive me."

He grunted.

"I know it is my duty to be an obedient daughter, but Hans, I cannot help feeling as I do. How would you feel if suddenly you found your future laid out before you, without any possibility of choosing it for yourself?"

He stopped abruptly, glaring at her, and she blanched. Greta reached out and laid a hand on his arm.

"Please, Hans," she whispered, her eyes filling with tears once more. "Please, take me away from here. Do not make me marry him."

"It is your duty, Greta. I cannot help you."

Tearing off his jacket, she shoved it into his chest. "You are a coward," she choked out. "You are afraid of facing my father if he should discover where we have run off to. But I am willing to risk my life for your love, Hans. If you were honest with yourself, I think you would find that you love me just as much as I love you. The difference is that I am not ashamed to declare it."

She spun on her heel and stalked off, but Hans caught her

elbow. "Greta, it is not like that!" he said. "I told you before, I do not—"

"No, Hans, please! Do not repeat it. If you say it again, you may begin to believe it yourself, and then there will be no hope for me. I love you, Hans, and I am willing to wait as long as it takes for you to acknowledge that you love me as well."

"You will be waiting forever, Greta. I cannot make my heart love someone it does not."

She shook her head angrily and turned away again, but he caught her in his arms and pulled her close. She struggled against him for only a moment before burying her face in his chest.

"Greta," he said, his voice husky. "You are an amazing woman. Stubborn and headstrong, yes, but brilliant and beautiful and so many other wonderful things. You will make a wonderful wife someday, but not to me. You *must* accept that, Greta. I cannot allow you to hope."

He bent down and kissed her on the forehead. With a sob, Greta pushed against his chest and broke free from his embrace. Picking up her skirts, she turned and ran headlong for her home, stumbling and crying as she disappeared into the darkness.

Chapter 11

The rest of the week was the most miserable of Greta's life. Nothing could console her after Hans's rejection. At first, she locked herself in her room and refused to come out. The rest of the household, of course, thought her actions were still in defiance of her betrothal to Lord Ellsworth. But after missing supper two days in a row, Frau Rodenburg marched upstairs and demanded that she present herself. Greta complied, but was so cross during the meal that her father ordered her away to await him in his study.

"Margareta, it is high time you stopped moping about and accept your responsibility," he said as he shut the door behind him.

Greta was slumped in a chair near the window, staring dejectedly out into the darkness. Herr Rodenburg sighed.

"*Schatz*, I know this is not what you wish. But it is your duty and responsibility, as a Rodenburg, to—"

"Oh, hang my duties and responsibilities!" Greta cried,

jumping to her feet. "I wish I was anyone *but* a Rodenburg!"

The moment she spoke the words, Greta wished them unsaid. She saw the pain flash across her father's face before she heard it in his voice. When he spoke, his words were measured and calm, but the disappointment and hurt were there, lurking under the surface.

"You have been born into a life of privilege, and because it is so, you are under certain obligations. I thought that you had accepted our position as a family and the rights, privileges, and responsibilities that come with our standing. But your behavior on this matter has greatly disappointed both your mother and I, not to mention your future husband."

Greta could not meet his gaze. She tried to swallow past the lump in her throat, but it remained firmly in its place.

"Now, about Hans."

Her head snapped up, dislodging the temperamental curl that insisted on haunting her forehead.

"I knew you harbored a certain fondness for him when you were a child—anyone could see how you practically worshiped him then. But I never dreamed that your girlish infatuation would survive beyond the nursery." He frowned at her, and his voice grew stern. "It cannot continue, Greta. From this time forth, you will have no more contact with him. I have already spoken with his father, and he is in agreement. Hans will continue to learn his duties here, but he is not to speak with you, nor are you to seek him out. Violating these rules will jeopardize his future position, so see that you obey them."

The guilt Greta had felt at the harshness of her earlier words disappeared. She felt nothing but white hot fury. How dare her father dictate with whom she may associate! She opened her mouth to retort, but Herr Rodenburg held up a hand.

"I indulged your tongue once before, Margareta, but I will not do so again." There was an edge to his voice that Greta was not accustomed to hearing.

She glared at him, grinding her teeth together. Herr Rodenburg walked wearily to the chair behind his desk and sat down. Greta stood, reaching for the door with a trembling hand.

"Oh, and Greta," her father called out. She did not turn. "I have found a new tutor for you. Your French lessons will resume this week, as before."

Greta threw her shoulders back and stalked out of the room, not stopping until she had gained the stairs. Furious tears leaked out of her eyes and ran dripping down her chin, which only angered her more. Tears were a sign of weakness, and before last month Greta had prided herself that she rarely cried. But ever since the ambassador had arrived and turned her life upside-down, she had become a veritable watering pot.

Having gained the second floor, Greta stormed into her room, slamming the door so hard that the crystals hanging from the massive chandelier in the entrance hall rang and jangled together.

Herr Rodenburg rubbed his brow, feeling far more weary than his forty-six years. Greta had always been high-spirited and stubborn, but he never imagined she would so adamantly refuse to comply with his wishes. He pulled out his favorite pipe and tamped down some fresh tobacco. Lighting it, he leaned back, puffing slowly as he contemplated what to do.

He looked up at a knock on the open door, and saw Lord Ellsworth standing there. Motioning the viscount in, Herr Rodenburg stood.

Frederick shut the door quietly behind him. "I saw Fräulein Rodenburg just now, heading upstairs. She looked upset."

Herr Rodenburg sighed. "*Es tut mir leid*, Lord Ellsworth. Forgive me, but my daughter is less receptive to the idea of marrying you than I was led to believe."

The viscount shrugged. "She is young. It is natural that she would resist such interference in her life."

Herr Rodenburg shook his head and sat down once more, gesturing for his guest to sit as well. "She may be young, but she certainly knows her mind. I am afraid, Lord Ellsworth, that you may not desire her for your wife after all."

He looked over the edge of the desk at his guest, puffing on his pipe. Frederick's brow was furrowed in thought.

"I still feel as I did before," Frederick said at length. "Her tenacity shows a firmness of mind that is admirable, and under different circumstances, could be quite valuable."

Herr Rodenburg chuckled. "*Mein Freund*, you are an incurable optimist. But what would you have me do? I have never forced Margareta into anything before, and I am averse to doing so now. She has been stubborn at times, argumentative even, but she has always complied with my wishes in the end, and by her own choice. How can I force her into marrying you when she is so set against it?"

Frederick stood and paced to the window. Crossing his hands behind his back, he gazed out into the night. A sliver of moon hung high in the sky, perfectly reflected in the still waters of the pool. Frederick smiled to himself, remembering the incident he had witnessed between Greta and her sister there.

"Would you allow me to attempt to win her hand myself?" he asked without turning.

"If you feel you are up to the challenge, I don't see why not," Herr Rodenburg answered, rubbing his forehead.

"Good. Then I shall attempt to soften her heart in my own way, rather than coerce her into giving in to your wishes. If I succeed, we can proceed with the engagement."

"And if you do not?"

Frederick looked over his shoulder at his host, his brown eyes twinkling. "Then I suppose we shall see who is the more determined between us."

Greta awoke the next morning with a raging headache. She blamed her empty stomach and her overactive tear ducts, and climbed grumpily out of bed. Drawing the curtains, she beheld a glowering sky, perfectly suited to her mood.

Lisbet came in when she was still looking out at the gloom. "Fräulein, come away from the window—what if someone should see you!"

Greta moaned and moved towards her dressing room. Lisbet had laid out a lovely cream petticoat with a green-striped jacket for her. Lying beside the gown were a small set of paniers and the hateful stays, which Greta eyed with distaste.

With the help of her maid, she was dressed in half an hour.

Upon appearing in the breakfast room, she was relieved to find that her father and Lord Ellsworth were already gone—out for a morning hunt. Although Greta still had to endure her mother's pointed looks and Katarina's sly remarks, it was far less awkward without the viscount present.

After the meal, Greta gave directions to have her horse saddled, then retired to her room to don her riding habit. Her head still ached and she was not particularly in the mood for a ride, but she had to get out of the house. If she remained, another lecture from her mother was surely forthcoming, and she had not the energy to endure another such ordeal.

Greta's horse was waiting for her by the time she went outside. Franco was a four-year-old stallion, standing fifteen hands high. He had a glossy brown coat, but his mane, tail, and stockings were black. Taking a lump of sugar from the groomsman, Greta held it up and let Franco lick it from her gloved palm. She rubbed his nose and spoke soothingly to him in French, which was a habit she had fallen into of late. Herr Rodenburg had given Franco to his daughter as a foal, and Greta was quite fond of him.

Placing her foot securely in the stirrup, Greta swung her leg over the back of the horse and settled herself into the saddle. She felt at once the familiar thrill of freedom. Taking the reins in her hands, she nudged Franco into a walk, then into a trot, and upon clearing the gate at the end of the lane, finally let him run.

The thrill of riding a horse at a high gallop always took her breath away. The moment Greta felt Franco shift and lunge underneath the saddle, her breath caught in her chest and her stomach dropped to her toes. She let her horse have his head for several minutes before reining him in. Leading him off the road and into the grass, she walked him through the meadow as they both caught their breath. The day was still overcast and cool, but Greta could see the perspiration gathering along Franco's neck and she did not want to overtire him. They meandered through the meadow for a quarter hour while Greta gathered her thoughts.

If her father and Lord Ellsworth were out hunting this morning, Hans had likely accompanied them to handle the dogs. Had the men finished their hunt? Would they be heading towards the manor soon? If Hans was with her father, there would be no chance to speak to him. But perhaps when they parted ways, and Hans took the dogs back to the kennels... Greta stood up in the stirrups and glanced around. Not a sign of movement nor the sound of horses and dogs met her ears. Perhaps they were in the woods. She turned Franco in the direction of the trees and prodded him into a trot.

The clouds were growing thicker and the first few drops had fallen when Greta broke into the grove. If the men were still hunting they would certainly be turning back now. She decided to look around the woods for a few minutes before returning herself.

She had not gone far when a snap and a screech accosted her ears. Startled, Franco tossed his head and Greta nearly lost the reins. "*Doucement,*" she soothed.

Turning towards the source of the commotion, Greta edged her horse forward, searching the brush and the surrounding trees for signs of life.

"Eh now, Greta, what are you doing out here?"

Ernst stood up from where he was crouching in the bushes, not five paces from Greta.

"Oh Ernst, what a fright you gave me!"

He chuckled. "You? I was afraid you were your father. Nearly cut and run when I heard your horse coming."

Greta glanced down. Ernst was holding a dead pigeon in one hand and a large knife in the other. She frowned.

"Trapping is not allowed, you know."

He shrugged. "We need food."

"But Ernst, it is against the law! What if you were caught?"

Ernst grinned at her. "It warms my heart to hear you so concerned for my welfare, Greta."

"You are my friend, Ernst. I do not wish to see you hauled away by the *polizia*."

His smile faded. "It didn't seem to bother you at the dance."

She flushed. "That was… different."

"How?" He stepped towards the horse, looking up into her face. "If I am your *friend*, Greta, why did you not dance with me?"

"Ernst, please, you know that is not the way things are done."

"The way things are done is wrong."

He scowled and turned away, crouching down to reset his snare. Greta's eyes followed him, and she gasped when she saw a pile of animal carcasses beside him—mostly birds, but a few rabbits and squirrels as well.

"Ernst, you cannot use those snares! Especially not here. What if my father should find out?"

Ernst turned around, cocking his head. "And just how would he find out, Greta? Are you going to tell him?"

She made a sound of disgust. "Of course not."

"It doesn't seem fair, does it? That your father, with his guns and birds and dogs, is allowed to hunt whatever animal he

100

chooses, whenever he chooses, but that *we're* not allowed to use our traps and snares for the very same animals." He bent to retrieve his day's work. "I must be getting home. *Schönen Tag,* Greta."

"Ernst, wait!"

Greta nudged Franco in the flanks and followed after him. "Have you seen my father? He has been out hunting."

Ernst grunted.

"Ernst, please. I am looking for Hans—I think he was with them."

"Them? Oh, right—your bloody Englishman."

Greta bristled at his words. "He is *not* my Englishman. And don't swear."

Ernst rolled his eyes and kept walking.

"Please, Ernst. I must find Hans. Do you know where he is? Have you seen them?"

Ernst sighed and stopped walking. "I saw your father and *not* your Englishman earlier today, but Hans was not with them."

"Who was tending the dogs, then?"

"Peter Schneider."

"But… where was Hans?" Greta asked, confused. "He always manages the dogs when my father goes hunting."

Ernst shrugged and began walking again. "He probably cried off from work and spent the day with Julianna."

Greta flinched.

"Course, if *I* had a girl I was sweet on," he looked pointedly over his shoulder at her, "who wanted to spend the day with me, I'd probably cry off, too."

"And why would Julianna want Hans to miss a full day of

work? He could lose his position. That does not seem very kind of her," Greta said, her jaw tight.

Ernst stopped once again, staring at her incredulously. "Did he not tell you? Hans and I signed up as mercenaries. We leave for England in a week."

Chapter 12

The mournful notes of Mozart's 9th Concerto weighed down the air like a funeral pall. Greta played the second movement over and over again, infesting the household with her melancholy. After an hour, Frau Rodenburg's heels tapped a staccato rhythm across the polished floor of the music room.

"Really, Margareta, must you continue to play that horrid concerto? Is it not enough that you cried into your soup at supper last night, disrupting our entire meal? Select something else, or refrain from the instrument entirely."

She stalked away, and Greta glared after her. Her neck and back were aching as she rose from her place, rolling her shoulders. Perhaps she would rest for a time.

Leaving the music room, Greta walked slowly down the hall. The walls were covered in thick tapestries, with intricately carved moldings and gilt-framed portraits covering them from floor to ceiling. As she neared the grand staircase in the entrance hall, a large portrait of a much younger Herr Rodenburg caught her eye.

He was standing straight and tall, in a crisp military uniform of navy blue. He wore knee breeches of rich yellow, with a matching waistcoat and gold epaulets on his shoulders. A white sash stretched from his right shoulder down to his left hip, and a tricorn hat was tucked under one arm. He was smiling, and as Greta looked up into his face, it looked as though her own eyes were staring back at her.

Her father had served in Prussia's army long before she was born, and she had never really considered his military service. Now, with the man she loved only days away from going off to war himself, she saw her father with new eyes. Turning away from the portrait, she hurried to his study.

The door was open, but Greta knocked anyway. Herr Rodenburg looked up from his work.

"Why, Greta! Come in, *Schatz*."

"Papa," she asked, approaching his desk. "Did you know that Hans Schneider has joined the mercenaries hired by the British to fight against the American colonists?"

He studied her for a moment, then returned to the papers before him. "Yes, I did. His father told me of his plans several days ago. It is a pity—he would have made a good steward."

"Yes." Greta bit her lip. She waited for him to look up again, but he continued to read, leafing through his letters and occasionally making note of something. She cleared her throat.

"Papa, in light of his forthcoming departure, would you consider—"

"No, Greta."

"But Papa, I may never see him again! This may be my only chance to say goodbye!" Her voice caught on the last syllable, and she blinked, striving to hide her tears.

Herr Rodenburg looked up from his desk, his face a mask of determination. "Hans will come to say his goodbyes to the family on Friday—you will see him there, and can say whatever it is you wish to say to him then."

Greta marched from the study, trembling, but determined. When she arrived in her room, she sat down at her writing desk and penned a swift note.

> *Hans,*
>
>   *My father refuses to allow it, but I must speak with you. Can you meet me by the old oak at midnight?*
>   *Greta*

She folded the paper, sealed it, and rang the bell on the wall. A few minutes later, Lisbet came into the room.

"Fräulein?"

"Lisbet, I need you to deliver a message for me." Greta handed her the note, and she took it automatically. "There is no one else whom I can trust. Will you please deliver this to Hans Schneider, and bring me back his reply?"

"But, Fräulein!" Lisbet said with alarm, attempting to return the letter to her mistress. "Your father has forbidden it! You are not to have any contact with him, and the servants have been given strict instructions that—"

"*Bitte,* Lisbet, please. I *must* speak with him."

Lisbet sighed. She was several years older than Greta; closer in age to Frau Rodenburg than her daughter. But she had been with Greta ever since the latter left the nursery, and she was very fond of her. Greta's eyes were pleading, imploring her, and at last she nodded.

"*Sehr gut*, Fräulein. But only this once."

Greta hugged her, smiling for the first time all day. "I shall never ask you for anything again. Be sure that you find him as soon as may be, and Lisbet, do not come back without his reply, whatever he may say. Be sure that he reads it, and tell him you will wait for his response."

Lisbet nodded weakly and slipped the note into her pocket.

Greta did not know whom she was expecting to meet that afternoon for her French lessons, but it was certainly not Lord Ellsworth. She took two steps into the room and stopped.

"You?" she asked incredulously.

The viscount smiled. "Me." He held a chair out for her. "*Gallons-nous commencer?*"

"No." Greta turned on her heel and stomped from the room, not stopping until she reached her father's study. She rapped sharply on the door, not waiting for an invitation to enter.

"Lord Ellsworth?" she cried. "Papa! Why is he to be the one to teach me French?"

"Lord Ellsworth was the natural choice," Herr Rodenburg said calmly. "He speaks French fluently, his accent is impeccable— and even you cannot deny that he is by far the most qualified individual in the province at present."

"But Papa!"

"Margareta," he said sharply, "you requested that your French lessons be extended, and you *will* participate in them. Is that understood?"

Greta nodded stiffly, and was dismissed. She stalked back to the parlor and faced her new tutor.

"I am only here because my father insists upon it," she said brashly, sitting down and folding her arms tightly across her chest.

Frederick frowned. "I thought I understood from Herr Rodenburg that you had asked for a French tutor."

"*Je parle parfaitement le français*, Lord Ellsworth."

He laughed nervously. "Yes, I can see that. But if you speak French so well, why did you wish to continue your lessons?"

Greta was not about to admit the real reason for wanting her French lessons to continue, but the viscount was an astute observer. He took in the set of her jaw and the tightness of her shoulders before nodding.

"Unless… it was not the lessons so much as the company you wished to continue?"

Greta said nothing.

"Perhaps," he continued, "you would enjoy our lessons more if we became better acquainted."

"There is nothing more about you I wish to know, nor anything about myself I wish to divulge."

Greta knew she was being horribly rude, but she did not care. She was tired of everyone trying to force her hand. Was her life not her own to command?

Frederick put his hands behind his back and turned towards the window. "Then I believe we are at an impasse, Fräulein," he said. "Your father insists on these lessons, and I myself was looking forward to this opportunity. Yet you confess that you do not wish to participate." He glanced over at Greta, who sat in stubborn silence at the table. "Hm. How best to proceed?"

Refusing to acknowledge him further, Greta kept her eyes fixed on the view outside. Frederick stepped over to the table and perused the books there. Picking one up, he stepped into her line of sight, leafing through it. Greta turned her head.

"Have you read this book before?" he asked in French. She remained silent. *"It appears very interesting,"* he continued, looking over at her. Still she did not reply.

"If you will not speak in French, I believe we should try another language. Perhaps Italian?" he said, slipping into that tongue. *"Would that be more agreeable to you?"*

Greta's eyes flickered to his face.

"Ah! It appears you understand Italian as well. At least enough to gather what I am saying. Perhaps you would like to study Italian, instead of French?"

Greta looked away again.

"Your father told me you have studied Latin," he said, switching languages once more. *"But have you learned any Greek?"*

He waited, hoping for a response from her to guide his own. When she did not acknowledge him at all, he threw caution to the wind. *"If I told you how pretty you look, even sitting there with a scowl on your face, would you understand me?"* he said in Greek.

Greta turned with a curious look on her face. Frederick flushed. "What language are you speaking?" she asked.

"Ah!" he responded, relieved. *"You do not know what I said to you?"* he asked in Greek.

"It sounds familiar," she said with a frown, and his face relaxed. "But I do not think it is one I have heard before. Is it Hebrew?"

Frederick smiled. *"I wonder how long it will take you to guess? Clearly you are as intelligent as you are beautiful, so perhaps you will figure it out."*

Greta listened to his words intently. "It is similar to Latin," she mused. "But it is not—ah! I have it!" she cried. "It must be Greek!"

He chuckled. "Well done, Fräulein. You have a very discerning ear."

"Thank you. Will you tell me now what it is that you said to me?"

"Oh, it was nothing," he replied, setting the book back on the table and avoiding her eyes. "Speculating about all the languages you might be familiar with."

"I see." Greta rose from her seat and curtsied politely. "I believe that concludes our lesson for today, Lord Ellsworth," she said.

"Of course, if you wish," he said, bowing to her.

"I do." She smiled tightly at him, then gathered her skirts and walked towards the open door. She paused at the threshold. "Lord Ellsworth?" she called.

He looked up expectantly.

"I thank you for your compliments, but perhaps you should stick to French," she said in Greek.

Greta laughed at his startled expression all the way back to her room.

Chapter 13

Lisbet brought Hans's response shortly after supper. Greta hurried to her room, tearing open the note the moment she was alone.

Greta,

Do not think that you will be able to talk me out of it. I have signed a contract and will be leaving whether you like it or not. And if you wish only to make yourself ridiculous by again asserting my claim on your affections, I would rather not see you. I feel for you all the love of a brother and the affection of a childhood friend, but nothing more. Please do not risk the wrath of your parents by slipping out to meet me tonight, for I will not be there. I shall see you on Friday to say farewell.

Hans

The letter crumpled as Greta's hand fell into her lap. Her last hope was gone. Hans would be leaving, and he had no desire to see her before departing. Hot, angry tears spilled onto her cheeks, and she snatched up the missive again. *I feel for you all the love of a brother and the affection of a childhood friend, but nothing more*, she read again.

No! she inwardly screamed. *I* know *he loves me. I know he cares for me. He is only blinded by this infatuation with Julianna. Why can he not see that we are perfect for one another?*

She crumpled the letter and threw it to the floor. It bounced erratically towards the hearth, and in a fit of reckless anger, Greta picked it up and tossed it into the grate. The fire had just been lit, and the flames licked hungrily at the ball of paper. She watched as the letter disintegrated, feeling as though it were her heart turning to ash. When nothing was left, she slipped out of her clothes, climbed into bed, and cried herself to sleep.

When Friday came at last, Greta was not sure whether she was more relieved or upset. She both longed for and feared the moment when Hans's presence would be announced; when she and her family would say goodbye. How was she to behave? How could she possibly say goodbye, perhaps forever, to the man she loved?

The morning hours crept by. She was inattentive and irritable during her lessons, and at dinner she barely touched her food. When her father expressed his concern and asked what was troubling her, Greta merely answered that she was not hungry.

Frau Rodenburg said nothing.

It was late in the afternoon when he finally came. Greta, too depressed to even play, was languishing on a sofa in the music room when a servant came to announce that her presence was requested in the drawing room.

"Have we a guest?" she asked, her throat constricting.

"Yes, Fräulein. The elder Herr Schneider and his son are here."

Greta's legs trembled as she walked the length of the hallway and down another long corridor. The drawing room door was open, and she heard Hans's voice before entering the room.

He was dressed in ivory knee breeches with a navy blue tailcoat, and he held a matching tricorn hat in his hands. A bisque-colored waistcoat peeked out between the brass fasteners on his jacket, and his eyes were alight with excitement. He looked more handsome in his military uniform than Greta had ever seen him. She dropped into a curtsy, her knees shaking so badly she thought she might fall. Hans bowed, low and formal, but just before he rose he winked at her. Greta looked down, blinking away her tears.

"Ah, here she is," Herr Rodenburg called, smiling at his eldest daughter. Frau Rodenburg stood next to her husband, and beside her were Greta's younger siblings. Peter Schneider was at Hans's elbow, a mixture of pride and sorrow on his face. Lord Ellsworth, having been in conversation with Herr Rodenburg when the Schneiders' visit was announced, had been invited to stay. He stood across the room, watching the scene before him but not participating.

"*Guten Tag*, Fräulein," Hans's father greeted her.

"*Guten Tag*, Herr Schneider," Greta said.

"Hans, if you make half as good a soldier as you would have made a steward, you will do very well for yourself," Herr Rodenburg said.

"*Danke*, Herr Rodenburg."

"And if you find the mercenary life not quite to your liking, you are welcome to return to your post, at any time."

Hans looked taken aback. "Again, I thank you, Herr Rodenburg."

Herr Rodenburg dismissed his thanks with an informal wave. "You are practically family, Hans! We shall all miss you."

He extended his hand, and Hans shook it firmly. Herr Schneider looked as though the buttons on his waistcoat might pop off, and he clapped a hand onto his eldest son's shoulder.

"Good luck, Hans," Frau Rodenburg said, nodding cordially. Johann ran from his mother's side and threw his arms around Hans's waist.

"I wish you were not going," he mumbled, his face buried in Hans's coat. Hans removed himself from the boy's grasp and knelt down, pulling him into an embrace.

"This is not goodbye forever," he said. "I shall be back. Until then, I am counting on you to help with the dogs. Your father is training some fine new hunters—think you can manage them until I return?"

Johann's face lit up. "You bet I can!" He scrambled back to his place, a wide grin stretched across his face.

"*Auf Wiedersehen*, Hans," Katarina said, dropping into an elegant curtsy.

"*Auf Wiedersehen*, Fräulein Rodenburg," Hans replied, equally formal. He bowed low, and she giggled.

All eyes now turned to Greta, who stood on the other side of her father. Hans took a step closer to her.

"Goodbye, Fräulein," he said, his face solemn.

Greta tried to reply, but the words caught in her throat. She nodded instead and blinked back her tears, extending her hand. Hans took it and bowed again, brushing his lips across her knuckle. He looked up at her, his blue eyes boring into her own.

With a sob, Greta threw herself into his arms, and this time, Hans was ready. He caught her in an embrace and held her close, ignoring the surprised exclamations of her parents and the yelp of his father.

"Do not go, Hans," she whispered. "Please, do not leave me."

"I shall never leave you, Greta. I am always there, in your heart."

"Margareta!" Frau Rodenburg cried. "Come here this instant!"

"Hans…" his father warned.

"I love you," Greta breathed.

His only reply was a quick squeeze, and then he released her. Frau Rodenburg snatched Greta's hand and jerked her away, her face livid. Herr Rodenburg's normally placid look was replaced with a scowl.

"Hans, I think you should go," he said curtly.

Hans ducked his head and turned to his father, who stood anxiously by his side. He glanced at Greta, but her face was hidden in her hands. He could hear Frau Rodenburg's voice hissing at her daughter, and his fists clenched. It took every ounce of strength he possessed not to turn around and tell Frau Rodenburg just what he thought of her, once and for all. What could she do to him? Throw him out? He was already leaving—what did that matter to him?

A movement out of the corner of his eye caused Hans to turn, and he found himself looking into the eyes of Lord Ellsworth, across the room. The viscount was watching him intently, his eyes flicking back and forth between Hans and Greta.

Hans blew out his breath. *Leave it alone, Hans,* he told himself. *She will be fine.* With a curt nod to the viscount and another glance at Greta, he turned and left the room.

Chapter 14

Time passed slowly for Greta. With Hans gone, all purpose seemed to have left her life. For two days she shut herself in her room, refusing her lessons and any interaction with her family. Only after her mother threatened to have her horse and all her instruments sold did she finally emerge. Her eyes were red and swollen, and the dark shadows beneath them bore testimony of the sleepless nights she had spent since Hans's departure. She ate very little and spoke even less, which caused her father much alarm.

"*Schatz*, have a little more soup," he coaxed her.

Greta made an effort to move her spoon around inside the bowl, but did not raise any of the steaming liquid to her lips. Herr Rodenburg frowned.

"Margareta, you cannot go on like this," he said.

Frau Rodenburg cleared her throat, and Herr Rodenburg looked up at her. She raised her eyebrows at him and he sighed, turning his attention back to his own meal.

When the food had been consumed and the dishes cleared away, Greta stood and excused herself, but before she could sail away her mother arose as well.

"I shall be glad of your company in the drawing room this evening," she said pointedly, "for we have not seen much of you these last few days."

Greta bit her tongue and merely nodded, noting that both her father's and the viscount's eyes were trained on her face. She curtsied to the gentlemen and followed her mother from the room.

The next hour, spent in her mother's company as they waited for the gentlemen to join them, was agony. Restless energy coursed through her veins, and she paced the length of the room a dozen times, purposely avoiding her mother's gaze. Frau Rodenburg sat on the settee and sewed, remarking every so often how pleasant the viscount was and how glad she would be to visit his estate in England after they were married. Greta knew her mother was baiting her, but she refused to be drawn in, saying nothing unless asked a direct question.

"Margareta, did you hear me?"

"I did, Mama."

"And what do you think? Shall we order your trousseau out of Berlin, or would you rather send directly to Paris for your gowns?"

Greta swallowed the spiteful words in her mouth and said instead, "It matters not to me at present. When the time comes that I am to be married, I suppose I will have an opinion."

Frau Rodenburg pinched her lips together as Greta resumed her pacing.

At last the gentlemen joined them, and Herr Rodenburg

wasted no time imploring his daughter for some entertainment. "Shall we not all retire to the music room? Greta, won't you favor us on the pianoforte this evening?"

Grateful for a chance to escape, Greta readily agreed. But as she turned to the doors, Frau Rodenburg called from her place on the settee, "Let us send for an instrument, Margareta. You have neglected the others of late, and this room is far more comfortable."

Greta froze, not daring to look back at her mother.

"What would you like to play, Margareta?" Frau Rodenburg continued, ringing a bell. "The pianoforte can wait. Would you like the harp brought in for you?"

Trembling, Greta slowly turned around. A footman entered the room and bowed to Frau Rodenburg.

"Fräulein Rodenburg will be playing for us this evening," she said loftily. "Bring in whatever instrument she requests."

Greta could see the triumph in her mother's glance. Frau Rodenburg knew full well that the only instrument Greta wished to play was the pianoforte, and there would be no moving *that* into the drawing room. Narrowing her eyes, Greta inclined her head. *Two can play this game*, she thought. Smiling grimly, she turned to the servant. "Fetch my viola, please."

Shocked surprise flashed across Frau Rodenburg's face, quickly replaced with deadly fury. Greta waited for the eruption, certain it would come, but her mother said nothing. She glanced at the viscount, curious what his reaction would be, but his face was unreadable.

Soon the servant returned with the wooden case holding the instrument, and a long leather pouch containing its accessories.

Greta removed the viola, bow, and a small block of rosin. After treating the hairs on her bow, she set it aside and began turning the pegs on the instrument to get it in tune. After a few attempts she made a face.

"Bring me my fork, please," she said to the footman.

He left the room again, and soon returned with a small bundle. Greta unwrapped the silver tuning fork from its velvet casing, knocked it soundly on its stand, then set it upright in the base. The note hummed in the air, growing more faint as Greta continued to adjust the lead pin, plucking on the string. As the tone ceased, Greta picked up her bow and drew it across the thinnest string, mimicking the sound almost exactly. She played a quick succession of notes, made a slight adjustment to one of the pegs, then placed the instrument under her chin and started to play.

She was not nearly as adept on the viola as she was on the pianoforte, or even the harp or mandolin. Something about the way she drew the bow across the strings never seemed quite right to Greta, and it annoyed her. But she did not care about that now. She cared only that she had bested her mother at her own game.

Frau Rodenburg sat in tight-lipped silence throughout the entire performance. Her mother had vehemently opposed the idea of her learning to play the instrument, but Herr Rodenburg insisted. Their daughter was so talented, he claimed it would be a sin not to encourage her musical abilities. And, he argued, though female violinists were rare, they were by no means unheard of. The viola, however, remained a rather sore subject with Frau Rodenburg, and she dissuaded its use whenever possible. Greta now played with reckless energy, knowing full well how angry her mother must be at her choice of instrument. Though she was still distraught over Hans's departure, the music wove its spell as it always did, and the weight on Greta's heart lifted. After her second concerto, she let the instrument drop to her side, grinning at her father.

"*Schatz*, that was wonderful!" he said, applauding.

"Thank you, Papa."

"Magnificent performance, Fräulein," Lord Ellsworth said. "I have never heard a woman play the violin before, but it is clearly a skill not only gentlemen can claim."

Greta glanced nervously at her mother, but Frau Rodenburg either did not hear or was still too angry to speak. Turning back to the viscount, Greta nodded.

"Thank you, Lord Ellsworth, but this is a viola. And I assure you, women can play it just as well as men can."

"Of course. And shall you favor us again?"

His expression was open, his eyes alight with anticipation. Greta refused to let her heart soften towards the viscount, but she lifted the instrument once again to her chin and launched into another song.

Lord Ellsworth and his host watched the bird overhead circling lower. Soon Herr Rodenburg whistled, stretching out his arm to the falcon, who landed heavily on the coarse leather glove.

"A beautiful creature," Frederick remarked.

"One of my finest," Herr Rodenburg replied.

He slipped the hood over the bird's head and handed him off to his steward. Removing his glove, Herr Rodenburg motioned to Frederick, who held their guns. Three hunting dogs trotted at their heels as they strode off.

"How goes the experiment?" Herr Rodenburg asked.

Frederick grimaced. "Not as well as I would like."

Herr Rodenburg chuckled. "I told you she was stubborn."

"That is certainly a portion of it," the viscount acknowledged, "but I believe there is more. Her friend, Hans…"

"Do not concern yourself about Schneider," Herr Rodenburg said. "I have spoken with Greta about him. She knows what is expected of her."

Frederick shook his head. "That is what concerns me. If she has already lost her heart to another, it will make my task far more challenging. Perhaps impossible."

Herr Rodenburg took his gun, walking in silence as his servant commanded the dogs. After a time he looked over at his companion.

"Do not lose hope just yet, *mein Freund*. Hans is gone, and Greta will soon forget him. Though I cannot help but feel that we might need to postpone the ceremony. I do not think she will be ready as soon as we hoped."

Frederick shook his head. "I do not want to set a date. Let it occur when she is ready and willing."

"And what will you do in the meantime?"

"I will stay in Brandenburg as long as I am able. King George has requested that I meet with Herr Offenbach in Müncheberg to discuss our concerns, and I've arranged an audience with him on Friday. I may be gone a few days."

Herr Rodenburg nodded. "That might prove advantageous for

your suit. By the time you return, perhaps my daughter will be ready for some company."

They walked on, skirting a small wood as they stayed close to the open grasslands. The summer was drawing to a close, and the warmth provided by the afternoon sun was thin. Soon it would be autumn, and the landscape would shed its colorful garments in favor of browns and golds.

"Tell me," Herr Rodenburg said, glancing at the viscount. "Why are the English still recruiting mercenaries?"

Frederick shook his head. "I wish I knew."

"You do not think it wise?"

"Certainly not. Do you?"

Herr Rodenburg frowned. "I believe the war in America is a lost cause," he said. "England would do well to admit defeat and remove themselves from the colonies. Let the rebels govern themselves if they have a mind to."

"That is precisely how I feel," Frederick said. Herr Rodenburg looked at him curiously.

"Lord Ellsworth, there are times when you astound me. For an Englishman, you have a great deal of humility," he said.

Frederick laughed. "I shall take that as a compliment."

The men looked up as the dogs began barking, and soon a pair of pheasants rose into the sky, their wings beating the air with a furious staccato. Frederick took aim and fired, and the smaller bird fell to the earth.

"*Sehr gut*," Herr Rodenburg said. "Nice shot."

"Thank you."

Herr Rodenburg called to the hounds and they came loping back, the fallen bird hanging from Rolo's mouth.

"Perhaps it is because I have seen so much of the world," Frederick remarked, returning to their conversation. "I am loyal to my country and my sovereign, but I also know when they are in the wrong."

"And you feel them to be wrong in this case?"

"Yes," Frederick said firmly. His look was grave. "The colonists have not been treated fairly, and their demands have not been unreasonable."

"You think not?"

"Wishing for representation in parliament and tax funds to be spent in their own communities? Those are hardly points worth arguing. Any rational man in the same situation would side with the colonists."

Herr Rodenburg was nodding. "Even if it meant admitting defeat?"

"Yes."

"Strange," Herr Rodenburg said, his eyes full of mirth. "You do not strike me as a man who would give up easily."

Frederick laughed again. "I only admit defeat when it comes to war. In matters of love," his grin broadened, "I never concede."

Chapter 15

Several weeks had passed since Hans's departure. The shades of the forest were changing, and splashes of crimson and gold were reflected in the deep waters of the *Straussee*. Greta had finally swallowed her grief, and spent the better part of every morning writing letters to Hans. She had received no response yet, but, knowing that he was busy with his training, she cheerfully continued to compose and post letters nearly every day, confident a response would come very soon.

Life fell into the same routine as it had before, and Greta's French lessons with Lord Ellsworth resumed. Only, instead of studying French, they often spent the hour arguing in various other languages. The viscount never again assumed his pupil did not understand what he said to her, and for the most part, she did. At first, his attempts to draw her into conversation were futile— she was as tight-lipped and obstinate as ever. He soon found, however, that certain topics led to an almost instantaneous reaction. He therefore spent his time with her complimenting her mother, criticizing her country, and ruminating on the very ladylike habits of English women he knew—including the habit they had of falling in love with foreign soldiers.

Frau Rodenburg continued to promote any appearance of intimacy between her eldest daughter and the viscount. Walking parties, impromptu recitals, private carriage rides; if her mother suggested the activity, Greta was certain to be thrust at the viscount at the very first opportunity. Her resulting rudeness to their guest did not go unpunished, and several threats were carried out by her mother. This did not help warm Greta's heart towards the viscount, but they at least had the effect that she was now civil, if not kind, to him.

Weeks passed without any news from Hans, and Greta's former melancholy returned twofold. Her depression made her irritable, which resulted in a heated outburst at her mother, a sharp reprimand from her father, and a gloating look from her sister.

After pounding viciously on the pianoforte for over an hour, Greta's anger was finally spent. Her wounded spirit cried out for comfort, but she knew not where to find it. Hans was gone. Her parents were against her. Trina was a nuisance, Johann was a child, and Juli was competition. She sighed, moving to a window in a far corner of the room. The world outside was drizzly and gray. Rain poured down the glass in haphazard streaks, the drops colliding with one another in their haste to pool on the sill. Sitting down with a huff, Greta put her chin in her hands and stared out into the gloom.

Frederick watched her from the open doorway, his hands clasped behind his back. Despite her reluctant acceptance of his presence in the house and as her new language tutor, Greta remained somewhat of a mystery to him. He wondered what was going through her mind when she got a sudden, mischievous grin on her face, or when her eyes narrowed but her lips spoke sweet words. Her heart was easy enough to discern—one had only to listen to the music that poured from her fingertips to know what her feelings were. She played the pianoforte in various moods, but he had observed that usually the harp was only played when she was sad, the viola was often played to spite her mother, the dulcimer to spite her sister, and the various other instruments were only brought out occasionally. Usually they were called upon when she was feeling bored, or at the request of Herr Rodenburg, who had varied musical tastes. Yes, Frederick felt it was a simple thing to understand her heart; he only wished he could discern her thoughts as easily.

She had been sitting at the window, staring sullenly out into the rain, for a quarter hour. Frederick walked slowly in her direction, his eyes never leaving her face.

He was a few paces away when she looked up and saw him there. "Your Excellency," Greta said, getting to her feet and smoothing out her skirts. Frederick smiled weakly.

"Fräulein, I have told you before that you do not need to address me so formally."

A corner of Greta's mouth drew up. "True. But neither do you have to bring up my mother at every French lesson." She raised one eyebrow, and Frederick laughed.

"*Touché*, Fräulein." He glanced past her, at the darkened world outside. Greta turned as well.

"It always reminds me of home," he said softly.

She made no response. They stood there in silence, watching the rain track down the window, listening to the soft *tat, tat* on the glass.

"Do you miss it?" Greta asked at length.

"Hm?"

"Your home. Do you miss it?"

He did not answer right away, and his hesitation caused her to look up at him. "I miss England," he said at last, "but not my home."

"Why not?"

He looked down into her eyes. They were darker today, more slate than the soft, dove gray he was so accustomed to seeing. He answered her question with one of his own.

"Would you miss your home, if you went away by choice?"

A crease formed between Greta's brows as she considered his question. "I would miss my music. My instruments."

"Is that all?"

A smile tugged at the corner of her mouth. "And my horse."

He laughed softly. "Of course. But those things are not what make this your home, are they, Fräulein?"

She thought of her parents and younger siblings. "I suppose not," she said slowly. Then, raising her eyes to meet his, she asked, "Is that why you do not miss your home? Because of your family?" Her mind reached into the past, at the ride they had taken through the woods. She tipped her head to one side. "Are they the reason you wished to escape?"

Frederick clasped his hands behind his back once more, staring out the window. "I am an only child, Fräulein. An only *son.*" He glanced at her to see if she understood.

"You will inherit," she said slowly. "Because of the laws of primogeniture."

He nodded. "Yes. After I was born healthy, my parents never even considered having another child. Even after my mother passed away, and my father could have remarried, he did not. I am the only heir."

Greta thought of her own family: first herself, then Katarina, and lastly Johann. She frowned. Johann was the only son, and the youngest child. Frederick was nodding as the pieces fell into place in her mind.

"I have known all my life what is expected of me: by my parents, by my country, by my king. And it is not what many would consider to be a difficulty. After all," he smiled wryly, "what is so difficult about living on a beautiful estate, having plenty of servants, and being admired by one and all?"

"I never considered that your appointment might not have been of your own choosing," Greta murmured.

"You are mistaken, Fräulein," he said. "While His Majesty the King *did* appoint me an ambassador, it was my choice to pursue such an occupation."

She frowned. "I do not understand."

The viscount's look softened. "It is a temporary appointment, Fräulein," he said. "When my father dies, I shall return to England."

"What about your duty to the king?"

"I will have a new duty when that time comes," he said, moving away from the window. "And it is not one I would choose."

They lapsed into silence once more. Greta turned the

viscount's words over in her mind, picking them apart to get at the feelings underneath. She knew them well—had she not felt the same stifling, controlling effects of her own birthright? She had not expected to find an ally in the viscount, but the feeling of camaraderie was there.

At last, Frederick cleared his throat. "If you will forgive me now, Fräulein, I have some business to attend to." He made a slight bow to her and turned to leave.

"Lord Ellsworth," she called, and he looked back. "*Je voudrais recommencer nos cours de français*," she said.

He laughed quietly. "Our French lessons have continued with very little interruption, Fräulein," he said.

"I meant, I would like our lessons to be more educational," she said, coloring slightly. "I believe I am a little rusty. Especially with my translation."

He nodded. "As you wish, Fräulein. We shall—"

"Greta," she broke in. "My friends call me Greta."

He looked at her for a long time, before a slow smile spread across his face. "As you wish, Greta," he said with a bow.

"Fräulein, a letter has arrived for you."

Greta looked up from the passage she was translating, at the outstretched arm of the servant standing beside her. A dirty piece of paper lay on a silver tray, the direction written in a tidy hand she knew very well. Jumping to her feet, Greta nearly knocked over her chair. "Forgive me," she called to the viscount, snatching up the letter and running from the room.

Hans! her heart sang. *Hans! Hans! Hans!*

Bursting into her room, breathless from her flight, Greta broke the seal and unfolded the paper. A flash of disappointment coursed through her upon seeing its length, but her hungry eyes would not be withheld.

London, England
28 October, 1779

Dear Greta,

Thank you for your letters. I am not sure who has written more faithfully, you or my mother, and I am heartily glad to hear that things are well at home. Have you been into the village lately? Juli does not write nearly so often as you, and I am anxious to have word from her.

Greta smirked. It did not surprise her that Julianna did not write.

Life in the service is as I expected, though perhaps not as glamorous as Ernst had imagined. I was prepared for hard work, long days, and poor rations. But they feed us well, and that makes the rest quite tolerable.

Our instruction here is nearly finished, and we shall soon be leaving for America. We have been training with four other Prussian units, though I do not recognize anyone else from home. Though our unit captain is a fellow Prussian from Brandenburg, our head commander is British, and I do not believe he thinks very highly of us. I am sure that Ernst could lick him in a fight if he wanted to, but of course that would lead to Ernst's court-martial, so I am trying to keep his temper in check. He has already mouthed off one too many times for his own good, even if the insults he flung were deserved.

Greta rolled her eyes. *Ernst will never change*, she thought.

We do not have much time to ourselves, but in quiet moments at night, I sometimes find myself thinking of you. We were always such good friends, Greta. Do you remember that time when we were children, when we climbed up into the fir tree at the edge of the woods? We went up so high, and the limbs were so close together, and your hair became tangled in the branches. You were so frightened that you would be stuck up there forever!

Greta laughed quietly to herself, reaching up to gently touch the curls atop her head. She did indeed remember the incident, including Hans's helpful suggestion that they cut her hair loose with his penknife. Thankfully that had not been found necessary.

We had such good times together, Greta. I miss those days. I miss you, Schwesterlein.

Please give my affections to Johann and Trina. And would you please check on Juli for me? I know she must be lonely, with both Ernst and myself gone. Perhaps you can visit her and cheer her up a bit. I would love to hear how she is doing.

Yours affectionately,
Hans

For a long time Greta sat staring at the paper before her. She had anticipated Hans's first letter for weeks, but now, having read it, she felt more hurt than anything else. Hans had called her *little sister*, no doubt as a subtle reminder to her of his feelings. When she first read that he missed her, Greta's heart burst with joy, only to be plummeted back into disappointment by the very next sentence.

Her eyes scanned the page once more, indignation welling up inside of her at his words. He certainly had gall, asking Greta to visit Julianna for him.

Tossing the letter onto her bed, Greta made her way across the room and sat down at her desk. She pulled out paper, quill, and ink, and began to write.

Strausberg, Prussia
17 November, 1779

Dearest Hans,

I was very happy to get your letter today, and can answer your inquiries about Julianna without having to call upon her, for I saw her not long ago.

Greta bit her lip, tapping the feather against her cheek as she considered what to say.

Julianna seemed in excellent spirits, as did Auguste

Weisler, with whom she was walking when I chanced upon her. Our visit was short, but I can assure you that she is quite well and getting along wonderfully without you.

Sighing, Greta laid down her quill. She was angry and hurt, but she did not want to fight with Hans. Crumpling the paper, she retrieved Hans's letter and read it through once more, determined to begin afresh. This time, she noticed a small postscript at the very bottom of the page, where the paper had curled. She squinted, holding it closer to the light. In a small, almost illegible hand, she read,

Give my regards to that bloody Englishman of yours.
-Ernst

Chapter 16

"Would you like a drink, Lord Ellsworth?" Herr Rodenburg asked, pouring himself a glass.

The gentlemen were in the dining room, having just said farewell to Greta and her mother after supper. Frederick shook his head.

"No, thank you. But there is something I wish to discuss with you."

"Yes?"

"I must send a report to His Majesty King George about the political developments in Brandenburg. While I have already included what I have learned from Herr Offenbach in Müncheberg and Herr Schaeffer in Rüdersdorf, I was hoping to have more, ah, advantageous news to share."

Herr Rodenburg took a sip from his glass, waiting. Frederick cleared his throat.

"I know you met with the League of Princes in Berlin last week. Was anything decided upon?"

"Concerning what?"

"Allying yourselves to Great Britain, as we have discussed. Or taking preventative measures against France, perhaps?"

Herr Rodenburg was shaking his head even before Frederick finished speaking. "I am sorry, Your Excellency, but no one is willing to enter into another alliance with the British."

Frederick sighed. "I thought not."

"And we are not planning anything concerning France, either. So you may be easy on that account."

"I am not sure I can be easy about anything. If England is left without an ally on the continent and the people declare war in France..." Frederick blew out his breath. "You know our hands are tied. Fighting the colonists in America has claimed practically all of our military strength, and most of our resources."

Herr Rodenburg shook his head. "You should have pulled out years ago."

"I wish that we would pull out now. Then we might be able to do something about France."

"Why do you feel the need to do something about France?"

Frederick frowned. "Something must be done. Most of Europe is still in an economic depression from the mid-century wars. The magnitude of the revolution brewing in France could devastate the entire continent."

Herr Rodenburg swirled the liquid in his glass. "Let France worry about its own. I do not think there is anything one can do, in such cases as these."

Frederick gawked. "Good heavens, man! Do you mean to say that you *want* a revolution in France?"

"Of course not. I am merely saying that I believe it is

135

inevitable. Anyone who interferes may be caught in the crossfire. No one wants any trouble with France," he said. "Least of all you."

"We are having enough trouble with the Americans as it is," Frederick said. "Of course, we might be able to end the conflict in America sooner if our old allies *here* would lend us their support."

Herr Rodenburg chuckled. "Lord Ellsworth, that is your country's entire dilemma. You never wish to back down from a fight. When you get in over your head, instead of admitting defeat, you eagerly appeal to your neighbors and connections for an ally in your cause."

"And does not Prussia do the same?" Frederick retorted.

Herr Rodenburg shrugged. "The Empire wishes to retain its lands, but Prussia is far more cautious in such cases as these. With all due respect to our former allies," he nodded at his guest, "there is hardly any reason for us to join your cause now. You said yourself it is practically impossible."

Frederick ran a hand slowly through his hair. "That is true."

"And furthermore, if Prussia *did* enter into another alliance with England, what would that do, but free up your own navy and resources to launch an attack on France? With whom I already told you, we do not wish to become entangled."

"Herr Rodenburg, you are a man of incredible understanding," Frederick said, admiration coloring his tone.

Herr Rodenburg bowed his head and smiled. "Thank you, *mein Freund*. I have worked hard to become so."

"I am honored to be called your friend. And look forward to an alliance between us of a different sort before long."

"How are things progressing on that front?" Herr Rodenburg asked, as he motioned for his guest to follow him out of the room. Frederick stood and walked with his host down the hall.

"Not as quickly as I would like," he said. "But she is young. It may take some time."

"You seem to be making remarkable progress, from my estimation."

"Remarkable, you would call it?" Frederick asked, amused.

Herr Rodenburg chuckled. "You may not feel it, but I certainly can—knowing my daughter as well as I do. How are the French lessons coming along?"

"Better. We have finally progressed to speaking French."

Herr Rodenburg laughed, and the ornate drawing room doors were opened for them. Both women looked up as they stepped into the room, and Greta stood. She looked relieved.

"*Schatz*, you look pleased to see us," Herr Rodenburg said, brushing a kiss on his daughter's cheek. Greta smiled and squeezed his arm.

"I am always happy to see you, Papa," she said. Turning to the viscount, she asked, "*Aimeriez-vous me rejoindre à la salle de musique?*"

Surprised but pleased, Frederick smiled. "I would like that very much."

"And what shall I play for you?"

Frederick waved a hand in the air. "Surprise me," he said, offering her his arm.

They walked off in the direction of the music room, and Herr Rodenburg turned to his wife with a smile.

"Well, my dear? What do you think?"

Dorothea stood slowly, running her hands gently along the folds of fabric at her waist. She drifted to her husband's side, a look of shrewd satisfaction on her face.

"I think that despite her repeated denials, our daughter may be a viscountess before long."

Michaelmas had come and gone, the harvest was over, and preparations were being made for the Christmas holidays. The house was filled with the sweet aroma of *Stollen* and *Plätzchen*, and servants were sent out into the forest to find the *Tannenbaum* to place in the entrance hall. The fir tree would be decorated with clusters of fruit and nuts as the holiday, and the Rodenburg's famous Christmas Eve ball, drew near.

Greta came downstairs one December morning, humming quietly to herself. The skirts of her gown rustled softly as she walked, until she stopped with a jerk at the bottom of the stairs. Music was coming from down the hall, but it was not the harp or the dulcimer. Her mother so infrequently played the piano, and Trina flatly refused to, that Greta was astonished to hear its gentle tones drifting towards her. Stepping lightly down the corridor, she peeked around the open door to the music room. Sitting at the pianoforte—*her* pianoforte—was Frederick.

His was not the sound of a practiced hand, but he was not unpleasant to listen to. Greta recognized the melody of one of Mozart's earlier sonatas, though the tempo was somewhat too slow. She listened for several minutes, watching Frederick's face as he methodically played the keys. Soon the song ended, and she stepped around the doorway into the room.

"That was lovely," she said.

Startled, Frederick looked up, getting quickly to his feet. "Greta," he said. "I thought you would be out for your morning ride."

"It is too cold this morning." She cocked her head, looking at him curiously. "Why did you not tell me you could play?"

He laughed nervously. "One could hardly call my clumsy attempt at a song proper talent," he said. "I only learned so that I might, on occasion, accompany myself."

"Accompany yourself?"

The color on his face deepened. "When I sing."

"Oh!" Greta's shock melted into a laugh. "Forgive me, Lord Ellsworth, for my surprise. Only imagine! All these months I have been entertaining *you*, when you were every bit as capable of entertaining all of us."

He laughed, relaxing. "You have not heard me sing. Perhaps you would consider it a punishment, rather than an entertainment."

She made a face at him. "I highly doubt that. But let us not quarrel over the matter—let us hear you now."

She sat down on the bench and looked up at him expectantly, her eyes bright. "What would you like to sing?"

"Er, well now." He clasped his hands behind him, shifting his feet. "I am partial to Handel myself. Do you know his *Messiah*?"

A grin flashed across her face. "It is one of my favorites for the viola."

She retrieved the music and sat down again. "Which song?" she asked, leafing through the pages.

"The Trumpet Shall Sound, in part three," he said.

Greta found her place and began to play. She rarely played Handel on the pianoforte, and her eyes remained trained on the music as Frederick started to sing.

His voice was clear and strong, a decided bass. Greta's amusement soon turned to astonishment as he sang through the first several measures. She had rarely heard men sing, but even with her limited experience, she knew she was listening to a man of incredible talent. Glancing up, she saw that his eyes were closed, his head tipped back, his face calm. He looked more comfortable than she ever remembered seeing him before.

Halfway through the piece, Frederick's voice suddenly broke off. Greta paused, looking up at him. He had a sheepish look on his face.

"I am afraid that is all I can remember," he said.

"Oh," Greta said, surprised at the disappointment she felt. "Would you like to look over my shoulder at the music?"

"No, thank you, Fräulein."

"Perhaps another time, then."

"Yes. I mean, no. I do not sing for company," he said, color creeping up his neck.

"Why ever not? You sound wonderful."

"Thank you. But I have not received much training. And it is such vanity, I think, to put oneself forward in company when there are other, more qualified individuals to entertain. Such as yourself," he said with a serious nod.

Greta gaped at him. "Do you mean to say that you have received *no* formal training?"

"My mother had me tutored as a boy, for a time, until my

father put a stop to my lessons."

"Why?"

Frederick shrugged. "I believe he felt that singing was a bit too feminine a pursuit for his son."

"And you complied with his wishes, even though it brings you such joy?"

Frederick looked taken aback. "How do you—"

Greta's vibrant smile flashed across her face. "I love my music, Lord Ellsworth. I know what that feeling looks like, and I saw it upon your face."

He nodded once, and they were silent, considering each other. At last Greta stood.

"Well. I certainly hope you will favor us with a song, one of these evenings. Your father is not here to forbid you," she teased.

Frederick smiled. "No, he is not. But I—"

They were interrupted by the arrival of a footman at the door. Greta bid him enter, and as he approached them, he bowed and held out a tray to the viscount. "This has just arrived for you, sir," he said.

"Thank you."

Frederick took the letter, a slight crease drawn between his eyes. "Forgive me, Fräulein," he said. "But I must see to this immediately."

"Of course."

They bowed to one another, and Frederick strode off, tearing the seal and unfolding the note before he had even left the room.

"You have my condolences, Lord Ellsworth. Er, Lord Rockwell, is it now? When shall you depart for England?"

Frederick stood with his back to his host, staring out the study window. "Before Christmas, in all likelihood."

"So soon?"

Frederick turned, a sad smile on his face. "Yes. My duty is there now."

Herr Rodenburg nodded, reaching for his pipe. "True. But I had hoped…" His voice trailed off and he looked up at his guest expectantly. Frederick—now the Earl of Rockwell—turned back towards the window.

"Your daughter has softened considerably towards myself," he said. "But I do not believe I have yet earned her love."

"Do you think, perhaps, with you leaving…?"

"No. If we force the betrothal now, she will resent us even more, and all of my work will be undone. Let us be patient, a little while longer."

"Frau Rodenburg will not be pleased," Herr Rodenburg frowned.

Frederick turned around, an amused smile on his face. "Why ever not? Frau Rodenburg was happy to see her daughter marry a viscount, but now, with only a slight delay, she will be the wife of an English earl. Surely Her Highness can exercise the patience that outcome will require."

Herr Rodenburg chuckled. "That is true. But tell me, how do you anticipate continuing your courtship with Margareta when you are in England and she is here?"

"I will ask her to write to me," Frederick said, taking a seat across from his host. "With your permission, of course."

Herr Rodenburg nodded, waving a hand dismissively in the air. "Of course."

"And when things settle down for me in England, I will be back to see her."

"When shall that be?"

"Not before the spring. While I am sure that my father left his affairs in perfect order, there is always a great deal of paperwork to complete and meetings to arrange when one inherits."

He said it with perfect mildness, and Herr Rodenburg smiled sadly.

"I am sorry that you do not feel the loss of your father more acutely, *mein Freund.*"

Frederick nodded. "Thank you. He was a good man, my father, but..." He sighed, shaking his head. "I see the efforts you are making with your own children, Herr Rodenburg. They are quite admirable. Surely they would miss you if anything were to happen to *you.*"

Herr Rodenburg leaned back in his chair, puffing slowly on his pipe. "I would hope so."

The men fell silent, each turning to their own thoughts. At length, Herr Rodenburg sat forward and cleared his throat.

"Well. Christmas is but a fortnight away, and you were to be the guest of honor at our annual ball. Shall you leave us before then, or might I persuade you to stay?"

Rubbing a hand across his eyes, Frederick sighed. "I would like to stay, of course. But I do not know if that is wise."

"Stay." Herr Rodenburg insisted, rising to his feet. "After all, the late earl would have wished you to do your duty, would he not?"

Frederick slowly drew his hand away from his face, his eyes slightly narrowed. "That is true," he said, unsmiling.

Herr Rodenburg beamed. "*Gut!* You shall stay, and we will arrange for your removal after the holiday."

"Immediately after."

"Of course, of course." Herr Rodenburg said, waving his pipe in the air. "But more than one lady has been known to fall in love at a ball. Perhaps Greta will fall prey to your charms then, eh? And what will you do when that happens?"

"I do not think your daughter's head is one to be turned at a ball."

"But what if it were?"

Slowly, the Earl of Rockwell got to his feet. "I will stay for the ball," Frederick said deliberately. "And will arrange to leave first thing the next morning."

"But what if *she* wanted you to stay—would you reconsider?"

"What are you playing at, Herr Rodenburg?" Frederick said sharply. "Do you believe you can bend your daughter to your will by sheer determination? Surely you know her better than that."

"I know my daughter very well indeed, Lord Rockwell," he said.

"Then you must know how absurd it sounds to speculate that she is so fickle as to attach herself to a man merely because he was her dance partner."

The men stared at one another, a clear line drawn between them.

"Herr Rodenburg, you must be satisfied with my plans for your daughter as I explained them to you," Frederick said. "I will be leaving for England directly after the Christmas Eve ball, and that is final."

He bowed briefly and left the room, leaving Herr Rodenburg staring frostily after him.

Chapter 17

"*Guten Morgen*, Fräulein. And Happy Christmas."

"*Guten Morgen*, Herr Zeller."

Greta shut the door behind her and approached the elderly man behind the counter.

"Have you another letter to post?" he asked, his eyes twinkling. Greta grinned.

"Why else would I be here?"

The old man laughed, and reached a wrinkled hand out to take it from her. "Off to England with this one, too?" he asked.

"No, to America."

"Hm," Herr Zeller put his spectacles on, squinting at the direction. "Ah, yes, to the colonies. Herr Schneider and Herr Gottfried are well, I trust?"

"*Ja*, they are well. Though I confess that I worry for them."

Herr Zeller smiled kindly at her. "We all worry for them, Fräulein. The sooner those English can get their colonists under control and send our boys home, the better. Though it won't be in time for Christmas," he said, frowning. Then, brightening a bit, he asked, "What are your plans for the holiday, Fräulein?"

"Tomorrow will be our annual Christmas Eve ball. And Lord Ellsworth—er, Lord Rockwell—will be leaving for England on Christmas Day."

"Ah, yes, the English ambassador. Are you glad to see him go?"

Greta shook her head. "There was a time when I could not wait to be rid of him. But he is my friend now. I shall be sorry to see him leave."

After paying for the postage, Greta bid Herr Zeller good day and left the shop. Stepping out into the crisp winter air, she drew a breath, her nostrils pricking. A light snow had fallen a few days prior, and though the sun was out, it was frightfully cold. She pulled the hood of her fur-lined cloak over her head and slipped her hands into her muff, shivering.

Though her father had offered her the carriage, Greta enjoyed her walks into town. It was now too cold to ride her horse, but her restless heart still longed for exercise, and the few miles to town and back were a welcome escape. Once or twice Frederick had offered to accompany her, and though she would have liked his company, she did not want to give her scheming mother any further fuel. So she traveled to town alone, and enjoyed every minute of it.

Walking down the frozen street, she passed only a handful of people brave enough to bundle up against the chill. A few called out to her as she passed, and Greta smiled and returned their greetings. Turning the corner in the main square, her eye caught on a young lady in a beautiful red cloak. It was Julianna, on the

147

arm of Auguste Weisler, the innkeeper's son.

Julianna spied Greta at almost precisely the same moment and called out to her, a broad grin splitting her face. "Margareta!" she called.

Greta smiled and waved, but did not stop.

"Have you heard from Hans? I've had a letter, just the other day, and he said—"

Greta's stomach clenched, and she hastened her pace, pretending she had not heard. Her last letter from Hans arrived over a fortnight ago, and though it still contained a great deal about Julianna, there was a note of exasperation in his words. It appeared that Hans was far more faithful in his letters to the baker's daughter than *she* was faithful in writing to *him*.

The walk home was beautiful and calm. The icy blue sky held only the faintest trace of color, while the landscape around her glistened like a million-faceted gemstone. Greta kept a brisk pace to ward off the chill, her breath trailing behind her in wispy clouds of silver.

With crimson cheeks and nose she finally arrived home, her spirits only slightly dampened by the encounter with Julianna. Christmas Eve was tomorrow, and she was looking forward to the holiday and the ball with great anticipation. Hans may be gone, but at least she had a friend in Frederick.

Frederick. Greta wondered idly when she had begun to think of him as "Frederick" and not "the viscount," "the ambassador," or "Lord Ellsworth." It made it infinitely more convenient at the moment, considering his new title. She did not have to remember how to address him—he was just Frederick now.

"Greta! There you are."

Greta turned at the sound of his voice and smiled. *"Guten Tag*, Frederick. I was just thinking about you."

He stopped short, clearly surprised. "About me?"

"Yes. I was musing on your change of address, and how glad I am that I can simply call you Frederick, and not worry myself over forgetting that you are no longer Lord Ellsworth, but Lord Rockwell now."

"Oh, yes. It *is* most convenient, I suppose." He smiled. "Have you been to town already?"

"Yes, I am only just arrived home." She reached for her handkerchief to wipe at her dripping nose. "But you can probably see that for yourself."

He laughed. "Come, let us get you someplace warm. There is a good fire in the music room." He offered her his arm, and she took it with a smile.

"Was there something you wished to speak with me about?" she asked.

"Yes, there is." His look turned serious. "But let us wait to speak of it until we are settled somewhere more warm. And private," he added.

For the first time ever in his presence, Greta's stomach lurched into her throat. Why did he want to see her alone? And why was he acting so formal? She swallowed, feeling faint. "Of... course," she murmured.

She walked with him down the hall, growing more nervous with every step. What could he have to say to her? She was still adamantly opposed to the idea of an arranged marriage, and though her father had never said anything to suggest that the intended marriage had been canceled, she wondered if Frederick

149

had withdrawn his desire for the match. He certainly did not seem intent upon wooing her. But perhaps that is what he wanted to speak of? Greta felt ill at the thought. Two months ago, she would not have thought twice about refusing Frederick to his face. But now that they were friends... they *were* friends, were they not? Why could things not remain as they were?

Frederick walked beside her in silence, and she was relieved that he made no move to close the music room doors behind them. Greta released his arm and stretched her fingers towards the flames, grateful not to be looking at his face as she waited for him to speak. Frederick walked a few paces towards the window, his hands behind his back.

"As you know," he began, looking out at the glittering landscape. "I shall be returning to England in two days."

Greta twisted her hands together, staring intently at the dancing flames. "Yes."

"I had hoped to remain in Prussia longer, but my duty now calls me home."

They were silent, the only sound in the room the popping and crackling of the logs in the grate. Greta could hardly hear it over the pounding in her ears as her heart hammered in her chest. Should she speak now, before he asked for her hand? Her nerves were strung as tightly as the strings on her viola, and suddenly it angered her. Why must he ruin everything? Her opinion of their supposed engagement was hardly a secret, and if he thought that she had changed her mind, simply because they were now on friendly terms, he certainly did not know her very well.

Determined to speak her mind, Greta turned to face him, just as Frederick blurted out, "Will you write to me, Greta?"

She snapped her mouth shut, effectively disarmed. "Write... to you?"

"Yes. Since we will not be able to continue our French lessons in person, I thought maybe we could continue them by post. Of course, it does not mean..." He cleared his throat. "I know it is uncommon, and even frowned upon, for single young ladies to correspond with gentlemen who are not their next of kin, or to whom they are not—"

"Yes," she said, interrupting him. "Yes, I will write to you, Frederick."

She smiled, her relief at his inquiry nearly tangible. She would not have to reject Frederick to his face, and perhaps, with him leaving for England, she would not have to refuse him at all.

Frederick looked as relieved as she felt. "Thank you, Greta. I have discussed it with your father already, and he heartily approves."

"You spoke with my father about it?" The uneasy feeling crept back into Greta's stomach.

"Yes, last week." Frederick saw her alarm, and he hastened to add, "But only to ask his permission to correspond with you. We did not speak about—"

"Lord Rockwell," Greta said solemnly. "I am grateful for your friendship, and thankful for your assistance regarding my language lessons. I will write to you as your friend and former pupil, but nothing more. That must be understood, or I cannot agree."

There was silence for an infinite moment, but then he smiled softly. "Of course."

Perhaps she imagined it, but Greta thought he sounded

151

disappointed, almost sad, as he agreed with her.

"Was there anything else you wished to discuss?" she asked, stepping away from the fire.

"Actually, there was one more thing."

Greta steeled herself. "Yes?"

With a deep bow, Frederick extended his hand. "Might I have the pleasure of the first dance tomorrow night?"

Greta laughed, bursting the bubble of tension between them. "Frederick, you know it is my duty as my mother's daughter, and *your* duty as the guest of honor, to stand up together for the first dance."

Frederick's lips twitched. "I know. But the last time we danced together at a ball, you did it against your will." He lifted his brow, as if daring her to contradict him. She blushed. "This time," he continued, "I should like very much to know that you are standing up with me by your own choice."

Greta dropped into an elegant curtsy, bowing her head so deeply that her nose nearly touched her skirts. The curl that never remained in its proper place bobbed across her forehead. "I would be happy to dance with you, Lord Rockwell."

Standing straight once more, she laughed. "There! Now let us shake hands, and be friends."

Frederick took her outstretched hand and brushed a kiss on the back of it. "Friends," he said. "Though perhaps…"

But Greta had withdrawn her hand, and before he could finish the thought, she was gone.

Chapter 18

The Rodenburg's Christmas Eve ball was a tradition the townspeople of Strausberg had enjoyed for many years. The surrounding gentry and many of the *bourgeoisie* were often in attendance, but Frau Rodenburg clung tenaciously to her nobility, and refused to invite any paupers. Greta realized this was the first year Ernst had not been around to grumble over her mother's prejudice, and she found, much to her surprise, that she missed it.

Shortly after breakfast, there was a knock on Greta's bedroom door. She was sitting at her desk, composing a letter to Hans, when her father walked in.

"*Guten Morgen, Schatz.*"

"Papa!" Greta stood and went to embrace him. "I was not expecting you. Does my mother need me?"

"No," he said, smiling indulgently, "I have a gift for you." He motioned to the servant behind him, who set a large box down on the bed. Lifting the lid, Greta cried out in delight.

"A new dress! Oh, Papa, thank you!"

Reverently, she withdrew the beautiful evening gown from the box. It was made of pale yellow silk, which shone with a beautiful luster in the morning sun. Embroidered roses in olive and crimson thread climbed up the bodice, blossoming in large bouquets along the sleeves and the hem. Intricate lace and satin ribbons adorned the edges of the fashionable elbow sleeves. An enormous skirt, large enough to fit even her formal panniers, billowed and puffed as Greta held the dress to her figure, turning around. Tiny golden threads, woven into the embroidery, sparkled and flashed in the light.

"The dressmaker in Paris used spun-gold thread for the embroidery," Herr Rodenburg said proudly.

"It is beautiful, Papa. *Danke.*"

Carefully laying the dress on the bed, Greta went up on her toes to kiss him on the cheek. His smile softened, and he drew her into his arms.

"Only the finest for my Margareta," he said. Greta sighed and closed her eyes, leaning against his chest. He pressed his cheek to the top of her head.

"*Schatz,*" he said, and Greta felt his deep voice rumbling in his chest, "you seem to have formed a friendship with Lord Rockwell. Or reached a truce, at the very least."

Greta pulled back so she could look up at him. "We are friends, but nothing more," she said with emphasis.

"Of course, of course," Herr Rodenburg said, smiling indulgently. "But he will be leaving us soon. Are you not sad to see him go? Do you not wish that he would stay?"

Greta lifted her chin. "His duty is in England now. He told me so himself."

"Yes, but if you pressed him to stay…"

"I will write to him," she said quickly, feeling the ground slipping out from under her. "He said that you gave your permission."

"I did."

Greta's knuckles were white, the skin stretched taught. "Is this why you gave me the dress? As an engagement gift?" she threw at him.

Herr Rodenburg blew out his breath. "Margareta," he said, reaching for her. But she stepped away.

"*Schatz*, I do not want to force you—"

"Then there is nothing more to say."

Silence filled the room, heavy and thick, as father and daughter stared at one another. At last Herr Rodenburg turned away.

"I am glad you like the dress. I look forward to seeing you in it tonight," he said softly.

He left without another word.

Frederick Greenwood, the Earl of Rockwell, carefully tied his cravat for the third time. He could hear the sounds of the orchestra warming up in the ballroom downstairs, and his pulse quickened. It would not do for the guest of honor to arrive late, but neither would it do for him to arrive looking unkempt and disheveled.

He blew out his breath in frustration. He had always preferred to tie his own cravats and had already dismissed his valet.

Tonight, however, his nerves must be getting the better of him, for try as he might, the knots would not lie smoothly across his neck.

Defeated, he crossed the room and pulled on the bell cord. A few minutes later, a soft knock sounded on the door.

"Come in," he called.

His valet, a portly gentleman only a few years older than himself, came into the room.

"You called, sir?"

"Yes, Hastings, I need you to tie my cravat."

His servant raised his eyebrows, but selected a fresh cravat from the armoire and set to work. "I cannot remember the last time you asked me to tie your cravat, sir," he said.

"I cannot remember the last time I was so nervous," Frederick replied, looking over his valet's head at his reflection in the glass.

Hastings chuckled. "If I might be so bold, sir, it seems only natural for you to be nervous."

"Oh?"

"Yes, sir. Women have always made men nervous. They still do me."

Frederick raised an eyebrow. "And what makes you think Fräulein Rodenburg makes me nervous?"

His valet looked up, grinning. "There now, is she the reason? I was referring to her mother, Frau Rodenburg."

Hastings finished his work as Frederick shook his head, chuckling. "You are a sly one, old friend."

"Begging your pardon, sir. I only meant to make you smile, and help to ease your mind."

"That you have. And you have tied my cravat beautifully. Thank you."

His servant bowed and stepped away, and Frederick looked over his appearance once more. Satisfied, he shrugged into his jacket and strode out the door.

The first carriages had just arrived when he took his place beside Herr Rodenburg in the entrance hall.

"At last," Herr Rodenburg murmured. "We were beginning to worry."

Frederick peered around his host at Frau Rodenburg, who stood in tight-lipped silence beside her husband. Her face was forward, not looking at him.

"My apologies," Frederick said, inclining his head.

A flash of golden fabric caught his eye, and he caught sight of Greta standing on the other side of her mother in a stunning gown that shimmered in the light. For a moment he was struck completely speechless. Never before had he seen her looking more radiant, more beautiful than she did tonight. She caught his eye and grinned.

"Is everything all right?"

Herr Rodenburg's question cut through Frederick's mind, drawing him back to the moment. He straightened.

"Yes, quite. Please forgive my tardiness."

Herr Rodenburg raised his brow at Frederick, then turned and glanced at his daughter, a smirk on his lips. Before he could comment further, the front doors opened and the first guests of the evening were introduced.

For the next half hour, Frederick smiled and bowed politely as he greeted the ladies and gentlemen invited for the evening. At a quarter to eight, it was time to join their guests in the ballroom. Frederick offered Greta his arm.

"You look beautiful this evening," he murmured, as they followed her parents down the hall. Greta smiled.

"Thank you, Lord Rockwell."

He laughed under his breath. "I am still getting used to that. The first time Herr Rodenburg addressed me thus, I looked around, expecting to see my father."

A torrent of light burst upon them as they entered the ballroom, born from the tiny flames of a thousand candles. Skirts swirled, heads bowed, fans waved, and the general hum of nearly a hundred people filled the room. All eyes turned to look at them, and the murmuring died down.

"*Meine Damen und Herren*," Herr Rodenburg said, lifting his arms high. "Thank you for coming tonight. We are pleased to celebrate with you on this blessed Christmas Eve, and would like to thank our dear friend and honored guest Frederick Greenwood, the Earl of Rockwell, for joining us."

Scattered applause met these words, and Herr Rodenburg paused. "Lord Rockwell has spent the last several months in our community," he continued, "but unfortunately, his time with us has come to an end. He will soon be leaving to return to England."

A gentle hum filled the room as the guests reacted to this news. Frederick smiled politely and inclined his head at those who acknowledged him. Beside him, Greta shifted from one foot to the other, watching her father intently.

"Tonight we honor him, but for now, let the dance begin!"

A general cry of pleasure arose from the crowd, and Frederick saw Greta visibly relax. He extended his hand to her as the orchestra began to play.

"Shall we?"

Greta's smile was nearly as brilliant as the chandelier overhead. Her gray eyes were bright with anticipation, flashing in the candlelight like molten silver. She took his hand as he led her to the floor, his heart pounding.

The steps of the minuet were slow and graceful, and they circled one another as the violin played. He reached for her, and as she took his hand, he squeezed it gently. All eyes in the room were upon them, and Frederick could hardly tear his own eyes away from her. She was breathtaking, all silver and gold in the candlelight. He focused on the steps of the dance, trying not to lose himself in her eyes.

"You have improved," Greta breathed as she crossed in front of him. Frederick allowed himself a smile. They twirled in unison, steps apart, then came together once more. Greta's fingertips brushed his own as they reached towards one another, their feet light as their bodies swayed, turning and rotating in the steps of the dance. When they were opposite one another, Frederick never let his eyes stray from her face. Greta, however, often dropped her gaze, smiling at the floor, and he wondered what she could be thinking.

The music continued, and they circled one another with mincing steps, each rotation drawing them closer to each other and the end of the song. The moment Greta rested her hands in his own, Frederick saw her draw a sharp breath, her cheeks coloring slightly as their eyes met.

"Are you all right?" he murmured.

She merely nodded, looking down once more. She was no longer smiling.

They were close now, no longer holding hands at arm's length, but clasping them together with elbows bent, their bodies almost touching. Though Greta's chin was up, her eyes were lowered, as if she were looking down her nose at their entwined hands between them. Frederick felt the tension building between them, and he willed her to look up at him, desperate to read her thoughts.

The crescendo of the music signaled their final turns, retracing their first steps of the dance. They broke apart, to bow to one another and the crowd gathered around them, but just before they did, Greta glanced up at Frederick, her thick, golden lashes framing her silver eyes.

He did not even realize he was holding his breath, until her look drew it out of him in one long sigh.

They bowed to the room, then turned and acknowledged each other by the same motion. Polite applause and murmured compliments floated on the air, but Frederick was hardly aware of them. Greta had withdrawn her hand and was quickly retreating, even as the floor filled with other dancers to form the first set of the evening. He followed after her as she made her way back towards her parents.

"You danced beautifully, Lord Rockwell," Frau Rodenburg purred. "And what a lovely couple you made, standing up together. Was it not so, my dear?"

"A most handsome couple," Herr Rodenburg agreed, smiling at the earl.

"Thank you," Frederick said, his eyes on Greta. She stood beside her mother, her hands clasped behind her, her face turned away. Why would she not look at him?

Herr Rodenburg took his wife by the hand and led her onto the floor, leaving Frederick and Greta standing awkwardly apart from one another. Frederick bridged the gap between them and lowered his voice.

"Greta, what is wrong?"

Greta shook her head emphatically, and the unruly curl came loose from her pins. "I am... tired, Your Excellency."

Frederick's eyebrows shot up. "Your Excellency?"

"Yes. Forgive me, but I am unwell. I... I have a headache. Forgive me," she said again, darting out of the room.

Frederick stared after her as the violins played, wondering what he had done to upset her.

Greta leaned against her bedroom door in the darkness, her pounding heart keeping time with the lively Scottish air drifting up from downstairs. She closed her eyes, but Frederick's face was immediately before her, and she snapped them open again.

Her heart took off at a gallop, and she scowled, crossing over to the bed. Pulling off her gloves, she sat down to remove her slippers. As her toes touched the floor, she shivered, pulling her feet up instead and wrapping her arms around her legs. Resting her chin on her knees, she gazed into the fire.

Greta, what is wrong?

Frederick's words echoed in her mind, and she closed her eyes, knowing she would see him there. His kind face, so full of concern as he peered down at her, made her smile. *Dear Frederick!* The endearment popped into her head without a thought, and slowly her smile faded.

That is what was wrong. Terribly, horribly wrong.

He was *not* dear Frederick. He was the Earl of Rockwell, the English Ambassador sent by King George and invited to stay by her father. He was nobody of consequence, at least not to her, and she could not understand why her heart insisted on doing pirouettes as they danced tonight.

Greta unfolded herself from the bed and went to the window, shivering as she hurried across the room. Her toes curled against the cold, and she hugged herself, rubbing her arms for warmth. Outside, the gibbous moon cast an avenue of light across the lawn, broken only by the shadowed claws of the barren trees.

What had happened? Somewhere between hello and goodbye, Frederick had become more than a friend. *No*, Greta thought, her jaw tight. *He is* only *a friend. Nothing more. My heart belongs to Hans.*

Hans. The thought of him brought an aching loneliness, the fluttering feeling for Frederick that had filled her breast melting away at its intensity. Hans was her love. He was her dream. Somewhere, out in the wide expanse of the world, he was fighting an enemy with whom he had no quarrel, his safety no concern to the men who had him in their charge. Shutting her eyes against the thought of him, bloodied and bruised, she placed her bare palm against the window.

In a moment, her hand was as cold as the glass, and she pressed it to her still warm cheek, opening her eyes. Her reflection stared at her with wide, silver eyes, one curl brushing her forehead and another grazing her neck. What did Hans see when he looked at her? Was it the same thing Frederick saw?

Moving away from the window, she reached behind her, struggling with her laces. She did not want to call Lisbet, she merely wanted to get out of her dress and crawl into bed. Her confusion during the dance left her feeling vulnerable and raw, and until her head could sort through the madness that raged in her heart, she wished to see no one.

Giving up on her dress, she climbed onto her bed and curled into a ball, shutting her eyes tight against the memories that rose unbidden in her mind: Frederick singing as she played. Hans kissing her cheek. Frederick offering his arm. Hans laughing as they walked together. Back and forth in a dizzy charade, Hans's and Frederick's faces fought for dominance in her mind, until she at last fell into a fitful sleep, dreaming of the man she refused to love.

Chapter 19

Frederick left on Christmas day, just as he had planned, and Greta was more relieved to see him go than she cared to admit. She still was not sure what had happened at the ball, but something had changed. The air between them was different as they danced, but she was afraid to examine her feelings too closely, lest they reveal what she was not willing to admit.

January came to Strausberg on an icy wind, chilling the land and freezing the lake. The young people of the village took advantage of the cold to form skating parties on the *Straussee*, which Greta joined as often as she could. Sometimes Johann came with her, and she even convinced Trina to leave her books and join them once. It was good exercise and great fun, but it made her terribly lonely for Hans. She'd always gone skating with him.

The weather grew even colder in February, but Greta had fur wraps, warm blankets, and letters from Hans to keep her warm. The war in America grew more desperate every week, and she anxiously awaited news that the British had surrendered or a truce had been reached, for that would mean Hans could come home.

One afternoon Greta curled up on her bed, rereading Hans's most recent letter. It had arrived only last week, but she had read and reread his words so often that the paper was beginning to tear at the folds.

Charlotte, Carolina, America
January 10, 1781

Dear Greta,

Your letter arrived just before Christmas, and I confess that it lifted my spirits tremendously. Conditions here are bleak indeed, and there was certainly nothing else to celebrate. Hearing from you, and learning of all that has been going on in Strausberg was bittersweet. It made me ache with loneliness for home, but at the same time, your cheerful words brought comfort and peace to my heart. Thank you, my faithful friend, for your letters. You know not how much I treasure them.

Greta's cheeks grew warm. Hans's words stirred in her the hope that he was at last beginning to recognize his feelings for her. *Hans treasures my letters.* It was little enough in the way of encouragement, but it made her heart sing nonetheless.

She reread over the rest of the letter. Hans complained about their treatment and their rations, and mentioned that they would be marching north to join a larger company of soldiers soon. He did not specify where, but since Greta knew little of the geography in America, it did not signify. There were also a few bitter lines by way of complaint about Julianna. She had not written for months, and he was beginning to think she did not care for him at all. When Greta first read those words, she rejoiced to know that the seed of doubt had at last taken root in his mind. It had just been announced in church that Julianna was engaged to Auguste Weisler, and though Greta had hinted at Julianna's fickleness in her previous letters, Hans had always excused Juli's behavior. A wedding, however, was being planned for the springtime, and Greta knew that Hans would not be able to deny the truth any longer.

Along with letters from Hans, Greta had received one letter from Frederick. It was posted from France, as he awaited passage across the channel into England. She was at first afraid to read it, lest Frederick address the night of the ball and insist on an explanation for her behavior. What could she say to him? How could she explain the confusion their dance had wrought in her heart? Thankfully however, the only mention he made was in his parting words:

> *I have thought often of the dance we shared on Christmas Eve, and look forward to dancing with you again.*

His words were harmless enough. Had not other gentlemen expressed a similar sentiment to her before? *Frederick is not like other gentleman, though,* her heart murmured upon first reading the missive. She had scowled, folding the letter and shoving it into her desk. She was glad that he had instructed her not to write until she heard from him again, after his arrival in England.

Surely by then her head and her heart will have reached an agreement about Frederick, and their correspondence could be as uncomplicated as she wished it to be.

Chapter 20

American colonies
January 1781

"Hold!"

Hans stopped, grateful for the rest. His neck and back ached from the day's march, and he could feel where a new blister had formed on his right foot. He shifted his weight to his left leg, craning his neck to see the front of the line. Their destination, the American fort Ninety-Six, was at last in view, which made the command to halt mildly confusing. They had been marching for several hours on little food, and he was anxious to get into the fort —which was being held for the British by American loyalists— and enjoy a hot meal and some rest.

"Eh now, why are we stopping?" the man behind him said.

Hans hissed quietly. "Hold your tongue, Ernst, or you'll get us both in trouble."

Ernst grumbled his way into silence, and Hans's mind

wandered back to when they had both enlisted. Careless, arrogant, hungry for adventure—how little they knew of the life of a soldier, then! Their naiveté did not last long, for the gruesome sights of war had quickly sobered them, though not in the same way. Years of abuse had transformed Ernst into one of the most ruthless soldiers in the regiment, and though he cared for his friend, Hans was repulsed at the bloodlust he'd seen come over Ernst during battle. The war had certainly hardened Hans, but it had completely demonized Ernst.

Hans was pulled from his thoughts by a horse and rider approaching from the fort, heading straight for Colonel Banastre Tarleton, their commanding officer. After several minutes of discussion, the newcomer gestured to the north, but Colonel Tarleton made a sweeping motion with his arm, taking in the troops before pointing at the fort.

The messenger shook his head, and pointed again in the other direction.

Colonel Tarleton was still for only a moment before turning his horse around. "Company, to the north, march! Double time!"

Hans gawked. "He cannot be serious," he muttered, even as he swung himself around and started marching in time with his fellow soldiers.

"What's happened? I thought we were going to the fort?" Ernst muttered from behind him.

"Just keep your head down—I'm sure we'll be stopping soon."

Hans was wrong. After marching for seven hours to get to Ninety-Six, they were forced to march another four hours in the opposite direction. Rations were low and tempers were short, but Tarleton kept them going with nary a break until well after sundown. At last the order was given to make camp, and the men dropped, exhausted, to the ground.

Their rest would not be long.

The next four days were some of the most brutal Hans had ever spent. Marching from before sunrise to after sunset, with little rest and even less food, made for volatile tempers in every quarter. The soldiers grumbled openly, and their captains, just as exhausted and nearly as malnourished as their men, did little to stem the insubordinate mutterings.

"Schneider! Schneider, wake up. The order's come to move."

Hans rubbed his bloodshot eyes with a dirty hand. "It's the middle of the night," he slurred.

The soldier shrugged. "Colonel's orders."

He moved off to wake the others, and Hans got to his feet. He swayed for a minute, exhaustion and hunger making him unstable, but steadied himself and ran a hand through his tangled curls. Stowing his bedroll, he picked up his musket, forming into a line with the other soldiers.

It was three o'clock in the morning when they started marching again. By this time, word had trickled through the lines that Morgan's army, whom they had thought to meet at the fort, had in fact fled north, and Colonel Tarleton was in hot pursuit. Another British army, led by General Charles Cornwallis, was ahead of them both. It was clear that Tarleton hoped to trap Morgan between them, and claim a much-needed victory for the sinking British army.

The sky was getting light when the colonists were finally spotted. A shout went up, followed by others, and soon the captains were calling orders to form into lines.

"Attack formations, men! First line, drop and fire!"

The motley crew of American soldiers sent a volley of shots into the advancing British before the line in front of Hans had even dropped to their knees. Two men fell over while the rest fired at command. The rush of battle sent Hans's heart skittering, but outwardly he was calm as he waited for the order to fall back and reload, which was also the signal for him to ready his firearm. The command came, and the line of soldiers in front of him moved out of the way as Hans stepped forward, dropping to one knee and putting the musket to his shoulder.

Without warning, the Americans suddenly turned and fled, and the shouted order from his captain barely reached his ears over the cheers of his fellow soldiers.

"Infantry, charge!"

Ernst ran past Hans in eager pursuit, the gleam in his eyes obvious even in the dim morning light. Gripping his gun, Hans took off after his friend, the soldiers around them shouting as they pursued their enemies. Every so often an American soldier would stop long enough to fire a haphazard shot into the ranks of their pursuers before continuing pell-mell around the east side of the hill.

Dizzy with exhaustion, Hans gulped down the frigid air as he ran, glancing up the hill when a movement to his left caught his eye. Two lines of armed militiamen appeared on the crest of the small embankment, their guns taking aim at Hans and his fellow soldiers. Hans lunged after Ernst, who was running around the hill and could not see the threat above him.

"Ernst!" Hans shouted, his voice lost in the blast as the Americans fired two volleys, one after another, into the sea of red and blue coats.

The soldier directly in front of him grunted, falling backwards onto Hans. Hans caught him before he hit the ground. "Are you all right?" Hans yelled above the din. But the man did not answer. A dark stain was spreading outward from a hole in his chest, and Hans lowered him to the ground. There was nothing he could do for him.

All around him, men were shouting as they ducked and weaved through the smoke-filled air. Bodies littered the ground, their uniforms dark with dirt and blood. Hans's eyes frantically swept the battlefield, ducking instinctively at every shot he heard, looking for his friend.

"Ernst!" he screamed, the bitter taste of gunsmoke coating his tongue. "Ernst!"

The tide of the battle had shifted in an instant. With half their officers dead on the ground, the British and Hessian soldiers were frantically retreating back the way they'd come. Hans was shouldered violently as a panicked soldier ran past him, and the force of the blow turned him almost completely around. There, not ten paces from where his eyes landed, he saw Ernst on the ground.

He was not moving.

Choking in the acrid air, Hans stumbled to where Ernst lay, dropping to his knees by his side.

"Ernst," he said thickly. "Come on, *mein Freund*, get up. You cannot stay here!" A bullet slammed into the ground near his feet, and he pulled on Ernst's shoulders, grunting as he turned him over. Ernst's half-open eyes were glazed in death, his cocky grin now frozen on his face. A chill that had nothing to do with the freezing January air filled Hans's heart.

A sudden blow to his face whipped his head violently to the right. Dazed, he reached a hand to his cheek, only to pull it back a moment later, his fingers sticky with blood. Warmth and wetness was quickly spreading down his neck and underneath his collar, and he struggled to get to his feet, panic and confusion replacing the grief he felt for his friend.

The right side of his head was burning, like the devil had branded him with a white-hot iron. He pressed a hand to his ear, but drew it back in horror when his fingers encountered a tangled mass of flesh where his ear had been. Suddenly dizzy, he dropped to his knees. He blinked, and the battlefield blurred, grew clear, then dimmed once more.

"Schneider!"

A Hessian soldier from Hans's regiment shook him violently on the shoulder. *"Raus hier!"*

The man ran off, the shouts of militia and the whiz of artillery crowding into Hans's consciousness like the rushing of a tidal wave. Energy coursed through his limbs as he got to his feet, running after his fellow soldier.

The desperate will to live kept him running, even though his bleeding, half-starved body wanted to collapse. Only a few more paces until he reached the shelter of the trees, until the bullets flying past him would find purchase in heavy oak trunks instead of fragile human flesh.

A snakelike root reached out of the darkness, catching the toe of his boot and sending him headlong into the dirt. His chin slammed into the ground and he tasted blood, the searing pain on the side of his head exploding with the impact. Struggling for breath, he pushed off from the ground, only to collapse in a heap when his arms gave way. The spike of energy that fueled his retreat leaked out of him like the blood that poured from the wound in his head.

The muffled sounds of war faded away, replaced by a ringing in his ears. Despite his desperate race for survival, he felt strangely calm at the thought of dying. His eyes flickered shut, and Ernst's laughing grin swam before his face, twisting and contorting into a death mask. Hans squeezed his eyes shut, blocking out the image of his dead friend, when another face drifted into his mind. It belonged to someone he had not seen in many months, but the sight of it stirred something deep within him. Golden curls fell gently across a creamy forehead, and a pair of dove-gray eyes smiled up at him.

"Greta."

Her name fell from his lips like a prayer, and as his consciousness slipped away, he felt a pair of arms around him, holding him tight.

Chapter 21

10 February, 1781

Dear Fräulein Rodenburg,

I have at last arrived in Kent and have the pleasure of writing to you from my own home. Somehow it feels strange to be back in England after so many months abroad. It is quiet—too quiet—and I find myself listening for the sounds of the pianoforte, even though I know you are not here to make it sing.

Greta smiled. She was curled up before the fire in the music room, having been practicing a new song when a servant arrived with a letter from Frederick. How strange it felt, to hear him speaking of her music when she had just been playing!

It is rainy and gray here, but I am so busy settling the affairs of the estate that I hardly have time to despair about

175

the weather. I should be preparing to go to town for the opening of Parliament, but I fear I may not attend this year. Perhaps in the spring I will make an appearance. If your father accepts my invitation to bring you and your mother for a visit, we shall certainly go to town and taste the delights of the season.

A season in London! The idea sparkled in her mind, winking and flashing like a jewel as she turned it over. She had heard much of the goings-on there, and was curious as to what was true and what was embellished. Would her father accept? Would she see for herself what the fuss was all about?

Greta curled up on the window seat, reading over the rest of his letter. He spoke of his journey, of the plans he had for the estate, and of missing her company. Near the end of the second page, he penned a few lines which gave Greta pause.

Your father is likely keeping you abreast of the war in America, since you have friends engaged in battle there, so I will mention only briefly what you likely already know. It appears that we have taken a multitude of heavy losses in the Carolinas. I know you will not rejoice in our defeat, but it now looks quite certain that the colonists will win. I hope that your friends are well, that this war will soon be over, and that they might return home safely.

Rising from her seat, Greta went across the hall in search of her father. As expected, she found him in his study, enjoying a book and his pipe. He looked up when she rapped on the open door.

"*Schatz!* Come in, come in."

Greta came around the desk, looking over her father's shoulder to see what he was reading. It was a thick volume, and when he noticed her curious look, he showed her the cover.

"*The History of the Decline and Fall of the Roman Empire, Volume I,*" she read.

Herr Rodenburg laughed at the face she made. "It is quite engrossing, I assure you. But I trust you did not come for a history lesson on Roman politics?"

She smiled. "No. I came to ask what you have heard concerning the war in America."

Herr Rodenburg frowned. "Has something happened?"

"Not really. But I received a letter from Fre— Lord Rockwell today, and he mentioned something about the war being over soon."

Her father raised his eyebrows, and Greta felt her cheeks grow warm. "I see. May I read what he wrote?"

Greta handed her father the letter. "It is near the end."

She stood silent as her father scanned the final page. "Hm," he said when finished. "Yes, I have received a similar report."

"So the colonists have defeated the British? Is the war over?"

"No. Nothing has been settled, though it is looking more certain everyday."

Herr Rodenburg passed the letter back to Greta, who returned to the music room in high spirits. With Julianna getting married, the ambassador back in England, and the war in America nearly over, she was certain there would be a happy ending for her and Hans in the future.

Tucking the letter into her pocket, she sat down before the piano, letting her fingers sing the happiness she felt in her heart.

A week after receiving Frederick's letter, Greta followed her parents into the dining room for the evening meal. The day had been overcast and cold, and her spirits were as depressed as the barometer in her father's study. Just as they were sitting down to supper, Gregor Schneider burst into the room, with a footman hard on his heels.

"Herr Rodenburg!" the boy cried, clearly distraught. "You must come, you must!"

"*Ruhig!* Forgive me, sir, he would not wait," the footman broke in, out of breath.

"Please, Herr Rodenburg!"

"Calm down, child," Herr Rodenburg said, waving off the footman. "What is the matter?"

"My father has collapsed!" Gregor said, beginning to cry.

"Collapsed!"

"*Ja.* He is at home. But he is not moving, sir. I fear that he is dead!"

Herr Rodenburg jumped to his feet, calling to his servants even as he strode out the door. Greta stood and made to follow him.

"Where are you going?" her mother snapped.

"To find out what has happened."

"You will do no such thing. Let your father handle it."

But Greta was already gone, her mother's threats ringing in her ears. She ran to her room and snatched a cloak, then hastened downstairs and out the door.

The familiar path to the Schneiders' house was covered in a thin layer of snow. Greta had not taken the time to exchange her slippers for boots, and they were soaked through in a matter of moments. Clenching her jaw against the chill, she looked down the path. In the darkness, the Schneiders' home glowed with a brilliance she had never seen before. Every window was lit, indicating that something of great importance was happening therein.

The sight terrified her.

Her lungs sucked in the freezing night air as she half ran, half stumbled in the darkness, her legs screaming in pain from her frenzied flight. At last she staggered onto the front steps, clutching her belly and gasping for breath.

She knocked briskly on the door, but received no answer. Boldly she opened it, and her ears were at once accosted with the sounds of crying, wailing, and shouting. Her father's deep voice came from another room, alternately calling out directions and speaking soothing words to someone she could not see. Greta forced her frozen feet to move, walking towards the commotion.

Stopping in the doorway to the parlor, she saw her father, crouched beside the motionless figure of Peter Schneider, who lay on his back in the middle of the room. Frau Schneider sat on the sofa, her face buried in her apron, wailing uncontrollably. One of her daughters sat beside her, tears streaming down her face as she tried to comfort her mother.

"Wolter, has your brother gone for the doctor yet? I need another compress. Sophia, fetch some more water. And be sure that—Greta!" Herr Rodenburg spotted her as he shouted instructions to the children. "What are you doing here? Go home at once."

"But, Papa…"

"*Geh!* Gregor, take her home."

Greta stumbled backwards, tripping on the hem of her cloak. Gregor Schneider reached a hand out to steady her.

"Gregor," she whispered as they left the room. "Is it… is Hans…"

A sob escaped from the boy's throat. "Papa received a letter from America. Hans and Ernst have been killed."

Chapter 22

Pain unlike anything Greta had ever experienced stole the next several weeks of her life. Her grief was suffocating. Crushing. Consuming. She felt as if she was drowning, without the blissful relief of ever actually dying.

Herr Schneider recovered from the shock he received upon hearing the news, but as he remained too weak to resume his duties, a new man was hired. Every time Greta saw the new steward around the estate, she felt as though she were being dragged under the water again. She wondered if she would ever resurface.

It was hard for Greta to believe that life outside her pain-filled world continued, but continue it did. Winter gave way to spring, and the snowy fields soon became sodden quagmires. Though her parents had refused to allow her to mourn publicly, Greta wore a black petticoat each day, sandwiched between her other skirts. She asked Lisbet to hem it shorter than the others to prevent discovery, and although no one else knew, Greta was glad to honor the memory of Hans in her own way.

Lord Rockwell sent her a heartfelt letter of sympathy upon hearing the news of Hans's death. It both comforted and tormented Greta, to hear Hans spoken of with such kindness by a man whom he had openly scorned. But she was grateful for Frederick's solicitude, and sent him a letter in reply telling him so. Hans may be gone, but at least she had Frederick. He listened without judgment, offered comfort without condescension, and condolences without pity. She missed him, and was glad when he wrote of coming to visit in a few months.

Amidst the terrible sadness hanging over Strausberg came a poorly timed wedding—that of Julianna and Auguste. Though Julianna wept upon hearing the news of Hans's death, it was clear that her heart had long been attached to another. She would not hear of postponing the wedding, and was even brash enough to complain that having the Schneider and Gottfried families in black at the ceremony would be bad luck.

The wedding was set for March twentieth, because Julianna insisted on being married the first day of spring. Greta stood obediently with her family in the churchyard, thankful that the clouds overhead were thin, for she had left her umbrella at home. Greta allowed her mind to wander as the priest droned on about the marriage covenant and the responsibilities each spouse had to the other. Julianna and Auguste stood facing each other at the door of the church, the priest standing just behind them in the vestibule.

"Our duty is to the Lord," he said, addressing the small crowd gathered to witness the ceremony. Greta had not been paying very close attention, but at the word *duty* she raised her head. It held bitter memories for her, and as it fell upon her ears she winced. Hans had claimed it was his duty to leave Prussia and fight for another country, but his error had cost him his life. Greta swallowed. What had the priest said about duty? She strained her ears, striving to hear more clearly.

"It is only through our acceptance of His will that we can find true joy and fulfillment in this life." The priest looked down into the earnest eyes of the two young lovers. "In binding your lives together through matrimony, you now have a duty to each other as well, and you will be held accountable for the discharge of those responsibilities."

Greta stared at the priest, stunned. His words reverberated in her head, understanding lighting her mind like a rocket. Over and over Greta turned the words in her mind, struggling to grab hold of the light she had found, and what it meant.

Cheers and well wishes burst from the crowd, and Greta realized with a start that the ceremony had ended. She looked to Auguste and his bride, the joy that emanated from them as they walked among their friends and family nearly palpable. Dazed, Greta followed after her mother, not knowing or caring where they went.

"Greta!" Katarina hissed, after Greta bumped into her. "Watch where you are going!"

Greta looked at her younger sister with new eyes. Though she wore a familiar scowl, Greta knew it was only ever aimed at her —rarely was it ever directed towards their parents. Katarina had always been a dutiful daughter. Content with her place in life and obedient to a fault.

Exactly the opposite of Greta.

And yet, as the eldest, the choices Greta made would dictate the course of Katarina's life, and to an extent, that of Johann as well. The magnitude of such responsibility fell suddenly, heavy and hard, upon her heart.

"Forgive me," she said, turning away. The crowd was pressing in on the happy couple, and Greta stepped out of the way, where she could ponder on the ideas swirling like eddies in her mind.

The sun broke through the gauzy film of cloud overhead, flooding the churchyard with weak spring sunshine. Herr Rodenburg stood next to Auguste and his parents, offering his congratulations and advice. Frau Rodenburg waited beside him with a condescending smile, her chin just high enough that her eyes appeared half-closed. Greta knew she should go to them, but first she stopped to congratulate the bride.

"*Herzliche Glückwünsche*, Frau Weisler," Greta said with a curtsy.

Julianna turned away from another guest to speak with her. "*Danke*, Fräulein Rodenburg. And thank you for coming." She smiled sweetly, lifting her brow. "Tell me, when shall I have the pleasure of celebrating your own nuptials?"

"My... own?"

"Of course. I thought you were engaged to that Englishman— the viscount...?"

"He is an earl now," Greta said stiffly. "Lord Rockwell."

"Oh, yes."

"And we are not engaged."

Julianna looked surprised. "Are you not? I thought it was a settled thing."

Sighing, Greta shook her head. "No. Nothing is settled. But let us not talk of that, and let us not quarrel over the past." She swallowed. "Frau Weisler—Julianna—please forgive me for my pettiness. For my jealousy. If Hans were here—" She choked on her words, and Julianna grasped her hands.

"There is nothing to forgive. Hans would not wish to see us quarreling, were he here." She was composed as she said it, but her eyes were shining.

Greta nodded, swallowing the lump in her throat. "You make a lovely bride, Juli. I am very happy for you."

"Thank you."

Greta stepped away to let other well-wishers greet the bride. Her father looked up as she walked to his side. Frau Rodenburg was already on his arm.

"Margareta, are you ready to go?"

"Yes, Papa."

Their friends and neighbors bowed in respect as the Rodenburgs passed, making their way to the carriage. Greta looked at each of them as if seeing them for the first time. Dozens of faces, dozens of names, each of them striving to fill their place in society as best they could. They looked happy, all of them, and the priest's words drifted back to her mind. *It is only through our acceptance of our duty that we can find joy and fulfillment in this life.*

Greta lifted her chin, resolve filling her heart, the brightness of hope flooding out the pain.

She knew what she must do.

Chapter 23

Greta's fingers slid deftly up and down the keyboard, her lips gently parted in a smile. It had been weeks since she had played anything other than melancholy concertos and depressing overtures, and it felt good. Cleansing. Healing, even.

The music softened in a ritard, and Greta lifted her hands from the keys, brushing away the curls on her forehead.

"I have always loved that song."

She looked up at her father, who stood in the doorway. He smiled and came to sit beside her on the bench.

"Pachelbel was a master," Greta said, caressing the keys.

"And you do him a great deal of credit."

She smiled and leaned her head against his shoulder. "Papa," she asked, fingering the lace on her sleeve. "What made you decide to marry Mama?"

Herr Rodenburg looked thoughtful. "Marriage is a complicated process in our world at times. Those of us who are born into privileged circumstances, are ofttimes required to marry within a very limited circle, if our position in society is not to be compromised."

"But did you *always* know that was your duty? Did you never wish for something else?"

"I always understood what was required of me. The alternative —disinheritance, poverty, shame—was not at all appealing. I certainly hoped that I would be attracted to my wife, and feel affection for her, but it was a secondary concern only."

Greta rubbed the lace between her fingers, feeling the delicate threads that were woven together. "I never understood that before," she said slowly. "But I think I do now."

She took a deep breath. "Before Hans went away, before he even joined the army, I think, he and I quarreled. About duty."

"Duty?"

"Yes. Hans claimed that in joining the army, he was doing his duty to his country. But I disagreed. I said he had a higher claim —the duty to his father, and his family—that he had ignored in pursuit of what he thought would bring him happiness."

Her father nodded. "I see."

"But," Greta's voice caught, and she swallowed. "Happiness did not come for Hans. Or his family. Or me."

Her voice broke on the last word, and she buried her head in her father's shoulder. He wrapped his arms around her as she wept, rubbing her arm in silence.

At last she sat up and dried her tears, her voice surprisingly strong as she said, "The priest told Auguste and Julianna that happiness is to be found in the doing of one's duty. Hans's choice to shun his first and most important duty cost him his life. But I do not want it to cost me mine."

187

Her father frowned. "*Schatz*, your life is not in danger."

"Not my life, no. But I am in danger of losing a life of happiness if I persist in my stubborn ways." Taking a deep breath, she squared her shoulders and turned to face her father. "I am ready to accept my betrothal to Lord Rockwell."

If Herr Rodenburg was surprised at her declaration, he did not show it. He looked at his daughter for a long time, his eyes searching her face. She stared back at him with calm determination, a serenity in her countenance he had never seen before.

"Are you sure, *meine Liebling*?"

"Yes." Greta looked down, twisting her hands in her lap. "I am well aware that my attitude and actions regarding marriage have been selfish and irrational. But I understand better now. And I am ready to accept my responsibility, as a Rodenburg. As your daughter."

Herr Rodenburg smiled, his gray eyes crinkling at the corners. "I am proud of you, *Schatz*. And I think you will be very happy."

Greta nodded, but a portion of her spirit was screaming inside, fighting against the shackles of her birthright. She forced a smile, striving to calm the turmoil within.

Herr Rodenburg stood and offered Greta his hand. "Come," he said, "let us tell your mother."

Frau Rodenburg heard the news with great elation. The usual displeasure she felt towards her eldest child evaporated, and she sang Greta's praises with all the insincerity of an unattached parent. Greta smiled and nodded, allowing her mother to flatter and praise her with wanton abandon. At length, Frau Rodenburg's raptures gave way to more practical matters.

"We must order your gown from Paris," she said. "As well as the rest of your trousseau. And as soon as may be—it will take time to have them all made up. When would you like to be married?"

"It does not matter," Greta said mildly.

"I think we can have everything arranged in a month or two. We shall plan the wedding for late in May. And you shall be settled in your new home before summer."

Greta's stomach twisted at those words, but she clasped her hands tightly in her lap, willing them not to tremble. *My new home.* Despite the fear and uncertainty of what that new home would be like, a tiny sliver of excitement wormed its way into her heart. She would get to see England. Perhaps other parts of the world, too. Places she had only ever read about, only ever dreamed of actually visiting.

And she would be with Frederick. Comfort filled her breast at the thought. She knew Frederick. He was a good friend, and he cared for her. Would that be enough? Would his affection and her respect be enough to ensure their happiness?

"Your father said he will write to Lord Rockwell this afternoon," Frau Rodenburg said, cutting into Greta's thoughts. "Only think! My daughter, the wife of an English earl." She was positively purring.

"Does it please you, Mama?"

"*Meine Liebling*, it is what I have always wished for you! To be so advantageously married, both in wealth and in consequence? There is nothing more that I could have wished for."

Not even love? Greta smiled, striving to hide her pain. Though she was determined to pursue her new course with as much vigor and passion as she could muster, Greta still mourned the loss of her childhood fancies. She grieved for Hans, and for the world she had imagined living in with him. All her life, she had secretly hoped and prayed and prepared to love and be loved by him, as his wife. But that dream would never be. Hans was dead, and no amount of tears would ever bring him back.

Chapter 24

Frederick wrote a beautiful letter to his betrothed immediately upon his receipt of the news from Herr Rodenburg. Greta received it a few weeks later, and found a quiet spot in the garden where she could read it undisturbed.

9 April, 1781

Dearest Margareta,

You know not the pleasure it gives me to address my letter to you thus. I confess that I was surprised—nay, shocked!— upon receiving the missive from your father, indicating your change of heart and your desire to attach yourself to me in matrimony. I returned his letter with one of my own, stating all that is proper and amiable to say at such a time. But from you I will not be so sedate. Greta, you have made me the happiest man alive. I have admired you almost from the very beginning of our acquaintance, from the moment I saw you throw your sodden handkerchief at your sister.

Greta gasped. How did he know about that? She frantically searched her memory, recalling the incident with Katarina in the garden. Greta had fallen into the reflecting pool, and... ah. Her father's study overlooks the back gardens; the gentlemen must have been within and been witness to the events outside. She shook her head and smiled, returning to the letter.

> *You have such spirit, and a genuine passion for life, that I could not help but be drawn to you. Every day, every moment spent in your company drew me farther under your spell. Your wit, your beauty, your talents, your charms—all combine to make you the loveliest creature I have ever known...*

Greta's cheeks were pink by the time she finished the letter, and she glanced nervously around, afraid that someone might be watching. It was the first time she had ever received such a letter in her life, and Frederick's words stirred feelings inside of her she had never experienced before. If she had ever doubted his affections, she certainly could not doubt them now—not when they were written so plainly before her.

Pressing a hand to her stomach to stop its fluttering, she smiled, and began to read the letter once more.

The next several weeks were some of the busiest of Greta's

life. She was measured and remeasured for the dozens of dresses her mother had ordered. Parties, outings, and visits occupied most of her waking hours, and when she at last fell into bed at the end of the day, her dreams were riddled with flowers and dresses and churchyards. Swimming through the murky lens of her subconscious, Frederick's face hovered.

The Earl of Rockwell came back to Prussia early in May, and his presence unnerved her so much that Greta hid in her room, claiming a headache, all the day of his arrival. Her mind was made up on the matter of her marriage, but in her heart, she still grieved for Hans. Pasting on a smile for company and pretending that she was joyfully anticipating their union seemed too great a task to bear.

Arising early the next morning, Greta dressed for a ride and went out to the stables. As she turned the corner of the house, she nearly ran into Frederick, returning from his own ride.

"Greta!" he said, reaching out to steady her. She flushed and stepped back.

"Guten Morgen, Lord Rockwell," she said. Then, flushing, "Frederick."

The hesitation in his face as she addressed him melted away as she spoke his name. "Good morning, Fräulein," he said, touching the brim of his hat. The formality of the gesture made Greta smile, though her stomach twisted nervously.

"Are you going for a ride?" he asked.

"Yes."

"May I join you?"

She glanced at the whip in his hand. "Have you not just finished your own ride?"

"I did. But I would be happy to accompany you. My horse is not overtired—another walk through the woods will not harm him."

She hesitated. "I had planned to ride hard."

"Then I shall saddle a fresh mount," he smiled.

They stood in silence for a moment, until Frederick stepped back and motioned towards the stables. Greta brushed passed him, her step quick because her nerves were strung so taut. Frederick kept pace with her.

"I have never been on this part of the continent during the springtime," Frederick said as they walked. "It is beautiful."

Greta said nothing.

"It is a great deal colder and wetter in England at present."

Still, she did not respond.

"Have you been out riding much lately?" Frederick persisted. At this, Greta was forced to reply.

"Not often. The weather has only recently warmed enough to ride with any regularity. And I have been busy at home."

"Oh? What has occupied your time?"

She stopped, and he did, too. "Arrangements for the wedding," she said flatly.

"Oh, yes. Of course."

She flushed—what was the matter with her!—then started briskly off again. He caught her by the elbow, and her stomach jumped into her throat.

"Greta," he said, his voice soft in the still morning air, "about the wedding. I am well aware that…" He sighed and released her arm. Greta wrapped her arms around her waist, holding herself together.

"I am sorry for the loss of your friend, Herr Schneider," he said gently.

At that, the color drained from Greta's face.

"Perhaps I am wrong," he continued, more slowly, "but I cannot help but assume, since your agreement to our betrothal came so soon after his death, that you have agreed to marry me only because you are now unable to marry another." His eyes searched her face, and Greta drew a deep breath, turning away.

"Hans was very dear to me," she said slowly. "And his death did have much to do with my decision. But it was more than that."

He waited, and after a moment she looked at him. "Before he left, Hans spoke to me of duty. His duty, and my own. He spoke of honor and responsibility, and though I would not hear him at the time, after his death, I considered his words more carefully. I realized that running away from my duties and responsibilities would never bring me happiness, and that was a sobering thought." She watched him, wondering what his reaction would be.

"Honoring one's duty is an admirable trait," he said after a thoughtful pause. "But I hope your choice does not lie in duty alone."

His voice and brow lifted, turning his statement into a question. She shook her head.

"No. While I had hoped to marry for love," she looked down, willing herself not to blush, "uniting myself with a friend is the next best thing. My father feels it is a good union, and I trust him."

"I see."

Though he smiled at her, she could see a tightness around his eyes that spoke of disappointment. She could not say it surprised her, but it saddened her nonetheless. It appeared they would begin their life together equally disappointed in the circumstances of their union. She sighed.

"Well," she said, "would you still care for a ride?"

He nodded, and they continued to the stables in silence. It was not a comfortable silence, but neither was it vibrating with tension. It seemed complacent, the honesty shared between them providing understanding, if not relief.

"You expressed a desire for a hard ride," Frederick said, when they were at last seated on their mounts. He raised his brow. "Would you care for a race?"

Greta smiled. "I would like that very much."

They led their horses down the lane and across the field to a large meadow, where there was plenty of room to run. Greta's horse pawed anxiously beneath her, sensing her tension.

"I believe I should warn you, Frederick," Greta said, adjusting her grip on the reins, "that although I have agreed to marry you, I have no intention of letting you win."

Frederick grimaced. "Of that," he said, positioning his horse next to hers, "I have no doubt."

Chapter 25

"Greta! Come in, my dear, come in."

Greta stepped into her father's study, arranging her skirts carefully as she sat down. She folded her hands in her lap and looked up expectantly. "You wished to see me, Papa?"

"Yes, *Schatz*, I did." Herr Rodenburg cleared his throat. "You are getting married tomorrow, Greta, and there are a few things I wish to tell you, about marriage."

"Oh!" Greta's face turned crimson, and she half rose from her seat, as if she would run from the room. "My mother has already spoken with me. You do not need to trouble yourself. I am—"

"*Ach du lieber Himmel!* For goodness' sake, Greta sit down! It is nothing of that sort that I wish to discuss with you."

Herr Rodenburg's face was tinged pink, and Greta sat back, breathing deeply in an effort to settle her nerves. They gnawed at her insides, making her feel ill.

"I am glad that your mother has already informed you of... er, *that* aspect of marriage. But it is something else entirely that I wish to see you about."

She waited, still too embarrassed to speak. Herr Rodenburg clenched his pipe between his teeth and paced in front of her, his hands clasped behind him.

"Greta," he said, perching on the corner of his desk. "What have I taught you about the balance of power in politics?"

She blinked, surprised by his question. "It is a state of equilibrium," she said, "between two or more political entities. Regarding international relations, it refers to the balance between allied countries, which prevents any one of them from gaining too much power over another."

"Precisely. And what happens, Greta, if that balance is upset?"

"If one political entity becomes too strong, they have the ability to enforce their will upon others."

"Just so. Now Greta, how do you think this applies to marriage?"

She frowned, concentrating. "It means… that there should be a balance between the parties engaged?"

"Exactly!" Her father pulled the pipe from his mouth, leaning towards her. "Marriage is a *union*, Margareta. Not a dictatorship."

"But I always thought that the husband ruled. Mama always said—"

"Your mother is old-fashioned," Herr Rodenburg interrupted, puffing on his pipe once more. "After we were married, and I began asking her opinion about things, she was horrified." He chuckled. "She has since learned to indulge in my 'fancies' as she calls them, and humors me with her thoughts on occasion." He frowned. "I did not realize she was instructing you otherwise."

"I—" Greta frowned as well. "Hm. Now that I think of it,

Mama only ever spoke of the honor and duty I owed to my parents. And to you, particularly. I suppose I took that to mean I was to honor and obey my husband in all things, just as I was meant to be obedient to you."

"You are to respect your husband, just as your husband ought to respect you. It may be a more radical way of thinking in this day, but it is the right way of thinking. That is one thing that has always impressed me about Lord Rockwell—he respects you, and treats you as an equal. That is why I was so desirous of the match in the first place."

Greta did not know what to say. After a moment, she reached down to smooth her skirt, fussing with the hem.

"Nervous?" her father asked.

She looked up and smiled. "A little."

"*Gut.* I would be worried if you were not a little nervous."

"Were *you* nervous, Papa?"

"As if my coattails were on fire."

She laughed, relaxing a bit. "It is good to know I am not alone. Lord Rockwell does not seem at all nervous."

"That is because he loves you."

Herr Rodenburg's look softened, and he reached out to her, taking her hand. "I can tell by the way he looks at you, *meine Liebling.* And I am glad of it. It means that you will be well-provided for, and cherished, always, as you deserve."

Greta's eyes filled with tears. "As you have done."

"Yes." He cleared his throat, looking down. "Yes, as I have done. Because I love you, Margareta."

"And I love you, Papa," she whispered.

Herr Rodenburg patted her hand, but Greta stood up and flung her arms around his neck, holding him tight. Startled, but not displeased, he embraced her in return.

Chapter 26

Four months earlier

Hans groaned, the pain in his head causing his stomach to turn. If his head hurt this badly, he must still be alive.

The thought was not as comforting as it should have been.

As consciousness slowly returned, he realized he was lying on his back, not on his face where he fell. He opened his eyes. He was no longer outside, either. The room around him was dark, but he could just make out the underside of a roof high above his head. Gingerly he reached a hand up to examine the gaping wound where his ear had been.

It was bandaged.

"Oy, we've got a live one here."

The voice was not loud, but it carried in the stillness. Hans heard shuffling steps coming towards him, and he turned towards the sound.

"Hello there, I am Doctor Fieldstone. How are you feeling?"

"Like my head was nearly blown off," Hans replied in English. His voice came out as a croak, and he licked his cracked lips.

"Yes, well, it very nearly was. I am afraid I could not do much about your ear, although I patched it up as best as I could." His voice turned serious. "You lost a great deal of blood. Here, have some water."

He held a tin cup to Hans's lips, who drank it quickly. "More," he rasped.

"Only a bit. You are near starvation; you must go slowly."

He gave Hans another small drink, then set the cup down and proceeded to examine him. After a moment, Hans spoke.

"You are American." It was not a question.

"Yes."

"Then I am a prisoner?"

The doctor looked at him for a long moment. "Yes. But I assure you, you have received the best of care. I do not discriminate between patients."

Hans said nothing, and the doctor finished his examination. "You are weak, but if we can keep out the infection, you will live. I will get you some food. Do you think you can feed yourself?"

Hans ignored his question. "Where are those who died in battle?"

The doctor sighed. "Buried."

"Where?"

"In mass graves, near the battle sites."

"Where am I now?"

"In the hospital."

Hans narrowed his eyes. "How long will I be here?"

"Tomorrow you will join the other prisoners, as we need the space here for those more seriously wounded." The doctor stood. "But do not think you can escape from here. Guards are posted at every door and window, day and night. You are weak and cannot make it far." He looked down into Hans's angry eyes and sighed. "I will bring you some food."

The next day Hans was taken to the far end of the town, where hundreds of British soldiers and their mercenary allies were being kept in a large warehouse. He was dizzy and disoriented, and his head hurt abominably. He was given a torn piece of canvas tarp to use as a bedroll, and he took it to a far corner of the large room and lay down.

He never wanted to get up again.

Grief at Ernst's death, along with anger and humiliation at being wounded and captured filled his heart. He was hurt in body and spirit, and wished more than once that his life had been taken on the battlefield. At least then he would not be suffering now.

Time passed slowly for Hans. Most days he lay on his makeshift bed, sitting up to eat and drink when rations were brought to him, but otherwise ignoring what went on around him. Gradually his strength returned, and at first, his wounds seemed to be healing well. But within a week infection set in. He tossed and turned in a feverish delirium, hearing voices that were not there and seeing faces that were no more. His dreams were riddled with bleeding men, exploding cannons, and the agonizing moans of the dying. But scattered between the chaos of his thoughts, when his fever would subside and allow his body to rest, his mind would recall the sound of Greta's laughter, or the brightness in her eyes whenever he came into a room. The stronger he grew, the more frequently her face appeared. She represented all that was beautiful and good in the hellish world he inhabited, and he clung to her memory, desperate for relief.

When Hans at last regained his health, he was an altered man. Not only because of the scar now stretching across his face, but because of the twisted lens through which he now viewed the world. He felt that everything good had been taken from him—ripped from his life like the bullet that tore through his ear. Bitterness, anger, and guilt festered within him, distorting his thoughts and tainting his memories.

A month after the battle that had taken Ernst's life, Hans was finally healed—his physical injuries, at least. Finding himself a prisoner did nothing to improve his mental and emotional wounds, and soon he was watching the American guards with hatred in his eyes, wondering which of them had murdered his friend. By the middle of March, having been imprisoned nearly two months, Hans realized something was terribly wrong.

There had been no mail. For anyone.

At first, he supposed that mail was slow in coming because the whereabouts of British prisoners was constantly shifting. But that excuse could no longer hold water. No one at home had heard from him in months—surely they would be concerned for his safety. Did they know of Ernst's death? Were they aware he was a prisoner? How many letters had they written that were lost somewhere, not knowing where he was? He no longer hoped that Juli would have written him, but surely his mother, and Greta...

Greta. Immediately her face came to his mind, laughing at the scowl now etched on his features. He sat down on his bedroll, closing his eyes and letting the memory of her wrap around him. He thought of her laugh, and her beautiful eyes. He imagined her as she had been when they were children, dancing away from him as he chased her towards the lake. Suddenly she morphed into the woman he left behind, and his heart beat faster as he imagined her perfect lips, the curve of her form... His thoughts of Greta grew tainted, polluted with lust and greed from his broken mind. *Greta is all I have left,* he thought. *I must find a way to get back to her. I cannot let anyone take her from me.*

At last he decided to approach one of the guards. The American soldier watched him warily, gripping his rifle as Hans sauntered towards him.

"What do you want?" the guard barked when Hans was still several paces away.

"I have a question."

"Yes?"

"Why have we not received any mail?"

His question surprised the guard, whose face twisted into a sneer. "So you've noticed, eh?"

Hans's fingernails dug into his palms, anger flashing from his eyes. "You've been withholding it from us?"

"What's the matter?" the man jeered. "Have a sweetheart back home who's forgotten you?"

Hans's fist was a lightning strike, colliding with the guard's nose with a vicious *crack!* Blood poured from his face, his painful yelp drowned by the string of German curse words Hans hurled at him. It took four other guards to pry him off the unfortunate soldier, clubbing him with the butts of their guns until Hans's face was bloodied and bruised.

It took weeks before Hans recovered. His rations were cut and he was locked up in a makeshift cell with a few other prisoners, his wounded mind obsessed with thoughts of Greta. Somehow, when he was well again, he must find a way to send her a letter.

Chapter 27

On her wedding day, Greta awoke with the dawn. She lay in bed, watching the light creep across the ceiling and gradually fill the room. A tumult of emotion washed over her as she thought of what the day would hold, and when at last she rose from her bed, her nerves settled in her stomach like a many-fingered flame, scorching her insides with the fire of uncertainty.

Breakfast was a subdued affair. Greta had no appetite and wished to remain in her room, but her mother insisted that she sit at the table with the family. Lord Rockwell was also there, seated across from her. She kept glancing at him over her plate, and every time she caught his eye, a jolt of fear—or was it excitement?—coursed through her. He smiled, and Greta wondered if he truly felt as calm as he appeared.

When the meal was over, Greta retired to her room to dress for the wedding. Both Lisbet and Trueden, along with two other maids, were there to help with the enormous task. Layers and layers of fabric were piled upon her; the formality of the event adding far more clothing than usual. Greta made a face when her formal paniers were tied to her waist, but she did not complain when petticoat after petticoat was pulled over her head. Her dress, which had arrived from Paris only two days earlier, was made of ivory silk, with satin ribbons the color of an early summer sky trimming the hem and the sleeves. A long, formal train hung from the back of her shoulders, embroidered with flowers and birds in golden thread. Frau Rodenburg came into the room during the final preparations. Greta's long, blonde tresses were pulled up into the highest bouffant Trueden could manage, with ringlets framing her face and brushing the back of her neck. When at last her daughter was ready, Frau Rodenburg cupped her face with both hands.

"You look like a countess," she said, a rare smile on her face.

"Thank you, Mama."

"The carriage is waiting. Are you ready?"

Greta nodded, afraid to speak lest she burst into tears. She could hardly think, and all she wished for now was that the event was over and life could return to normal.

Only it would not return to normal. She would be a married woman. She would move to England.

Greta pressed a handkerchief to her mouth, hurrying after her mother.

Greta's wedding was very much like Julianna's, only finer. Nearly the entire community in and around Strausberg was Lutheran, and the customs regarding marriages were the same for all classes of people. Frederick, being English, requested that the priest allow him to say the vows of his own Anglican background, but otherwise the words the priest spoke were the same they had always been.

Greta stood in the doorway of the church next to Frederick, while the minister read aloud the words of his vow. Frederick looked down at her, and repeated after the priest.

"I take you to be my wife and my spouse," he said, taking Greta's hand. "And I pledge to you the faith of all that I possess; that I will be faithful to you and loyal with my body and my goods; that I will keep you in sickness and in health and in whatever condition it will please the Lord to place you, and that I shall not exchange you for better or worse until the end."

Greta's hands were trembling as she looked to the priest. "And do you, Margareta Maria Rodenburg, desire to take Frederick Mathias Greenwood as your lawful wedded husband?"

She swallowed, feeling suddenly ill. Glancing up, she looked into Frederick's eyes, warm and kind, and resolve coursed through her.

"Yes," she said.

The charged atmosphere in the churchyard noticeably relaxed, and the priest asked them to exchange rings. Removing her glove, Greta held her hand out to Frederick, who took it gently in his own. He slipped a delicate gold ring onto her finger, and Greta's heart beat erratically when he did not let go. Taking a shaky breath, she slipped a ring onto his finger as well, then dropped her hands to her side.

There. It was done. They were married. Relief coursed through her for one blissful moment, until she turned to face the waiting crowd and caught Julianna Weisler's eye.

Juli was looking at her knowingly, a saucy smile playing about her lips. In an instant, a new thought sprang into Greta's mind, turning her stomach and making her dizzy.

The wedding might be over, but the wedding night was still to come.

With the ceremony finished, the wedding party and their guests returned to the Rodenburg's estate to celebrate. Climbing the stairs to her room, Greta glanced down the east corridor to the guest apartments, where Lord Rockwell was staying. Her stomach flipped, and she hurried to her room to change. Her mother had told her what to expect, but Greta was nervous for what the night would hold.

No, she was more than nervous. She was terrified.

After Lisbet helped her change, Greta sat on the bed, staring out of the window. She did not want to join the others in the drawing room until it was absolutely necessary. When a knock sounded on the door, she did not even turn, but allowed her maid to answer it.

"*Guten Tag*, your lordship."

Greta whirled around, horrified to see Frederick standing in the doorway. Lisbet let him in, then slipped out of the room, shutting the door behind her.

Jumping to her feet, Greta moved away from the bed.

"Lord Rockwell," she said, clasping her hands together. She blushed. "Frederick."

Frederick smiled and came towards her. "Greta." His voice was soft, and he said her name with such adoration that she looked down, embarrassed.

"I did not have a chance to tell you earlier," he said, "but you looked absolutely beautiful today."

"Thank you."

She stood several feet away from him, and he noticed the space between them. He glanced at the closed door, then smiled gently.

"I know that we shall be required to present ourselves in the drawing room, but I wondered if I might speak with you before then."

She swallowed, nodding.

"Margareta," he said, clearing his throat. "I know you are aware of my feelings for you. Of my admiration for you, and my joy in your accepting my hand in marriage. But I do not wish… that is to say, I hope you will not…" The color rose in his cheeks, and he shook his head. Taking a deep breath, he looked her squarely in the eye. Greta had never seen him look at her so earnestly before.

"Greta, I know that you are determined to do right by your family, and your country. To do your duty. I admire that determination, and I understand that it is one of the principle reasons why you agreed to marry me."

"Frederick," Greta broke in, her voice weak. "You know that I care for you. You know it was not only–"

"Yes," he said gently. "I know. But I also know that you have resisted, even resented, the enforcement of your duty nearly all of your life." He laughed. "It was that headstrong defiance which drew me to you in the first place."

Greta looked down, not sure what to say. He went to her side, reaching out to gently touch her chin. "My dear," he said, "I understand what it is like to be born to a life one may not have chosen for oneself. A life filled with duties and expectations one is often forced to accept. But I will not force you."

He waited, watching her. But Greta only frowned.

"I do not understand what you mean."

He blew out his breath and turned away, clasping his hands behind his back. Greta recognized the movement as something he did when he was deep in thought, or nervous.

"I will not call for you," he said softly, looking out the window. "You will not be required to come to my quarters. I have no desire to…" His voice cut off, and suddenly Greta understood his meaning. The color drained from her face, and when he looked back at her, she was very pale.

"You do not wish to consummate our marriage," she whispered.

Slowly, Frederick shook his head.

"You have a duty to your heart, Greta," he said, taking her hands. "And that is more important than any duty you have to your husband."

"I do not believe my parents would agree," she said, laughing weakly.

Frederick smiled, lifting her hands to his face. He kissed one, then the other. "Whether they agree or not does not matter," he said. "This is *our* marriage, and we get to make our own choices in it. No more duty, no more expectations. Only love."

"Love?"

"Love is a choice, is it not? I chose you, because I love you. You chose me," he hesitated, but smiled nonetheless, "and while you may not love me now, I hope that someday you will. Until then, your choices are your own. And coming to my rooms can wait."

He stepped back, embarrassed once more. Greta felt strange, as if bonds which she had become accustomed to resisting had suddenly been cut loose.

"Now then," Frederick said brightly. "Shall we go down to dinner?"

Greta looked up at her husband with new eyes. Then, throwing her arms around his neck, she held him close. "Thank you," she whispered. "Thank you."

Chapter 28

The following morning, Greta bid goodbye to her family. Johann clung to her skirts and wept. "First Hans, and n-now you," he sobbed. "What if you n-never come back? What if y-you die as well?"

Greta crouched down and dried his tears with her handkerchief. "Hush now, it will be all right. I will not die. Where Hans went, there was a lot of fighting. But there is no one fighting in England. I will be back to visit soon. And you can come to my house, too."

Johann wiped his nose with his sleeve, earning a hiss from his mother. "I suppose so," he mumbled.

She gave him a hug, her throat tight. Beside him, Katarina sniffed in a most unladylike fashion, though her look was stoic.

"*Auf Wiedersehen*, Greta," she said, awkwardly embracing her sister.

"*Auf Wiedersehen*, Trina."

"Will you... will you write to me?"

"Of course," Greta said, surprised. "If you wish."

Katarina nodded emphatically. "I do. I do wish you to. It will be strange, to have you gone." She swallowed, striving to keep her face impassive. "I will miss you, Greta."

Greta reached for her sister again, and this time Katarina clung to her, crying. Greta soothed and comforted her, assuring her that she would write, and they could all come visit her later in the year.

The clock in the entryway struck the hour, and Greta looked to Frederick. He smiled and nodded. They needed to go. She turned to her mother next, and the women clasped their arms around each other.

"Do not squeeze me so tightly, Margareta—you shall muss your dress." Greta drew back, and her mother smiled, pressing a hand to her daughter's cheek. "Goodbye, *meine Liebling*."

"Goodbye, Mama."

At last she stood before her father. Of everyone in her family, Greta would miss him the most. She tried to say farewell, but the sentiment stuck in her throat, and she coughed instead, dislodging the tears that shone in her eyes. They went streaking down her face, and before she could pull out her handkerchief, his hand reached out and gently brushed them away. With a sob, Greta buried her face in her father's neck, soaking his cravat with her noisy tears.

"Honestly, Greta," her mother clucked. But Herr Rodenburg gathered his daughter into his arms, his own eyes shining.

"There now, *Schatz*, what is all this fuss? Hush now, it is all right."

"I will miss you, Papa," Greta sobbed.

"And I will miss you. I could not let you go unless I knew that you were going somewhere where you will be just as treasured as you are here. And I do."

Greta pulled back and looked at Frederick, who handed her his handkerchief. While Greta composed herself, the gentlemen shook hands.

"Take care of my daughter," Herr Rodenburg said, his voice thick.

"You may depend on it," Frederick replied. He placed a hand gently on Greta's back. "Are you ready?" he asked.

She nodded, drawing a deep breath. Taking her husband's arm, they led the party out of the room and to the waiting carriages. Her family's traveling coach stood in the drive, a team of four sturdy horses ready to pull it away. All of Greta's worldly possessions were neatly packed and stowed in another carriage, which would follow them on the long journey to the coast.

Frederick helped her into the waiting coach while her family called their goodbyes once more. She waved out the carriage window until they turned at the end of the drive and the house was lost from view. She sat back against the seat and heaved a sigh.

"I will miss it here," she said.

Frederick smiled sympathetically, but said nothing. The silence remained unbroken as they continued on their way, and Greta was grateful for the time to get her feelings in check. She had been afraid that being alone in the carriage with Frederick for so long would be strange and disconcerting. But at the moment it felt neither awkward nor uncomfortable. It felt safe, and Greta was glad to have him near.

As the carriage passed through the countryside, and then through the streets of Strausberg, Greta watched out the windows as the home of her youth passed by in a blur. The spire of St. Mary's shot into the sky over the rooftops, and she turned, frowning at her husband.

"Are there Lutheran churches in England?"

"Yes, there are many."

Greta released a sigh. "That is a relief. With so many things to get accustomed to in my new home, I would rather not worry about a new religion as well." She hesitated. "Unless you wish me to attend services with you?"

He smiled. "I meant what I said last night, Greta. I am your husband, not your ruler. If you desire to attend services at the Lutheran church in Rockwell, I will be happy to accompany you."

"I would like that very much. Thank you, Frederick."

He inclined his head, and she turned to watch as the rest of the town fell behind them. She tipped her head back to look up at the high stone wall as they passed out of the city once more, the movement causing her hatpin to dig into her scalp. With a sigh, she unpinned the piece of millinery and placed it beside her on the seat. "I cannot abide that contraption poking into my skull any longer," she said, brushing at the rogue curl on her forehead.

"I have no hatpins to complain about, but that seems a marvelous idea," Frederick said, following suit. He tossed his hat onto the seat beside him, then shrugged out of his jacket as well. Greta blushed to see him in his shirtsleeves, and had to remind herself that they were married.

Married. It was as foreign a feeling as the land to which they were traveling. She wondered when being married would cease to feel strange and begin to feel normal.

"Nervous?" Frederick asked.

"A little. More excited than nervous, though. I have always wished to see more of the world."

"I remember the first time my parents took me to London," Frederick said, leaning his head back against the cushioned wall. "Rockwell is a relatively small town, but as a boy, it seemed rather large. I was stunned when I saw the rooftops of London, stretching endlessly to the horizon. I asked my father if London covered the world."

Greta smiled. "My father took me to Berlin once, when I was a little girl. I felt very much the same. But that is as far as I have ever traveled."

"You have never been outside of Prussia?"

"No. My mother would have liked to go to Paris, but Papa was always content to stay home. He liked the comfort and familiarity of Strausberg."

"You would have liked to go to Paris, too."

Frederick smiled as he said it, and Greta felt a familiar warmth spread throughout her chest. It was the same feeling she got whenever her father finished one of her sentences, or they shared a look over the table that meant he knew exactly what she was thinking. It was comforting, and strange, to feel it now with Frederick instead of her father.

"Yes," she said, a lump forming in her throat. She looked out the window at the passing landscape, willing her tears not to fall.

Frederick watched her for a moment, then pulled out a book and began to read. Greta was grateful for the silence as she watched her world slip away behind them.

Although Frederick had offered to give Greta a Grand Tour of Europe for their honeymoon, she deferred, saying instead that she would rather get settled in her new home, and travel the world with him later. Their first stop was in Berlin, which was only a day's journey from Strausberg. There, they switched to hired horses and continued on their journey to the coast, stopping each night to rest, changing horses when needed.

From Berlin they traveled to Hanover, on the western edge of the Empire, and from thence to the French city of Calais. By the time they arrived at the coast, they had been traveling for two weeks, and Greta was exhausted.

The winds were not as favorable upon their arrival as they would have liked, so they were forced to stay the night and cross the channel in the morning. It was damp and gloomy when they awoke, and a steady drizzle fell while they crossed to England in the ship.

After ten hours, the English coast loomed out of the mist, sodden, gray, and decidedly *not* Prussia. Greta watched the rocky coastline grow larger as the ship drew closer, her spirits sinking as they neared the port. Was this to be her home? This gray, wet, foggy land? She shivered, but not from the cold. Hearing footsteps behind her, she turned to look up into Frederick's face.

"Well, what do you think?"

Greta turned back to look across the channel. "Is it always like this?"

He chuckled. "No. The fog will burn off later this morning, and the clouds may part as well. Usually the weather is quite nice this time of year."

She did not reply.

"It is only two days more to Rockwell. We shall be home soon."

Sixteen days after leaving Prussia, their carriage at last pulled up in front of Frederick's estate, just as the sun was beginning to set. Crimson streaks stretched across the golden sky, richer and more vibrant than Greta had ever seen. She stepped out of the coach, tipping her head back to look at the massive brick building looming overhead. It was larger than she had imagined, with dozens of paned windows stretching to either side of the double doors. Three stories above her, the slate-colored roof reached heavenward towards the rainbow sky. Frederick, with a rapturous smile, pressed a hand to the small of her back and gestured up the steps with the other. She lifted her skirts, counting the stairs to steady her nerves as she climbed towards the front door. It was opened by a liveried footman, and as she stepped inside, Frederick leaned down and spoke low in her ear.

"Welcome home, Lady Rockwell."

The words, though fitting, sounded strange. Her old title and her old life were behind her now, far away in Prussia. Now she must embrace her new role in her new home as Countess of Rockwell.

"Welcome home, your lordship," the butler said with a bow.

"Thank you, Preston. I trust you are well?" Frederick said.

"Very well, thank you, sir."

"Would you like a bite of supper, sir, or shall I have a tray sent up to your rooms?" a matronly woman with a severe-looking bun said.

Frederick turned to Greta, who was removing her gloves. "My dear? Would you care to have some supper, or would you like to rest from our journey?"

They had been speaking German ever since they left Strausberg, but of course the servants spoke English. Frederick had replied in kind, but when he turned to her he slipped back into her native tongue. She smiled at him.

"I think I would like to rest this evening. If that is agreeable to you?" she said, forming the words in English. It sounded strange in her ears.

Frederick beamed. "Of course."

The woman who had addressed Frederick stepped forward and curtsied stiffly. Her dark hair was streaked with gray. "How do you do, your ladyship. I am Mrs. Whigham, the housekeeper."

"How do you do, Mrs. Whigham," Greta nodded in reply.

"Would you like me to show you to your rooms?"

"Don't trouble yourself, Mrs. Whigham," Frederick broke in. "I shall take Lady Rockwell upstairs. Please see that her trunks are brought up immediately."

The housekeeper nodded briskly and began issuing orders. Frederick offered Greta his arm, leading the way up the massive staircase.

"I do not think your housekeeper approves of me," Greta murmured, glancing over her shoulder at the servants bustling in the entrance hall.

"Nonsense. Mrs. Whigham is a gruff old sort, but she'll warm up to you soon enough."

"I certainly hope so," Greta murmured.

As they ascended the stairs, Greta looked around her in wonder. Beautiful wood paneling and ornate paintings adorned the walls. Above her head, a massive chandelier hung, crowning the spiral staircase like a many-faceted jewel. When they arrived at the third floor, Frederick guided her down a thickly carpeted hallway, pointing out portraits of family members and explaining their relation to him. At last he stopped before an elaborately carved door.

"These will be your rooms," he said, turning the handle and stepping back to allow her to enter first.

Greta stepped into a beautiful room, decorated in shades of blue and cream. Directly across from where they stood was a large paned window. She walked slowly over to it, admiring the furnishings and glancing up at the muraled ceiling. The window looked out on the front courtyard, where a large fountain stood in the middle of a circular lawn, around which the drive wrapped. Turning back to face the room, she saw that Frederick remained by the door.

"Do you approve?" he asked with some hesitation. "I asked Mrs. Whigham to oversee the refurnishing of the room, but if anything displeases you—"

"It is perfect, Frederick." She smiled to show her sincerity. "I am sure I will be quite comfortable here."

Frederick relaxed. "I am glad to hear it. This room has rarely been in use, and was in sore need of attention."

"Oh?"

"This is the family wing, you see. My parents' bedchambers

were across the hall, but since I am their only child..." He shrugged. "The guest wing is on the opposite side of the stairs."

"I see." She turned around, admiring the rest of the room. A massive canopied bed lay against the wall to her right, and directly across from the foot of it, another door stood open. She took a step forward and peered into her dressing room. She could hear the outer door of that room opening and closing as the servants brought in her things. Another door lay against the opposite wall, tucked in the corner by the window.

"Where does that door lead?" she asked.

Frederick cleared his throat, tucking his hands behind his back. "That is the door adjoining my own chambers."

"Oh! Yes. Of course."

Greta smiled to hide her blush, and turned away as if to inspect the wardrobe. Frederick cleared his throat again.

"I shall send your maid to you at once, so that you might refresh yourself."

"Thank you, Frederick."

"You are most welcome. If there is anything you need, anything at all, please let me know. This is your home now, and I sincerely hope that you will be happy here."

He bowed to her and left the room, shutting the door softly behind him. Greta moved to the bed and sat down.

Home.

The word sat heavy on her heart as she looked around the foreign room that was now her only refuge.

Chapter 29

The days and weeks following their arrival became a vast, headache-inducing blur to Greta. Dozens of servants, even more than she had known in her father's house, had to be introduced to and approved by the new countess. After meeting the seventeenth footman she stopped trying to remember all their names.

"I am sure," she said to Mrs. Whigham one morning, with some exasperation, "that whomever is currently employed by the household is adequate."

"It is not for me to say, your ladyship," the housekeeper sniffed. "You are the mistress of this house now, and it is your duty to ensure that you approve of everyone working herein."

"Hang my duty," Greta mumbled.

Mrs. Whigham pressed her lips together in a hard line, reminding Greta of her mother. She sighed.

"Very well. Who am I to meet next?"

When she was not meeting servants or being taught how the household was run by Mrs. Whigham, Greta spent her time roaming the gardens outside. Frederick often joined her, providing a listening ear for her near-constant lamentations.

"Frederick," she said during one of their walks, after a particularly frustrating morning, "why on earth did you insist on French lessons, when it would have served me far better to practice my English?"

The earl raised his brow, an amused smile on his lips. "Do you think English lessons would have been better received?"

Greta's lips twitched. "Perhaps not. But they would certainly have proven useful now."

"My dear, you are too hard on yourself. Your English is very good, and improving every day."

"My understanding is, perhaps. But my accent is dreadful." She groaned. "I never thought much about it before, but now that I am here, and I see the hesitant looks which accompany most of my directions, it is quite disheartening. I am usually asked to repeat myself, which is both frustrating and embarrassing."

Frederick squeezed her hand, which was tucked through his arm. "Be patient, Greta. It will come in time. Have you learned the layout of the house yet?"

"I believe so. Though why there are certain staircases that only reach from the first to the second, or from the second to the third floors, is beyond my comprehension. It is the most impractical nonsense I ever beheld."

Frederick chuckled. "I have often thought the very same thing."

They returned to the house and retired to one of the parlors on the second floor, where some refreshment and the day's mail were waiting for them. Greta sifted through the cards, handing a few business letters to Frederick and peering through the rest, hoping for a letter from home.

There were none.

Sighing, she picked up a card addressed *To the Right Honourable Earl of Rockwell and Her Ladyship the Countess of Rockwell.* She turned it over and broke the seal.

"I do not understand why Mrs. Whigham insists that *I* answer the invitations instead of you. I haven't a notion who any of these people are," Greta said, unfolding the letter.

"Mrs. Whigham is an old-fashioned sort. Whether you know the parties or not does not signify to her. You are the mistress of this house, and therefore the task of accepting or declining their invitations falls to you. Besides," he added, his eyes twinkling, "I haven't any notion who most of them are, either."

Greta laughed, shaking her head, and continued reading. After a moment she paused, holding the paper up for Frederick's examination. "This one has just arrived, from Mr. and Mrs. Sharpeton. They have invited us to dine with them this evening."

"Reginald! He was in town when I was here last," Frederick said, taking the note.

"Friends of yours?"

"Yes. But I've not seen them in ages."

"Would you like to go?"

"Certainly. But is that agreeable to you?"

"Of course. It is time I met some of the neighborhood, I think."

"Reg and I are old friends, having grown up together. Mrs. Sharpeton is a charming woman, and quite accomplished. I think you will get along very well with her."

Greta raised her brow. "Accomplished, you say? Does she speak any German?"

"I should think so," Frederick said with a smile.

"Then it is settled." Greta stood abruptly, plucking the letter from him with a coy smile. "I shall send a reply directly, and we shall see if her German is any good."

The appointed hour arrived, but Greta was still in her room, fighting with the clasp of her necklace. She had already dismissed her maid and was on her way downstairs when she looked one last time in the glass. The diamond necklace she wore seemed suddenly gaudy and disproportionate—something her mother would have wanted her to wear for her first public outing. Instantly she reached behind her to remove the jewels, but the clasp stuck, and the longer she tried to open it, the more clumsy her fingers became.

"Greta?" Frederick's voice carried through the door from the hallway. "Is everything all right?"

Growling in frustration, Greta stomped to the door and swung it open. Frederick stepped back, startled.

"The carriage is—why Greta, what is wrong?"

"This blasted necklace will not come off. Can you help me, please?"

She turned, presenting him with the back of her neck. For a moment, Frederick did not move. Gently, he placed his hands on her waist and nudged her forward. Startled, Greta looked back at him, his serious eyes only inches from her own. Quickly she stepped away, color rushing to her cheeks. Frederick smiled and stepped inside the room, closing, though not latching, the door behind him.

"Forgive me, but I would rather not stand in the hallway."

"Oh. Yes, of course."

They stared at each other, the tension crackling between them like a fire.

"Why do you wish to remove the necklace?" Frederick said at last. "It looks lovely."

Relief coursed through her at his question. She did not know what she had expected a moment ago, but feeling his arms at her waist in such an intimate gesture… She shook her head, trying to focus.

"It is a beautiful piece, of course. And I am honored to be its owner now. But—" She paused, hoping her words would not offend him. Frederick was the one who had suggested she wear some of the family's jewels in the first place. "It is precisely the sort of adornment my mother would like to see me wear, to have *others* see me wear."

"Ah, I see."

She turned her back on him again, as much to solicit his help as to avoid the depth of his eyes. This time, Frederick removed his gloves, reached up, and gently undid the clasp. It took a moment for his larger fingers to manipulate the delicate metal, but soon he had succeeded in removing the offending article. Greta sighed in relief, feeling a weight far greater than that of the diamonds lifted from her shoulders.

"Is there something you would like to wear instead?" Frederick asked.

"Yes, here on the bureau."

Stepping forward, she opened her porcelain jewelry box and pulled out a thin, golden chain. An ornate silver cross encrusted with rubies hung from it, flashing in the candlelight.

"My father gave this to me," she said softly. "For my birthday last year."

Frederick nodded. "Very fitting." He smiled. "May I?" he asked, holding out his hand.

Greta nodded, handing him the necklace. Her ungloved hands brushed against his, sending tingles shooting through her fingers. Quickly she turned, her heart stuttering in her chest.

I am only flustered because of the diamonds, she chided, forcing herself to breathe in slowly through her nose.

Frederick undid the clasp, then reached over her head to place it around her neck. As his hands brushed her collarbone, her heart skittered, making her jump.

"Sorry," Frederick murmured. "My hands are cold."

She said nothing, and as soon as the necklace was secure she stepped away from him. Smiling tightly, she picked up her gloves.

"Thank you, my lord," she said, inclining her head.

A half-smile pulled at the corner of Frederick's mouth. "Not at all, my lady." He held out his arm. "Shall we?"

Greta took it, wondering why she suddenly felt dizzy.

Chapter 30

The Sharpetons lived on a relatively large estate on the other side of Rockwell. They had a house in town as well, but since the Season was nearly over, they had recently returned to the country, and were overjoyed to find that Lord and Lady Rockwell had arrived from Prussia. They welcomed them with open arms, and Mrs. Sharpeton took Greta under her wing immediately.

"My dear Lady Rockwell! How glad I am to make your acquaintance," she said as they sat down in the drawing room. "Frederick is a dear friend of ours, and we had quite despaired of him ever finding a lady to suit his interest." She smiled cheekily at Lord Rockwell, who was watching the ladies with some amusement. "If we had known he'd be tempted by a foreign beauty, we would have packed him off to the continent long ago!"

Greta smiled politely, not knowing what to say, but Frederick laughed. "Come now, Mrs. Sharpeton, I am afraid you will give my wife the wrong impression of me with that sort of talk."

"Well, we cannot have that," Mrs. Sharpeton agreed, turning

back to Greta. "Forgive me, my dear, but old friends like to tease, you know. But I really am very pleased to make your acquaintance. Tell me, have you been to England before?"

"No, this is my first time."

"Really! And have you been to town yet?"

"No, I have not yet been to London."

"Not been to London! Frederick, you beastly man, how can you have denied her the delights of the Season?" Mrs. Sharpeton cried.

"Now, now, Penelope, they have only just arrived," her husband broke in. "Give the poor man a chance to acquaint his bride with her new home before subjecting her to the vultures in town."

"Vultures?" Greta frowned. "I am afraid I am not familiar with that English term."

"Vultures are a kind of bird," Frederick explained. "But there are no actual vultures in London." He smiled. "He meant gossiping old women, I believe."

"Oh!" Greta laughed. "That is something I do understand. My mother is a vulture."

Mr. and Mrs. Sharpeton stared at Greta, but Frederick burst out laughing. Greta smiled at him, and a look passed between them that warmed her heart. She was glad that someone, at least, understood her.

"Well, I cannot speak in your mother's defense, but if she is, I am certainly glad that you have come to us here," Mrs. Sharpeton said, recovering.

Greta judged her to be about ten years older than herself, which meant she had not yet lost the bloom of her youth. She was not particularly handsome, but she had a pleasant face and a good figure, and she seemed to have a lively disposition. Observing the back-and-forth banter between the Sharpetons and Lord Rockwell gave Greta pause. They were obviously very good friends, with an easiness to their manners that was encouraging to see. Greta had been afraid of the strict societal standards for which the English were known, and it was a comfort to see that with close friends at least, her manners could somewhat relax.

Supper was soon announced, and Greta found herself amazed at the change she saw in her husband. She had not seen much of his humor, nor his easy manners while in Strausberg. But here, he seemed almost a new man. He laughed and joked with Mr. Sharpeton and his wife throughout the meal, making sure to include Greta whenever he could. She was grateful for his solicitation, but for the most part was content to sit and listen to the others.

When the women excused themselves to await the men in the drawing room, Frederick cast Greta an anxious look. "I shall be all right," she murmured, smiling her assurance before following Mrs. Sharpeton down the hall.

"You have a lovely house, Mrs. Sharpeton," Greta said as they sat down on the sofa together.

"Thank you. It is not as grand as your home, but it suits us quite well."

Observing the pianoforte in the corner of the room, Greta asked, "Do you play?"

"Tolerably well. Though there are many who are far more skilled than I."

Greta smiled. "I am sure you are too modest. Frederick

mentioned you were quite accomplished, which has piqued my curiosity—on one point, at least."

"Oh?"

Greta smiled. *"Sprechen Sie Deutsch?"*

"Oh!" Mrs. Sharpeton laughed. "I suppose I do speak a little, though I am quite rusty."

"Perhaps you would care to practice?" Greta asked in her native tongue. *"I would be happy to help if you wish to refresh yourself."*

Mrs. Sharpeton considered thoughtfully. "Hm. Well, considering how abominably I teased you upon your arrival, it would only serve me right to humiliate myself."

By the time the gentleman joined them, Greta and Mrs. Sharpeton were laughing fit to burst. Mrs. Sharpeton's German was indeed *very* rusty, and while at first Greta had tried to gently and politely correct her translation and pronunciation, it did not take long for her smiles to break through her careful façade, after which Mrs. Sharpeton felt free to laugh at herself.

"Frederick, do rescue me!" Mrs. Sharpeton cried when the gentlemen entered the room. "Your wife is more strict than my old governess, though I would not have believed it from the looks of her."

"That does not surprise me," Frederick chuckled.

"Well, enough of that, then," Mrs. Sharpeton said, her cheeks pink. "I have certainly been taught a thing or two, and now, my dear, you must favor us with a song," she said to Greta.

Finally feeling at ease, Greta inclined her head and sat down at the instrument. She played only two songs, though everyone implored her to play another, and by the time they left for home,

Greta felt she was well on her way to making two new friends.

"Well, my dear? Was the evening to your liking?" Frederick asked when they were in the carriage once more.

"Very much so. The Sharpetons are wonderful," Greta replied.

"They certainly are the best of people. I am happy to see that you and Mrs. Sharpeton got along so well."

Greta smiled. "It was good to become acquainted with her, but I found as much enjoyment in becoming acquainted with my husband as well."

Frederick looked surprised. "Indeed! Do you not feel that you have been acquainted with me before?"

"Not in the same way. I have never seen you with your own friends and peers, after all."

He nodded. "Yes, I suppose that is true. And?" he asked, his look curious, "what have you discovered?"

Greta cocked her head to the side, studying the man sitting across from her. "You have a quick wit and a wry sense of humor," she said. "And there is a dimple in your left cheek, that appears when you smile too broadly. I had not noticed it before."

Frederick, too shocked to reply, contented himself with smiling at his wife, and wondering if she would ever stop surprising him.

The next month passed far more pleasantly than the first difficult week. Less rain and more sunshine made for pleasanter days, and with her first social affair behind her, Greta was anxious to meet the rest of the neighborhood. Balls and parties, dinners and picnics; the more she saw of the neighborhood and its tenants, the more at ease she felt. Even Mrs. Whigham seemed to be warming up to her, which Greta counted as a very great victory.

Greta and Frederick were growing more comfortable, too. Soon after their arrival, Frederick had given Greta a new horse, and they went riding together nearly everyday. Their rides often began with a brisk trot, followed by a lengthy conversation, and ultimately ended with a race. Greta was usually the victor in these races, although she suspected that Frederick let her win on purpose.

One afternoon, Frederick went in search of his wife. She was not in the music room, nor in her bedchamber, and he was almost to the point of asking a servant for help when he decided to check the library. It was there, curled up on the window seat, that he found her.

For a brief moment, time stood still. The early summer sunshine shone on her hair, crowning her head with a halo of gold as she slowly turned a page in her book. Her lips were gently parted, as if on the verge of a smile, and as he watched her, a delicate laugh bubbled up from somewhere inside. He smiled. Greta had breathed new life into his home and made a place for herself in his heart. He marveled at his good fortune, finding such a woman to share his life with.

Greta glanced up just then, and seeing him standing in the doorway, stood from her seat. "Hello, Frederick," she said, smiling at him. "Were you looking for me?"

"I was," he said, his eyes focused on her face. Her eyes were bright and her face turned up, her perfect lips just asking to be kissed.

He coughed, and offered her his arm. "I have something I would like you to see in one of the drawing rooms downstairs. Is now a good time?"

"Of course," she said, setting down her book. "Although I hope it is not another assemblage of servants. I shall never learn all their names as it is."

"You do not need to learn all the underservants' names—only the principal ones," he chuckled.

"I may not need to, but I certainly intend to. *You* know all their names, and seem to know all about them and their families as well," she grumbled. "If you have done it, then I will do it, too."

Though he had said nothing to her, it pleased Frederick immensely to see the vigor and determination with which Greta had thrown herself into her new role and the responsibilities attending it. He hoped she was as happy and comfortable as she appeared to be.

Frederick led her down a long corridor on the main floor, stopping in front of a pair of gilded oak doors. Greta clapped her hands together, a smile wreathing her face.

"I have not been in here," she said. "The doors have been locked; Preston said it was being remodeled."

"It was," Frederick said, pulling a key from his pocket. "But now it is finished, and I would like you to be the first to see it."

He handed her the key, and a thrill coursed through her. Carefully she fitted it into the lock and gave it a turn. A satisfying *click* made her smile, and she looked up at Frederick, who nodded his encouragement. Opening the door, Greta peered into the room. A cry of pleasure escaped her lips, and she rushed inside, only to stop abruptly after a few steps.

It was a large, oblong room, with windows stretching from floor to ceiling along the entire far wall. To her right, a cluster of sofas and chairs sat before an elegant fireplace, next to which her harp had been placed. Directly in front of her, a large pianoforte stood open, with a velvet-cushioned bench positioned before the keys. Frederick stepped beside her, smiling softly.

"Your other instruments are over there," he said, indicating a collection of cupboards to their left. "I had hoped to have this room ready before your arrival, but the piano has only just arrived."

"I wondered if you had a music room," Greta said softly, her eyes shining. "I knew that the harpsichord in the second-floor drawing room could not have been the only instrument in the house."

He chuckled. "You have quadrupled the number of instruments in the house since your arrival, so it is only fitting that you have another sanctuary in which to play them."

Greta walked forward until she was standing before the piano. She let her fingers trail along the polished wood, the familiar excitement building within her. Sitting primly on the bench, she arranged her skirts about her and placed her fingers over the keys. Closing her eyes, she took a deep, steadying breath and began to play.

Frederick stood, amazed, at the burst of emotion that came from his wife. Greta's eyes were half closed, her fingers flying between the keys as her arms reached up and down the entire length of the keyboard. It was not a song he recognized, but he could tell from the passion with which she pursued each note that it was a favorite of hers.

Up and down, the music rose and fell, graceful trills mixing with pounding chords as she played. The song seemed almost a musical version of Greta herself—all passion and beauty, flower and flame. At last Greta slowed, and the song ended on a beautiful, high chord. She looked up at Frederick with bright eyes, one curl dangling over her brow.

"That was…" Frederick searched for the right word, at last shaking his head. "Brilliant. Astounding. What is it called?"

"It has no name," Greta replied, playing a single trill with her right hand. "I wrote it after Christmas."

"You *wrote* it?"

"Yes." Greta flashed him another dazzling smile, and Frederick knew in that moment, he could never let her go. He stepped closer to her, and the smile on Greta's face slowly faded. She looked down, brushing at the curl haunting her forehead.

"May I?" he asked, indicating the bench.

"Of course," Greta said, adjusting her position to allow him room beside her. He sat with his legs to the outside, so that their right shoulders were nearly touching. Suddenly nervous, Greta forced the curl behind her ear, then turned to look at him. His face was there before her, so close she could see tiny flecks of gold and green in his warm brown eyes.

Frederick reached a tentative hand out, and Greta sucked in a breath. His fingertips brushed her temple, dislodging the temperamental curl she had just tucked behind her ear. He watched it fall across her forehead, his look softening.

"It suits you," he said, his voice like velvet.

Greta's eyes were wide, her breathing shallow. Frederick was so close, his face filling her mind so she could hardly think. His hand trailed gently down her face, leaving a streak of fire along her cheek. He paused, and his eyes darted to her lips, then back up to meet her eyes.

For a moment, Greta thought he would kiss her. But before she could decide whether or not she wanted him to, he dropped his hand to his side and stood up.

The disappointment she felt was as surprising as it was real.

"I am glad you like the room," he said. "If you find that it needs any attention, please let myself or Preston know immediately."

He bowed politely and left the room, while Greta stared after him, wondering at the feelings which continued to grow inside her.

Chapter 31

Frederick closed the door to his room, releasing a breath he had been holding almost since leaving Greta in the music room. The temptation to kiss her had been stronger than ever before, but the vulnerability in her eyes had nearly undone him.

Could it be? Have I won her heart at last?

He shook his head and paced to the window, frustration clouding his mood. If it were true, and Greta were at last opening her heart to him, a kiss could spell disaster. What if she were merely lonely? What if he kissed her before she was ready, and then she felt obligated to give herself to him? *No*, he thought severely. *I cannot let that happen. Greta's happiness is far too important to risk on something as silly as my own desires.*

He sighed. While he had certainly admired and even felt the stirrings of love for her before they wed, he was surprised at how swiftly—and deeply—his feelings for her had grown since bringing her to England. Watching her here, away from the constraints of her family and home, was like watching a rosebud bloom for the first time. Every day she grew more confident in her new life, and every day Frederick lost a little more of his heart to her.

He sighed. Love was a complicated emotion. He knew he loved his wife, and her happiness and comfort meant more to him than anything else. At the same time, he was a man, and he could not deny the attraction and longing he felt when he was in her presence.

Blowing out his breath, he turned from the window and paced across the room, clasping his hands behind his back. His mind wandered back over the events of the last several months, and when he thought of the Christmas Eve ball, his steps slowed.

Could Greta have been fighting feelings for him, even then?

He did not have an answer, but recalling the look in her eye as they sat together on the piano bench confirmed to his heart that she certainly felt something now.

And something could certainly grow into much, much more.

Smiling to himself, Frederick left his room far lighter than he had entered it. His wife may not love him yet, but if he were careful, he knew there was a very good possibility that she would love him before long. All that remained to be seen now was whether she would recognize it before he did.

Six weeks had passed since their arrival in England, and Greta was finally beginning to feel at home. Frederick had been tutoring her in English, and her accent was much improved. This helped her relations with the servants, and soon she felt confident in her new role as mistress of the house. She was still getting used to being addressed as Lady Rockwell, and there was some difficulty in remembering the more strict societal rules of England, but all things considered, she was settling in quite nicely.

And then there was her relationship with Frederick. She smiled to think that this time last year, she thought him only a stuffy old Englishman whom her mother wished to impress. How much had changed since then! She sighed, allowing her heart to ache for the home and the people she missed. But the ache did not last long. Soon, a sweet tendril of hope bloomed in her breast, making her smile. There could be no denying the stirrings she felt in her heart for her husband. It confused and fascinated her to think that the arranged marriage she had so vehemently opposed, might blossom into true feelings of love. She was not there yet— not by any means—but the beginning was there, and she was curious to see what the coming months and years would bring.

Greta sat at her writing desk one morning, making a list of items she needed to get from town. Frederick had business to see to in London, and she wished for him to make certain purchases while he was there. As she wrote, a footman came in bearing the mail on a silver tray.

"Thank you," she said, taking the letters.

She riffled through the cards, setting aside the social invitations to answer later. A rather bulky letter, in a vaguely familiar hand, was addressed to her. She flipped the note over and saw the Strausberg family crest. A letter from home! Excitement coursed through her as she broke the seal and opened the letter. Another folded paper, dirty and worn, fell out onto the desk. Setting it aside, she started to read.

14 June, 1781

My dear sister,

I hope this letter finds you well. We are all in excellent health and miss you a great deal, though I believe our father misses you most. How is the weather in England? Does it rain all the time? Have you a handsome library in your new home?

Since beginning this letter something has arrived for you that you may find alarming. I am enclosing it here, though I do not know if it is the right thing to do. It is a letter, presumably from Hans, if I remember his handwriting correctly. It came in the post yesterday, and you are lucky that I intercepted it before our mother did, for she would surely have thrown it out. As it was, I have been collecting the mail all week, hoping for a letter from you. I hope it does not pain you to read his last words, but rather than make the choice for you, I decided to send his letter on and hope for the best.

Please write as soon as you can and tell me all about your new home. I remain

Your loving sister,
Katarina

Greta finished reading and slowly, almost reverently, picked up the letter from Hans. His steady hand was clearly recognizable, though the paper had seen some rough handling. She knew that the war made the post to and from the colonies quite erratic, but she never considered how it might feel to receive a letter from a deceased person, written before their death.

She clutched the missive in her trembling hand, silently praying for strength to read Hans's last words. Would they be filled with spite and censure, or would they be jovial and kind? She hoped for the latter as she broke the seal and unfolded the single sheet of paper. She was surprised to find it filled to capacity, for Hans had rarely written such long letters. Drawing a deep breath, she started to read.

My dear Greta,

I take up my quill to write you the heavy words I never thought I would: Ernst is dead, killed in battle. I myself have been captured, and am being held prisoner until such a time as the war is over or an exchange is made. But I am getting ahead of myself—I must go back, and then you will understand all.

So much has happened in the past five months, but I believe my last letter to you indicated that our regiment was to travel north from the Carolinas, but the morning after posting it to you, orders came that Lieutenant Colonel Tarleton was desperately in need of fresh troops, and we were immediately to set foot for where he was. We turned ourselves to the south, met up with his company the next day, and took to marching straightaway, without any rest. Colonel Tarleton was a mean sort, who treated us mercenaries like dogs. Ernst got a lashing the very first night for cheeking an officer.

We were to head off an attack planned against the British

fort Ninety-Six, but the information we had been given was misleading, and instead of defending the fort, our commander ordered us to pursue the American forces marching to the west. We met them at Broad River on January 17, and there we were massacred. I will not describe the scene of carnage that I saw. Our commanding officer managed to escape with a few other cowards, but the vast majority of our company, nearly 1,100 men, were killed or captured, Ernst among them. I myself was wounded and fainted from exhaustion and loss of blood. When I awoke, I was a prisoner.

For weeks we received no word from the outside world. No letters were allowed, either in or out, and I thought I would go mad. Did you know my fate? Was my family well? You know not how I was tormented, wondering what was going on. But at last a parcel of letters was delivered to us, months after they had been mailed. There was one for Ernst, from his mother, and a short note from Julianna. I read the letter from Ernst's mother, and wept to see her concern for his welfare and a desire to see him safely home. I asked for a pen and scrip to be able to write to her, informing her of his death, but I was denied. Juli's letter was dated early in January and said that she would be married in March. By the time you read this, she is certainly Frau Weisler.

I find that though I am angry, I am not hurt. She has not wounded my heart, for I realize that it was never mine to give her. As a child, it found a safe home next to your own heart, and in my stubbornness and pride I refused to acknowledge its residence there. Dearest Greta, forgive me.

I was stupid and blind, unwilling to see what you already knew, what you have known all along. The thought of you, and your love, has sustained me through this living hell, and I pray that your affections have not changed. Knowing you, I do not think they have.

I have been four months in prison now, and this is the first time they have given me paper and pen with which to write home. We have been moved to another location, where we are permitted far more liberties, and I hope to hear from you very often. Please write me back directly, that I may know this letter has reached you. Until then, I will dream of your face, and find solace in knowing that my heart is safe with you.

Yours,
Hans

Horror gripped her heart as Greta stood. The abrupt movement sent her head spinning, and she clutched the desk, breathing heavily. Hans was alive. *Hans was alive.* Rather than bringing comfort, the thought made Greta ill with despair, and she swallowed back the bile that rose in her throat. Snatching up the letter once more, she scanned its contents, her panic growing with every sentence she read.

There could be no mistake; Hans had survived. She clearly remembered that terrible day in February, when the letter came for Peter Schneider, informing him that Hans had been killed at the Battle of Cowpens. Yet here was proof that Hans was yet alive!

She glanced at the top of the page, searching for the date when the letter had been written. A sob caught in her throat, choking her.

It was dated May 16, 1781—three months after the letter arrived pronouncing him dead.

Chapter 32

Greta paced her room, wringing her hands and worrying her handkerchief until her fingertips were raw. *Hans was alive.* The thought rang over and over in her mind, until she was dizzy with joy and sick with anguish. Hans was alive, and even more incredible, he loved her. *He loved her!* The thought brought at once both elation and despair. Hans may be alive, and he may even love her, but she was no longer free to accept his addresses.

The thought brought on a wave of nausea.

There was a soft knock on the door, and Greta's heart stopped. She froze, halfway between the door and the window.

"Greta?"

Frederick's concerned voice drifted in from the hallway, muffled by the heavy door. "Are you all right?"

Greta swallowed, striving to keep her voice steady as she replied. "Yes. I mean, no. I am—"

The door opened, and Frederick stepped inside. "My apologies," he said quietly, "but when you missed dinner I grew concerned. Are you well?"

She turned away, trembling. "I fear I am not quite myself at present."

"You are pale, my dear," Frederick said, crossing to her and taking her hand. "Let me call for the doctor."

"No!" Greta said, nearly shouting in her haste to refuse. She flushed, and then added, more gently, "Do not trouble yourself. I am well enough. I only need some rest." She withdrew her hand and took a step away from him.

"Rest is all well and good, Greta, but if it is something more serious—"

"It is not."

Her curt reply and anguished eyes made Frederick uneasy, but he did not want to force her. "All right," he said quietly. "but if you are still unwell at breakfast, may I call for the physician?"

Greta nodded, anxious for him to leave. If she could only be alone...

Frederick's brow was furrowed. "Very well. I shall leave you now. Please let me know if there is anything you need," he said.

She nodded, shutting the door behind him as he left the room.

Greta did not sleep that night. She tossed and turned in feverish anguish, tortured by the knowledge of Hans's survival. When the clock in the hall struck the hour of two, she rose from her bed, wrapped a shawl around her shoulders, and padded softly out of the room.

The moonlight cast strange shadows across the stairs as she

made her way down to the music room. Opening the heavy doors, she slipped inside and set her candle on the edge of the pianoforte, sitting down before the instrument.

She did not play, but ran her fingers softly up and down the keys, silent music filling her heart. But it did not calm her anguished soul. *Hans. Frederick. Hans. Frederick.* Over and over their faces flashed in her mind, trapping her heart in a vicious tug-of-war. Oh, why did Hans's letter have to come now! If she had learned of his survival months ago, before Julianna wed, she would not have hesitated over what to do. She would have thrown caution to the wind and chartered the very next boat to America. But things were so different now. Now she was married, and what was more, she cared about her husband. She had never anticipated the stirrings of love that quivered in her breast for Frederick, and it was this that caused her such misery. If she did not care for him, she would have no regard for the scandal her leaving would create. But Frederick was a good man. A good friend. And before Hans's letter arrived, he could even have been more. Could she leave him now? Did she even want to?

The ghostly white and black keys of the pianoforte mocked her as she stared at them, desperately searching for an answer to her plight. But no answer came, and no peace, either.

Feeling betrayed by the one thing that had always brought her comfort, she rushed back to her room, throwing herself on the bed. The tears that would not come pressed upon her heart, making it impossible for her to sleep.

It was the longest night of Greta's life, and when morning came, she was no closer to knowing what to do than when she had first read Hans's letter. She went down to breakfast, where

Frederick took one look at her and shook his head.

"I shall call for Mr. Remmington," he said, rising from his seat.

"No, Frederick, please. I assure you, I am—"

"Greta, you are even more pale than you were last night. And you are trembling like a leaf! I am quite worried." He frowned. "I cannot leave for London, knowing that you are in such poor health."

Greta's heart sank. She was counting on him leaving as soon as may be, so she could gather her thoughts and determine her course in solitude.

"I assure you, I am quite well," she said, forcing a smile. Frederick looked grim.

"If nothing ails your body, then what is troubling your mind?"

Greta startled at his words, and he frowned. "Greta? What is it?"

"I…"

"Are you worried about your family?"

"No. I have had a letter from my sister, and she says they are all well."

"I am glad to hear it. What else did she say? Was there some news from home that has troubled you?"

What little color remained in Greta's face drained, and she clutched the chair in front of her for support.

"Greta!"

Frederick sprang to her side, wrapping an arm around her waist and taking her hand. He gently guided her to a seat and knelt at her side.

"Now I must know. Tell me, Greta, please! I am in agony

seeing you thus."

Greta looked down at his face, his eyes filled with concern, his brow furrowed in fear. She closed her eyes, pressing a hand to her mouth.

She must tell him.

"I had a letter from my sister yesterday. And enclosed within it was…" The nausea rolled over her again, "a letter from Hans."

There was silence, followed by a low sigh. "Oh, my dear," Frederick breathed, clasping her hand. "I am so sorry. It must have been a very great shock, to read his last words to you."

Glancing at his face, Greta could see that the fear in his eyes had turned to sympathy.

She shook her head. "That is not what troubles me."

Confusion clouded his look. "Reading his words did not disturb you? What can have caused you such agitation, then?"

"It was not what he wrote, but *when* he wrote it, that disturbs me."

Frederick frowned. "I do not understand."

"Frederick," Greta whispered. "Hans… Hans is alive. He was not killed in battle. He was wounded, and taken prisoner. His letter was dated the sixteenth of May."

Frederick did not move, an expression of shock frozen on his face. Slowly he got to his feet.

"That is," he struggled for the right word, "surprising news. But are you quite sure?"

She nodded. "Yes. I recognize his hand. He gave me all the particulars of what happened. He has been imprisoned since their capture, but he is most certainly still alive."

Frederick walked slowly to the window, clasping his hands

behind his back. "This news is certainly unnerving. But one to be celebrated, is it not?" He glanced at her over his shoulder.

"Yes," Greta said, his look giving her words caution.

"You must write to him, then," he said, turning back to the window, "informing him of our marriage."

When she made no reply, Frederick turned back to look at her. Greta's face was very grave.

"Frederick," she said, "there was more to Hans's letter than simply the news that he had survived."

"Oh?"

"He also said…" Greta blushed, twisting her hands in her lap, "that he loves me."

The silence echoed between them, filling the space like a poisonous gas. Frederick's eyes cut into her, piercing Greta's heart and forcing her to speak.

"I always hoped that he did," she said, looking down at her hands. "But he did not leave me with much hope. But now, knowing how he feels, it has made me wonder…" Her voice trailed off, and she shook her head. She did not want to hurt Frederick, but she *did* wish to be honest with him.

"What do you wonder," Frederick said, his voice flat.

"I wonder," she said slowly, "what the marriage laws are in England."

"Marriage is a holy sacrament, Greta. It cannot be undone."

"I am not speaking of divorce," she said quickly. "But surely there are provisions for marriages, such as ours, where… well, when the parties have not…" She blushed, clenching her hands. "Can an annulment be obtained?" she blurted. "That is, I have not decided anything yet, but…"

Her voice trailed off as she looked into Frederick's face. Never before had she seen such fury, and though she would not admit it, his look frightened her.

"Frederick," Greta said, her voice frantic, "you do not understand. All my life I have cared for Hans! All my life I have loved him. And now, knowing that he is alive, knowing that he cares for me..." She held out her hands, pleading.

"You are mistaken, my dear," Frederick said, his voice so low Greta could hardly hear the words he spoke. "I understand quite clearly." His eyes flashed, and he took a step towards her. "I *understand* that to which I have been deliberately blind, but I can hardly ignore the truth any longer. You married me only because Hans was dead, only because your chance at a life with him had been taken from you. Do you deny it?"

"Frederick, I—"

"*Do you deny it?*"

"I have no wish to deny it!" Greta cried, jumping to her feet. "You knew what my feelings were then, and you know what they are now. I have always loved Hans."

"Then why did you accept me, Greta?" Frederick said, his face like thunder. "If you did not care for me at all, why did you not refuse my hand and wait for another suitor?"

"If you think my father would have allowed me that luxury, you are a fool."

The words left her mouth before Greta could stop them, but instead of regret she felt only anger. The furious lines etched across Frederick's forehead smoothed out, and he covered the distance between them in a moment. His voice was hard and flat, falling harshly on her ears.

"Of course. I am forgetting. You did not choose me—you chose your father. It was his insistence to which you finally succumbed. Not me. It was never me."

Greta glared at him, though a tiny knife of guilt pricked her heart. Frederick watched her for a moment, then strode purposefully to the door and opened it.

"I am leaving for London. I shall see you when I return." He was halfway through the door when he paused and looked back. "That is, if you are even still here."

He shut the door, hard, behind him.

A week passed with no word from Frederick. Guilt over the pain she had caused him soon turned to anger, which was manifest in furious outbursts on the pianoforte. She went to bed each night with aching muscles from her musical tirades, but the pain in her heart was even greater. Worry and anxiety over Hans, Frederick, and the complicated mess in which she found herself filled her mind, stealing her rest until well past midnight, when she would at last fall into a fitful sleep.

Ten days after Frederick left, a letter arrived for her. But it was not from her husband.

It was another letter from Hans.

This one was not redirected from Prussia, but was addressed to her directly in England. Greta swallowed.

If Hans knew where she was, he must also know that she was married.

With trembling hands Greta broke the seal and unfolded the

255

paper, her eyes desperate for his words.

17 June, 1781

Dear Greta,

I am still confined to military prison, but we are now encamped at Bell's Corner, in what they call a prison town. They permit us far more freedoms than we have hitherto been allowed, and were it not for the guards, I should hardly feel a prisoner at all.

You can imagine the shock I felt at the letter I received from my mother last week, informing me that you are now married to that English ambassador. I understand from her message that you were all under the impression that I was dead, but even still, I wished to believe her misinformed. But the letter I have had today, from your sister, confirms my fears. Greta, I know how you feel about him. I do not know what possessed you to accept his hand, but I beg of you, consider your heart. You claim to have loved me all your life, and if that is true, do not give yourself to him. We belong together, Greta. Never were there two people more perfectly suited for one another than you and I. As soon as I am able, I will come to you. I swear it upon my life, Greta. Wait for me. Please. And write to me as soon as you can.

Yours,
Hans

Greta read the letter thrice, each time feeling as though she would burst, whether from agony or delight, she did not know. With her head spinning, she sat down at her desk and pulled out a piece of paper.

Chapter 33

"You've a letter, Schneider."

Hans looked up from the cup of soup he was eating, to the outstretched hand of one of his fellow prisoners. He took the letter and the man walked away. Spooning another bite into his mouth, he nearly choked as he glanced at the direction.

It was written in Greta's hand.

He shoved the letter in his pocket and gulped down the last of his meager meal. Dropping the tin cup and spoon onto his bedroll, he made his way to the shady side of the nearby church and sat down with his back against the building, swatting at the insects that droned in the lazy air. He pulled out Greta's letter and tore it open.

28 July, 1781

Dearest Hans,

*   I do not know how to adequately express to you the*

complete shock I felt upon receiving your letters. Of course I wept to know that the information we received regarding your death was false, but also because I am no longer free to receive your addresses. I love you, Hans. But you were rightly informed, and I am now married.

Hans cursed under his breath, his eyes narrowing.

News of your death rocked me to my core. I thought of you constantly, and your words regarding my duty came back to me. I felt that the most honor I could give your memory was to accept my duty and marry the man whom my parents had chosen for me. Believe me, Hans, if I had known you were yet alive, I would never have joined myself to him! Frederick is a good man, but you know that my heart has always belonged to you.

I have agonized over the position in which we now find ourselves, and can see no way out of it. The only shred of hope I can perceive is that my marriage has not yet been consummated, and an annulment may be possible to obtain. But Hans, how are we to proceed? You are a prisoner in America, and I am sequestered in a country estate in England. To complicate matters farther, Frederick knows of your survival, that you have written to me, and that I still care for you. He was very angry, and left immediately for business in London. He has been gone a week and I know not when he will return.

Please write to me as soon as you can and advise me on what I should do.

Yours,
Greta

Hans leaned his head back against the wall of the church, blowing out his breath. His thoughts were racing, and after a moment, he lifted Greta's letter and read it through once more. He glanced again at the date written on top: July 28. Today was the twenty-third of August. If he sent a reply, and waited for her response again, it might be October before anything could be done. By then, winter would be closing in.

He got to his feet, shaking his head. He could not, and would not, wait that long.

It was time to talk with Jackson.

Of the 829 soldiers captured at the Battle of Cowpens, only 512 remained imprisoned near Richmond, Virginia. The rest had either died of disease or, like many others during the war, managed to escape the various "prison towns" where they were sent. In such places, the captives were housed in hastily built barracks or churches, and were expected to work right alongside the town's residents for their sustenance, enjoying a life more closely resembling parole than imprisonment.

Hans returned to his bedroll in the churchyard to gather his military jacket. The flies that had congregated on his still-dirty cup drifted away as he picked up his coat. Kneeling down, he rubbed it, hard, in the dirt. Satisfied, he stood and headed towards the river. It ran from north to south, about a quarter mile beyond the churchyard, which sat on the edge of town. He lifted a hand to a Patriot soldier as he approached.

"Mind if I wash my jacket down in the river?" he asked.

The guard narrowed his eyes. "There's water in the barrels."

Hans shook his head. "Empty," he lied. "They'll be filling them after supper, but I'd rather clean off my jacket now so I can lay it in the sun to dry."

The guard appraised him for a moment, and Hans did his best to appear disinterested in the response he hoped to receive. Finally, the guard gave him a curt nod.

"Be quick about it. I'll be watching for you."

Hans waved his thanks and trotted for the river. His heart was pounding as he crouched on the bank and dipped his coat in the cool water. The river was narrow, but swift. He hoped it was not deep, for Jackson would not be able to swim with his hurt arm. Keeping his head bent, Hans raised his eyes and scanned the forest on the other side. There was a wide expanse of grassland they would have to cross before taking cover in the trees. Hans did not like it; if they were seen crossing the river, a well-placed shot could destroy their chance of escape.

Finished with his observations, Hans stood and wrung out his jacket. Turning back towards camp, he could see the Patriot soldier in the distance, watching him. Hans raised his arm, and the soldier turned away.

"Jackson? A word, if you will."

The young man looked up as Hans sat down beside him,

another cup of soup in his hand. Hans smiled, but the Englishman frowned.

"How is your arm?"

Jackson did not respond right away. He watched Hans with careful eyes, until Hans looked down and began eating his meal. "Fair," he said at last. "Though still useless."

"I see that," Hans said, nodding at the sling.

The men ate in silence for a few moments, Hans dipping his spoon into the thin liquid, while his companion tipped the cup to pour it into his mouth. Hans leaned forward slightly, and in a low voice asked, "Are you still looking for a way to Philadelphia?"

Jackson raised his eyes, looking around. The nearest soldier sat on his own bedroll a few paces away. A handful of guards stood watch over the prisoners, but the nearest was well out of earshot. He returned to his meal.

"What made you change your mind?" he murmured.

"I need to get to England."

"But you live in Prussia."

Hans shook his head. "I need to get to England," he said again.

"Where?"

"Kent."

"No good. My family is in Devon."

"What about your uncle? You said you had an uncle who—"

"My uncle's influence is not enough to get you to Kent. Even if he is a baronet."

Hans leaned in. "I must get to Kent," he said earnestly. "If I can get you to Philadelphia, can you help me get there?"

Jackson finished his meal and took a drink from a small canteen. Hans watched him, his frustration growing the longer he waited. At last his companion gave a brief nod.

"If you can get us to Philadelphia, I'll see what I can do."

It was not the confident response Hans had hoped for, but it was his only chance. He smiled grimly.

"All right," he said. "I have a plan."

Chapter 34

When Frederick left for London, Greta thought he would be gone a fortnight—three weeks, at most. But when the whole of August passed without even a line explaining his prolonged absence, the concern she had begun to feel evaporated. Did he expect to hear from *her?* Did he really think she would pine over him, and beg him to return? Greta let her anger fester until she no longer cared what became of her husband.

Frederick spent the weeks in London agonizing over what to do. His anger and frustration had soon melted away, leaving behind the wounds of betrayal and heartache. He loved his wife, which made her declaration all the more painful. If he loved her, should he let her go? Should he seek an annulment? The thought nearly drove him mad. He simply could not live without her.

When he at last returned the first week in September, he found his wife cool and indifferent, which, to him, felt even worse than her fury. He had hoped that his absence may have allowed Greta time to reflect and acknowledge her feelings for him, but in this he was sorely disappointed. Greta was barely civil and remained aloof, refusing to spend hardly any time in his company. Desperate and disheartened, Frederick let the month of September slip by, without any sign of reconciliation.

Mealtimes were now quiet affairs. Only when asked a direct question would either of them respond, giving a pointed answer in a civil tone, then retreating back into silence. Greta had flatly refused to go out in company anymore, choosing instead to spend her time pounding furiously on the keys of her pianoforte. Frederick spent most of his time alone in his study.

It was early in October when Greta received another letter from Hans. She read it alone in her room, with a locked door between herself and the rest of the world.

29 September, 1781

Greta,

I am in England, and I am determined to come to you. I am not afraid of your husband, but I do not wish to cause a scene if it troubles you. Tell me when and where I am to meet you, and I will be there.

Write to me at the direction below as soon as you can.

Ever yours,
Hans

Greta pressed a hand to her stomach, breathing deeply. *Hans is here.* Sitting down at her desk, she reached for a sheet of paper to send a reply, her heart pounding with every stroke of the quill.

Of course she would meet him. She loved him. She had always loved him.

Then why do I feel so ill?

She shoved the feeling aside, focusing instead on the words that would finally win her Hans's embrace. They would meet at night, of course, but where? Greta bit her lip. She should probably take her horse, as she was not sure what Hans was planning. The direction he gave was in the town of Tonbridge, which was but five miles to the southeast, so he was already close. *Gut.* She knew there to be an inn on the northern outskirts of the town, so she dipped her quill into the inkwell, ready to write her instructions.

For several minutes the only sound was the scratching of the quill on the paper. Greta willed herself to think of nothing but the words she wrote, nothing but the man to whom she had given her heart.

Finished, Greta folded the letter and sealed the paper together. She paused for only a moment as she pressed the Greenwood family crest into the soft wax, examining the oak tree whose limbs grew over and around the family's coat of arms. Frederick's face flashed into her mind, and she shook her head quickly, dispelling the image and the guilt that accompanied it. She unlocked her door and rang the bell for a servant.

In two days' time, she would be with Hans.

Frederick stood in the drawing room, his hands clasped behind his back, silently counting the gentle *tick, tick* of the clock.

Three hundred seventeen, three hundred eighteen, three hundred nineteen…

The door opened, and Greta strode into the room. Her cheeks were flushed and her dark eyes were bright as Frederick turned and bowed to her.

"Lord Rockwell," Greta said, nodding at her husband. "Shall we go in to dinner?"

"Not just yet, if you please," Frederick said, crossing the room to be near her. Greta stood stiffly where she was, a slight lift to her chin. Frederick sighed.

"Greta, I cannot go on like this," he said. "Please, can we not move past the polite civility of the last few weeks? We are not strangers; we are husband and wife, for goodness' sake."

"Lord Rockwell…"

"Frederick."

Greta paused. "Frederick," she said. "Before you left—"

"Margareta," he said, reaching for her hand. She pulled it out of his reach, and a spasm of pain flashed across his face. He closed his eyes.

"Forgive me," he said softly. "Forgive my harsh words and my arrogant pride. You know not how I have tortured myself, how I have wished to make amends without knowing how." His eyes were pleading as he opened them. "Please, Greta. Tell me that I have not lost you already."

Greta turned away, the pounding in her head echoing the ache inside her ribs. What could she say to him? That there was no choice to make? That she had chosen Hans a lifetime ago?

"There is nothing to forgive," she said flatly. "You are my husband. You had every right to speak to me in that manner, and you have every right to put me away now, if you so wish."

"But I do *not* wish, Greta. You know that. I have never wished to force anything upon you. All your life you have been forced to do what other people want. I never wanted that for you. For us. Please, Greta, I am begging you. Do not go to him. Do not choose him. Choose me."

Slowly, Greta turned around. His eyes were open, pleading. His look reminded her of a stray dog she had once found, desperate for love and a place to call home. She'd had a choice to make, then—about whether or not to claim the dog's affections.

She saw that she had a choice to make now, as well.

She took a breath, willing the tumult in her mind to cease. "We were not meant to be, Frederick," she said. "I belong with Hans."

Frederick drew in a breath, his eyes snapping, but his response was measured and calm. "And what of our marriage?"

There was silence for a long time. "Get an annulment if you can. I will cooperate," she said. "And then you can move on."

She strode to the door and opened it. "I believe it would be best if I dine in my room this evening," she said, shutting the door —and her heart—firmly behind her.

Chapter 35

Hans's reply came the next afternoon. He would meet her at the inn the following night, when the new day was an hour old. Greta's stomach felt so ill with nerves she could eat nothing at supper that evening. Frederick noticed that she moved the food around her plate but lifted very little to her lips, and he paused while eating his own meal. No longer hearing the gentle scraping of his utensils on the china, Greta looked up. The sorrow she saw in his eyes made what little was in her stomach threaten to resurface.

I belong with Hans, she told herself firmly. *He loves me. And I love him.* The uneasy feeling in her midsection eased a bit, and she sighed, feeling her muscles relax.

But Frederick loves me, too.

Greta tripped over the thought, wishing she could banish it from her mind. It clung tenaciously to her consciousness, pricking her heart and tainting every thought of her reunion with Hans.

At last the meal was over, and Greta stood to excuse herself from the room. "Goodnight, my lord," she said, not meeting Frederick's eyes.

He let her go without a word.

Feverish with excitement, Greta tried to calm herself while her maid removed the pins from her hair. Greta allowed herself to be undressed, and watched as her abigail pulled down the covers. After she left, Greta lay under the blankets for what seemed like an eternity, until the darkness crept across her floor like a cat and the house around her became still. Though she tried to rest, Greta's mind was racing with the intrigue of the night. By dawn, she and Hans would be miles away, the scandal created by her departure left behind for Frederick to sort through on his own.

Frederick.

His face was before her, and try as she might, Greta could not shake his image from her thoughts.

"He knew when he married me," she muttered through clenched teeth, rolling over.

Her heart twisted painfully, and she thrust him from her mind.

At length, the large clock in the entryway announced the hour before midnight, and Greta released a breath.

It was time.

Rising from her bed, she slipped into her half-stays and pulled on her riding habit, stockings, and boots. Quickly she folded a simple gown, a petticoat, a clean shift, and two pairs of stockings into a parcel. She sighed as she passed over her pretty satin slippers, but there was no telling how far she and Hans might be traveling, and practicality in her wardrobe was essential. When all was in readiness, she crept to the door and unlocked it, opening it slowly.

The house was dark and still as she made her way silently downstairs. Slipping through one of the back entrances, she ran for the stables, grateful for the half-moon that lighted her way. She eased the door open and spoke soothingly to the horses, who stomped at the disturbance. Within minutes, she had her horse out of its stall, saddled, and ready to go.

The night was chilly but the air was still, and her breath hung in wispy clouds around her head before disappearing into the blackness. Greta winced with every footfall, convinced that Frederick could hear the crunch of the leaves and the clatter of stones beneath the horse's hooves. Soon they were without the gates, and Greta edged her horse a bit faster.

The distance to the inn was covered in little more than an hour, the mist hovering over the ground slowing her progress some. As the light on the front of the building bobbed into view, Greta strained her eyes in the darkness for the little path that led off from the main road. It wove around the building to a little copse of trees, where Greta knew Hans was waiting.

At least, that is where she said she would meet him.

Having found the trail, Greta turned her horse down it. As she drew near to the sheltering trees, her ears searched for a sound that would alert her to Hans's presence. But she heard nothing save her own approach. Easing her horse to a stop, she slipped out of the saddle and walked forward, her eyes sweeping the shadows. For the first time since planning the reunion, a sliver of doubt crept into her heart. What if Hans was not coming to meet her, after all?

A movement to her left made Greta jump, but then Hans's soothing voice called out before her horse startled as well.

"*Ruhig!* Easy now, it's only me. Nothing to be frightened of."

Greta knew he was speaking to the horse, but in the instant she heard his voice, all doubt fled. The knot of anxiety in her stomach eased, and a thrill filled her heart.

Hans was here.

He came out of the darkness, still speaking quietly, and reached a hand out to pat the horse's side. His eyes were on Greta, and she searched his face, hungry to see him in the dim light. He was taller, and a full beard now covered his face. If she had not heard his voice, Greta knew she would not have recognized him. She waited, hardly breathing, for him to speak. At last his mouth quirked in a grin.

"Still riding astride, I see."

Greta glanced down at her riding habit, the tension between them bursting with her short laugh.

"Of course. You know me."

"I do."

They stood across from one another, a lifetime of memories hovering between them, until Hans's lips parted and he breathed her name.

"Greta."

His voice was *home*, and Greta melted into it. She took a step towards him, and when he opened his arms she ran into his embrace.

"Oh, Hans!" Her cry was muted, her face pressed into his neck.

"There now, Greta, hush. It is all right. I am here."

"I thought I would never see you again."

He pulled her closer, crushing her to him. "I told you it was not goodbye forever."

Greta closed her eyes, relishing the feeling of his strong arms around her. She could not tell where her body ended and his began. "Never leave me again, Hans. Please," she whispered.

"*Niemals*, Greta. Never."

They stood in the dark holding one another for a long time. At last, Greta stepped away to look up into his face. A long scar pulled at his right cheek, and there was something strange about that side of his head. She could not see it properly in the dim light, but he angled his head away when she tried to peer at it.

"I wondered if you would come," Hans said, his voice not as welcoming as it had been. "It is nearly two."

Greta blinked. How could he have doubted her? She let the remark drift into the misty darkness.

"I told you I would come." She paused. "How did you escape?"

He shrugged. "It was not overly difficult. A friend and I slipped away under cover of darkness, and he got us passage aboard a ship coming to England."

She knew it could not have been as simple as he made it sound, but she did not press him. "And once you were here, in England?" She looked him over more carefully, noting the fine, thick traveling cloak and new riding boots he wore.

"Jackson's uncle is a baronet. His family has been helping me." He shifted his feet, ready to change the subject. "I've missed you, Greta," he said softly, reaching a calloused hand up to cup her face. She smiled, leaning into him.

"I have missed you, too, Hans. Every day."

Hans nodded, gently rubbing her cheek. Slowly, his thumb

traced the contours of her top lip, and Greta closed her eyes, thrilling under his touch.

"Greta," he whispered.

When their lips touched, it was as if a live coal had been pressed to Greta's mouth. Passion, hot and powerful, spread throughout her body. Hans pulled her close as Greta wrapped her arms around his neck, pressing herself to him. His lips against hers were hard and forceful, and when Greta broke away to gulp down some air, she saw the look in his eyes.

They were desperate. Hungry. Angry.

All at once, an image of Frederick's face burst into her mind. His eyes, warm and kind, looked down on her, smiling. She blinked, and Hans was before her again.

He pressed his mouth to hers again, working his lips down her jawline to her neck. Greta shivered, pulling her arms from around his neck and laying her palms flat against his chest.

"Hans," she breathed.

He responded by pulling her closer, his lips more insistent. Greta was crushed against his chest, but instead of desire she felt a trickle of fear. "Hans," she said more forcefully, pushing against him.

Hans relaxed his grip and she broke free of his embrace, stepping away from him. His chest rose and fell, his breathing heavy. Greta wrapped her arms around herself, dizzy and confused. Something was not right.

Hans watched her for a moment, then took a step towards the horse. It was a massive black beast with a white star on its forehead. In the moonlight, its glossy coat shone in places like silver.

"This is a fine horse. Your husband must be even more wealthy than you thought."

Greta swallowed. "Yes."

The weight of those words hung in the air, dividing them. "Hans," Greta said softly, holding out one hand. "We thought you were dead. All of us. When the letter arrived for your father, it said—"

"It said I was dead. I know," he said flatly. "But whoever sent it was wrong."

Greta said nothing.

"So you thought I was dead, and moved on with your life. How long did you wait, Greta, before marrying your nobleman? An hour? A week?" His words were hard, full of bitter accusations. She frowned.

"That is not fair, Hans."

"Is it not?" he sneered, abruptly coming towards her. She instinctively stepped back, frightened of him for the first time in her life. "You were the one who said you loved me, *had* always loved me, and would love me forever."

"I do love you, Hans, but—"

"If you really loved me, you would not have married the Englishman."

"That is not true," Greta retorted, her own temper rising. "You were the one who told me to marry him, Hans. You were the one who denied my love when I first came to you. I would have followed you anywhere, Hans, you know that! All you had to do was say the word, and I would have left it all behind. For you, Hans. For us."

Greta's chest heaved, her pulse pounding in her ears. Hans

glared at her for a moment longer, then dropped his eyes and shook his head.

"I suppose it does not signify. You are here, and that is what matters at present."

He stretched a hand out to her, and she stepped carefully into his arms. He pulled her close and bent down, his lips brushing her collarbone. Greta trembled.

"Come," he breathed. "I have a room at the inn for the night."

Greta stiffened. "Should we not leave at once?"

"We can leave at first light," he murmured, his lips against her skin.

A ball of unease settled in her stomach.

"Hans, I am still a married woman. Does your friend know how we can obtain an annulment? What shall we do?"

Hans pulled back to look at her. "What does it matter? We shall be together, just as you have always wished." He drew her close again, pressing his lips to her mouth. Greta closed her eyes, letting the heat of his kiss take over her senses.

But Hans's lips became more insistent. One hand tangled in her hair, holding her head while he kissed her mouth. His other arm wrapped around her waist, his hand pressing into the small of her back, forcing their bodies together. The more urgent his kisses became, the more panic grew in her breast. All her life, Greta had dreamed of kissing Hans, of feeling his arms around her, of hearing his voice whisper that he loved her. But this was nothing like what she had imagined. This was not the Hans she had known.

And suddenly she understood.

Mustering all her strength and courage, Greta pried herself

from his grasp, pushing him away and stepping out of his embrace. She was gasping for air, one hand pressed to her throat, the other to her stomach.

"Hans, I believe I should go."

"Go?" His surprise did little to mask the desire she saw burning in his eyes. "Go where? Is this not what you wanted? Am I not the man you have always loved?"

She looked at him, searching for the man she had known. His dark curls were nearly invisible in the dim light, and the face beneath them was that of a stranger. In his eyes she saw not the mischievous, determined boy she had idolized, but an angry, spiteful man, whose eyes raked over her figure like a man about to feast.

Her stomach turned, and she closed her eyes. At once, Frederick's face was again before her: his gentle smile, his piercing eyes. She heard his voice in her mind, as if calling to her from a great distance.

Choose me.

She opened her eyes, resolve coursing through her.

"No, Hans," she said firmly. "This is not what I wanted. This is not what I want now."

He stared at her, and she took a deep breath. "I want love, Hans. I have always wanted love. And this is not love."

"Are you saying you don't love me?" he sneered. This time, his tone did not cut her. Rather, it strengthened the conviction growing in her heart.

"Love is not what I expected it to be," she said honestly. "I spoke truly when I said I loved you, given my understanding of what I thought love to be, then. But I have learned better now. It was not love that I felt for you. And it is not love that you feel for me now."

Hans shook his head angrily. Taking a step towards her, he said, "You think I don't know how I feel? You don't believe me when I say I love you?"

Greta met his angry gaze with a gentle one. "I believe that you are as confused about love as I once was. You said you loved Julianna, and that she loved you. Now you say that you love me, but I do not think…" Her voice trailed off, leaving a sharp silence between them.

Hans stepped forward, his eyes narrowed so much they were barely discernible. "Go, then," he spat. "Go back to your earl, to your wealth and consequence. That is all you have ever known, and all you are capable of caring for. I should have known better than to trust an *Edelfrau* with my heart."

His words did not sting as they once would have, and it gave her courage. Swinging herself up into the saddle, Greta pulled on the reins to turn her horse around. "Say what you will, Hans, but I am not going back for those reasons," she said.

"Then what are you going back for?" he sneered.

Greta sat up straight, looking down at Hans with eyes full of pity. "I am going back for love."

Chapter 36

Frederick awoke the next morning with a smile on his face. His dreams had been light and pleasant, filled with laughter and music and Greta.

Greta.

At once, the crushing weight of the troubles with his wife fell upon him. What could he do to save his marriage? He loved Greta, more than he ever thought possible. He wished for her love in return, and he had thought that she was beginning to care for him. But now it was too late.

He sighed as he climbed out of bed, shrugging into his dressing gown. The fire in the grate had not yet been lit, and he hardly wanted to think on the morose situation of his marriage in a chilly room. He rang the bell for his valet, but when ten minutes passed and the man did not appear, Frederick thought he ought to investigate the cause of delay. He opened his bedroom door, and a disheveled mass of arms and legs and hair tumbled into his room. Frederick jumped back with a yelp.

"Greta?" he asked, incredulous.

Greta groaned, picking herself up off the floor. She brushed the hair back from her face, but as soon as she saw Frederick's shocked expression, she scrambled to her feet.

"Frederick!"

She flung herself at him, and he caught her in his arms, struggling to make sense of the words pouring from her mouth.

"Oh Frederick, I am so sorry! *Vergib mir!* Forgive me," she sobbed. "I was wrong—oh, so wrong!—and I beg of you to forgive me."

"Calm yourself, Greta, I cannot understand you," Frederick said, her wild appearance causing him some alarm. Her riding habit—why was she wearing her riding habit?—was wrinkled, and her hair was in a disheveled mess, falling nearly to her waist in long, tangled waves. But Greta shook her head.

"You must understand me, Frederick, you must! I cannot bear it any longer. I could not allow myself to rest until I had told you everything, and begged for your forgiveness."

"Tell me, then," he said, pulling her gently to a chair in the corner. "But first let me get you some refreshment."

He glanced up to find his valet standing in the doorway, a look of relief on his face. "Forgive me, sir," his servant said. "I heard your summons, and I would have attended to you sooner, but when I discovered her ladyship on the threshold this morning..."

"That is quite alright, Hastings. Thank you."

"Shall I send you some tea, sir?"

"No," Frederick glanced down at his wife, "I believe we shall need something with a bit more strength."

His valet bowed and left the room, shutting the door behind

him. "Now," said Frederick gently, kneeling at Greta's side, "tell me everything."

She did. She told him of Hans's other letters, of her intent to run off with him, and the secret meeting they had planned and carried out the night before. Frederick listened intently, his brow creased in a frown, but he did not interrupt her. When Greta told him that Hans had kissed her, he drew in a sharp breath, getting to his feet, while Greta rushed to explain.

"But Frederick, it was good that he kissed me, because that is when I saw your face."

Frederick, who had turned his back on her, glanced over his shoulder, confused. "You saw my face?"

"Yes. And I heard your voice in my mind. And then I knew."

"Knew? Knew what?"

Greta stood, reaching for her husband. Frederick took her hand, turning to face her. She smiled at him, her gray eyes full of joy.

"I knew that I loved you."

The shock on Frederick's face was enough to make Greta laugh. "I knew I loved you," she said again, "and I knew I could never be happy with anyone else. But Frederick," she said, biting her lip. "I have wronged you. I have sinned, against you and against God, and I do not know if—"

"Greta, my darling," he interrupted. "You have my complete and total forgiveness. Let us never speak of this again."

"But, Frederick—"

"Hush," he said, bringing his hand up to stroke her cheek. Her skin tingled where his fingers brushed against it, and a fullness filled her chest, stealing her breath. He looked into her face, his eyes full of wonder.

"Do you really love me?" he asked.

"I do," Greta said, her voice confident. "You have shown me what real love is, Frederick, and I will spend the rest of my life proving my love to you. I will be the most devoted wife, the most proper Englishwoman, the most gracious countess, the most—"

"Enough, enough!" he cried, laughing. "All I want is you, Greta. Just as you are." He brushed the hair back from her face, fingering the golden locks. "I've never seen your hair down," he murmured. "It is like the reflection of sun on the water—all gold and silver and light."

Greta smiled. "Would you like me to wear it down for you more often?" she asked with a coy smile.

Frederick's eyes widened. "Would you?"

She snorted. "Of course not. A lady never wears her hair down. What kind of a heathen do you think you married?"

He laughed, pulling her into his arms. "The kind I should like very much to kiss right now."

"Then kiss me, Frederick. I am yours."

Frederick bent his head, brushing his lips against her brow. Greta closed her eyes, thrilling to the softness of his lips on her skin. He kissed her temple, her cheek, and the edge of her mouth. And then their lips met.

Where Hans's kiss had been full of passion and spark, Frederick's kiss was full of wonder and love. The fire in Greta's heart spread until her body was consumed with heat, her arms reaching around him, not letting him release her. His lips were soft and full, and she found her own lips reaching hungrily after his when he moved to kiss her cheek once more. He laughed quietly.

"Greta," he breathed, resting his forehead against hers. "You have made me the happiest man alive."

"You deserve to be happy, Frederick. I have never met a better man in all my life," she said, kissing his chin, his jaw, his neck…

He groaned, placing his mouth once again on hers. She responded immediately, wrapping her arms around his neck and pressing herself to him. With one arm around her waist, he reached down and swung her up into his arms. He kissed her all the way across the room.

"So what happens now, my lord?" Greta murmured, her lips still against his.

"Now we get you out of that ridiculous riding habit."

Greta laughed, pulling away to look at his face. "I knew it! The first time we went riding together, I could tell from your reaction that you did not approve."

He was smiling at her, and the dimple was there in his cheek. She reached a hand up, tracing it there.

"It is not that I did not approve," he said, "I only wondered if you would continue to ride astride, even in England."

"I will *always* ride astride, Frederick. Nothing can convince me to do otherwise. Not even you."

He laughed, laying her gently on the bed and kissing her again. "And that," he said, caressing the curl on her forehead, "is why I love you."

Epilogue

Five years later

12 July, 1786

My dear Katarina,

I was so happy to receive your last letter. It has been quite lonesome since you all went away, and little Frederick has asked for his Tante Trina nearly every day since. Lord Rockwell says he will have business on the continent next spring, but unfortunately we will not be able to accompany him, as we hope to welcome a new addition to our family shortly after the new year.

Papa wrote that they have hired two teachers for the new Gymnasium in Strausberg. What a blessing for the children in the village to have a secondary school in town! I hope the families in Strausberg are grateful to Papa for all he has done. And to Herr Schmidt for putting him in mind of it.

When you were here, you said that you had had several gentleman callers, but your letter made no mention of your beaux. Do any of them strike your fancy? Will we be celebrating your nuptials before long? While I sincerely hope that you will find affection and love in your own marriage someday, I know you have always been a dutiful daughter, and will surely marry whomever our parents deem worthy. You were always so obedient, Trina—I could have learned much from your example. Though I am happy to say that I have finally learned to appreciate all our mother strove to teach me while I was at home. Considering my position now, I find that she was right on nearly every point (but do not tell her so, or I shall never hear the end of it). I am finding that my place in English society is very much one in the public eye, and for as little as I cared about propriety and manners in Prussia, in England they are everything. I do not want my lack of decorum to reflect badly on either Frederick or my father, and I am determined to learn and follow the rules of my station with exactness.

Send my love to mother and father, and tell Johann that if he does not write to me by Michaelmas, I shall not send him a Christmas package as promised.

All my love,
Margaret Greenwood, Countess of Rockwell

Historical Note

While my depiction of the events leading up to and involving the Battle of Cowpens are historically accurate, it is important to note that there were no Hessian companies involved in that particular skirmish. Hessian soldiers were employed by the British throughout the American Revolutionary War, but I could not find a battle in which they were involved that worked with either the location or time where I needed such an event to occur. Rather than invent a battle, I simply inserted my character's company into a real battle that otherwise worked for my story. I hope any history experts reading this will forgive my use of artistic license.

Acknowledgments

More than anyone else, I am grateful to my Heavenly Father for His hand in my life. He has blessed me with strength of mind and body when I didn't think I had anything left in me. He has led people into my life with whom I have developed deep and lasting friendships. I am humbly grateful for all He has done to help me with this endeavor, as well as in every other aspect of my life.

I am grateful to my amazing husband John, whose kiss still gives me butterflies. There is a portion of every hero I write that is rooted in the wonderful man that he is. I am so glad I get to spend my life with him!

For my sweet children, I offer my heartfelt thanks and my most sincere apologies. Thank you for your understanding and encouragement when I was busy with my book. I love you all so much.

A huge amount of gratitude goes out to Sally Treanor, who I am honored to call one of my dearest friends. Thank you for your friendship. Thank you for your encouragement and feedback. Thank you for the late night chats and the brainstorm sessions and the commiseration when things weren't going right. You are such a blessing in my life and I am so glad we found each other!

Christine McKinnon has been my German language expert through every draft and revision this book has seen. Thank you SO much for your knowledge and expertise! Special thanks to Erin Olds for her help with the French words and phrasing as well. You guys have been key in helping the authenticity of my story, and I am so grateful for all your help.

Carrie Jacks, Erin Lewis, Erin Olds, Katie Richmond, and Sachiko Burton, thank you for putting up with my moaning and groaning about this book for the past three years. Without your help and encouragement I may never have finished it! And thank you to all the other wonderful members of the Columbia River Writers group who helped critique and offer feedback on certain aspects of the story.

Special thanks go out to Heidi Kimball, Joanna Barker, and Sally Treanor (again) for taking time out of your insanely busy lives to read my manuscript in its entirety and offer feedback on the story. You are all such brilliant writers and I am blessed to call you friends.

Rebecca Blevins, thank you for fitting me into your editing schedule and helping my story to shine!

And last but certainly not least, a huge thank you goes out to you, my lovely readers. When I wrote <u>A Heart Made of Indigo,</u> Lady Rockwell was a relatively small character whom I didn't know very well. I knew she was loving but strict, and that she had ties to Prussia, but I finished writing that book not really knowing what her story was. I often wondered about it, but it wasn't until I was almost finished with <u>Scoundrel In Disguise</u> that Margareta's story burst into my mind. It still wasn't fully formed, but I knew enough of it to go back through and drop hints throughout the book, which so many of you picked up on! Your emails and messages and reviews asking me to write her story were so encouraging. I know it has been a long time coming, but as you can see, hers was not a typical romance. That—combined with the huge historical issues I knew I would be dealing with at the time in history when it was set—made it a complicated book to write. I know it's not perfect, but I hope you are as satisfied to read her story as I have been to write it.

About the Author

Shaela Kay was born and raised near Seattle, Washington. She studied Theatre and English at Brigham Young University-Idaho, but left her studies in order to be a wife and a mother. When she isn't writing, you can find her quilting, crafting, or homeschooling her four children. She and her husband John live with their family in a little house along the banks of the mighty Columbia River. Visit her online at www.shaelakay.com